RED MOON RISING

RED MOON RISING

K. A. HOLT

MARGARET K. McELDERRY BOOKS
New York   London   Toronto   Sydney   New Delhi

MARGARET K. McELDERRY BOOKS
An imprint of Simon & Schuster Children's Publishing Division
1230 Avenue of the Americas, New York, New York 10020
For information about special discounts for bulk purchases, please contact Simon & Schuster Special Sales at 1-866-506-1949 or business @simonandschuster.com.
The Simon & Schuster Speakers Bureau can bring authors to your live event. For more information or to book an event, contact the Simon & Schuster Speakers Bureau at 1-866-248-3049 or visit our website at www.simonspeakers.com.
Book design by Sonia Chaghatzbanian and Irene Metaxatos
The text for this book was set in Adobe Garamond Pro.
Manufactured in the United States of America
0116 FFG
10 9 8 7 6 5 4 3 2 1
Library of Congress Cataloging-in-Publication Data
Holt, K. A.
Red moon rising / Kari Anne Holt.—First edition.
p. cm.
Summary: "When space-farmer Rae is kidnapped by the native inhabitants of her moon, she is trained to become a warrior. But can she attack her own people?"— Provided by publisher.
ISBN 978-1-4814-3626-7 (hardback)
ISBN 978-1-4814-3629-8 (eBook)
[1. Science fiction.] I. Title.
PZ7.H7402Re 2016
[Fic]—dc23
2015013521

For Georgia, the fiercest of the fierce

RED MOON RISING

A CLOUD OF DUST LIFTS OVER THE RISE AND I
stand, smiling and waving, even though Boone is still too
far out to see me. Unless he has his gogs on. But that would
mean he's gotten his gogs fixed and I doubt that. The cloud
moves closer and though I expect to see a horse's head bob-
bing within it, I do not.

It is something else entirely.

The head grows larger.

There is no boy.

It is not Boone.

I drop my flares into the dust at my feet. For a moment
I'm completely frozen. Then I leap onto Heetle and tell her
to go, go, go!

Perhaps he has not noticed me. Perhaps he is just flying

low, looking for food or exercising his beast. I urge Heetle to go faster. My hat flies out behind me toward the gorge and I swear into the wind. I will be in even more trouble now. I hazard a look over my shoulder.

He's still right behind me.

Right gum behind me.

No, no no no no no.

I kick Heetle viciously and she rears up, almost throwing me to the scrub. "Sorry, girl," I yell. I know she's already going faster than she's used to. Her flank is sweaty, her face lathered. She rears again, announcing her displeasure, then takes off so fast it's as if her tail is on fire. My skirts billow out, a violent flapping in the dust. I throw one more look over my shoulder. My hair whips across my face, having come loose from its braids. It slashes at my eyes, my mouth, but even through the whipping hair I see him inside our cloud of pink dust, not twenty hands behind me, and just above. His beast has a mighty wingspan, which is probably why he is gaining so quickly.

"Go, go, go!" I yell at Heetle. She is galloping like the wind. I swipe my traitorous hair out of my face, catching tears and snot along with it. This is not happening. I will not let this happen. I am not Rory. Don't think about Rory.

I lean into Heetle's mane, protecting my eyes from the flying dust and scrub, then remember my gogs. Of course. Stupid, Rae. Holding the reins with one hand, I pull the gogs up over my eyes. They are caked in dirt and grime, I can barely see out of them. The compass spins to the right direction. The homestead. We will be there soon. If we can just keep up this pace, we will beat him there. Barely.

Poor lathered Heetle. I did not put on her heat armor before I went out. I just wanted to meet Boone. Just one secret race before supper. But now. The suns are so hot, even though we are months from high summer. She is moving fast, but ailing, I can tell. And I am not so well myself. My breaths are jagged, harsh, my lungs filled with heat and dust and dirt and scrub.

I can't breathe.

Panic upon panic.

I cannot have an attack. Not here, not now. I hear his beast shriek into the air, the *whoomph* of her wings. Oh, gods. I start counting as I nudge Heetle even faster. Just like Aunt Billie taught me. One. Two. Three. Four. Calm yourself, Rae. Calm your breathing. Blackness and stars are edging into my vision. I cannot let an attack happen. I will not let it happen.

He is still behind me, but now almost over me, too. I crane my neck and see the red ropes of hair piled on top of his head in a tall spray that looks like a misplaced horsetail. I see his upturned turtle nose, his bony upper lip. He is so close.

Breathe, Rae, breathe.

Faster, Heetle, faster.

One, two, three, four.

The leaning, ramshackle metal walls of the homestead come into view and I want to feel relief, but panic claws at me. Even as we grow closer, I feel we are too far away.

Finally, within sight of the sagging, dusty front porch, I yank back on the reins and throw myself off Heetle. I'm gasping, my chest as tight as if I'm wearing a church dress four sizes too small. I smack Heetle's haunch and she runs. I don't know where; I don't think she does, either. Just . . . safely away.

I am screaming like I'm the one whose tail is on fire. "CHEESE!" I yell, my voice going as sharp and high-pitched as a night beetle's song. "CHEESE! CHEESE! CHEESE!" I scramble into the cabin, slamming the rickety door behind me. It is as if I'm putting a skirt in front of myself to protect against a maelstrom. The Cheese know no boundaries, no walls, no rules, I know this. My breath is coming so fast. I am seeing stars.

"Ramona?" Aunt Billie looks up. She sits by the cooling grate, mending my fancy dress. Papa is simultaneously reading from his prayer book and cleaning his light rifle.

"Ch—" I say, sputtering, running into the center of the tiny room, my hair wild around my shoulders, my hands flailing. Papa sets down his prayer book and takes my hand. His grip is strong, unwavering. My hand shakes in his.

"Cheese. Here. Coming." I point at the door with my other shaking hand and by now we can all hear the *whoomph* of wings outside. A screech goes up into the evening air.

In three swift motions, Papa yanks the apron from his waist, hands the light rifle to Aunt Billie, and pulls two handbows off the wall. They automatically size themselves to his fists. Temple peers around the doorway of the bedroom, her gogs hanging around her neck.

"What's going o—"

Papa waves to her to shush up and then motions at me to go to her.

"I'm staying and fighting," I whisper fiercely. "I'm thirteen summers now. I want to protect the homestead, too—" Papa holds a hand up and pinches his fingers together. I know this means, *Hush your gum mouth, noisy child.* I begin to protest but Temple runs into the room and grabs my hand, pulling me back into the tiny bedroom with her. She's barely nine summers, how is she so strong?

The screeching comes louder and then softer, so I know the dactyl must be diving figure eights around the house. Just like Boone said they did to his. The night they lost Rory.

My throat is so dry I can barely swallow. I push Temple away from me, but as soon as she's loose she's grabbed on to my arm again, keeping me in the back with her. I know what we're about to do, where we're about to go, and I don't want any part of it. I will not go willingly into the dark.

Aunt Billie's and Papa's breaths are coming so hard I can hear them echoing off the metal walls. Aunt Billie looks to me and Temple and nods twice. It's our signal. Just like we've practiced. I shake my head, so that my brain lobs back and forth between my ears, but Aunt Billie just nods twice again, this time more forcefully.

The Cheese raps on the plastic window in the front of the cabin. The window scavenged from the *Origin*. The one that didn't crack even when the ship dropped out of the atmosphere and landed in the gorge like a rock falling from space; the window that still has the small imprint of the Star Farmers Act seal from so many summers ago.

The Cheese presses his scaled face up against the cloudy plastic, leaving a smear of golden and silver paint. The dactyl swooping over the cabin screams again. And then, with a yank, Temple has me in the pit. The metal floor of the cabin, which was once part of the *Origin*'s hull, is pulled over the top of us. The hiding pit. For storms and raids. For children and babies. For weaklings. For girls.

It is pitch black in here.

I hear the zoom of the light rifle. The *zip-pew* of the handbows.

The darkness crawls all over me, even though Temple holds both my hands. She begins counting softly. I try to count along with her, but I can't catch my breath.

The only light is from the stars in my eyes as I breathe so fast. So fast.

And then the stars disappear.

And it is only blackness.

2

"IT'S SAFER THIS WAY," I SAY, ARMS ACROSS MY
chest.

"It's a disgrace." Aunt Billie's voice is low. Her lips
quiver with emotion as she picks up the piles of hair from
the floor and holds them in her hands like she is mourn-
ing something beloved and dead. "What will your papa
say?"

"I don't care what he says," I say, tightening my arms.
My heart pounds because this statement is not the exact
truth.

"I care what he says," Aunt Billie says, more to the hair
than to me.

"He is not a girl-child working the fields. He does not
have to worry that his hair gives him away to the Cheese.

Now that my hair is short, I will be safer while I work. I wish I could cut Temple's hair, too," I say.

"No!" Aunt Billie looks up sharply. "You will do no such thing. It goes against the gods, Rae. Have you never listened to one lesson in your life?"

"The gods did not have to worry about being stolen by soulless beasts, did they?" I mutter. I did not sleep during the night, still shaking from my encounter with the warrior Cheese. My hands only steadied when I picked up the sewing shears and sliced at my hair.

"Get to the fields," Aunt Billie says, her mouth a tight line. "We will discuss this later. With your papa."

I run my hand over my head. I already feel lighter and more free. It is lovely to have short hair. Even if it goes against the gods. I walk past Aunt Billie and she sighs deeply, swatting at my back. I turn, surprised. Is she that angry? But then I see she is only removing more strands of thick black hair. I keep my eyes low and try for a smile. Can Aunt Billie forgive this latest transgression? She does not smile back.

Out on the porch Boone and Temple stop talking as soon as they see me.

"Shut your gum mouths," I say. "I already heard enough from Aunt Billie."

They continue staring as I sit. I pull a little stone figure and my knife from my apron pocket. I try to ignore them as I whittle at the stone. The nose is not quite right, but at least the arms are finally functioning. Built with tiny gears

I removed from broken watches and other pieces, the arms are attached to the rock, and when I push them back they fly forward to clap hands. Or they're supposed to. One arm flies off, striking me in the eye, and the other lands perfectly, precariously, on the top of my head.

Boone and Temple start laughing so hard they're snorting. Boone rolls off the porch and lands in the scrub and that sets them off even more. I'm afraid one of them is going to suffocate on their own gum stupidness.

"I said, shut your pieholes." I collect the broken pieces of my figure and run a hand over my newly shorn head. It is hard to cut your own hair when your only reflection comes from a piece of broken glass.

I want to be mad at them for laughing. I do. But after a minute I can't stop my mouth from twitching up just a little. Boone has a smear of red dirt under his nose like a mustachio.

"You think *this* is funny?" Temple says, changing the subject. "You should have seen Rae last night. She just . . . she just . . ." And Temple mimics a faint, complete with the back of her hand held to her forehead. She lands in the scrub next to Boone.

They both bust out laughing again until Boone chokes out, "She fainted? Just like that?"

"Just like that," Temple snorts, "into a heap on the floor. Out cold."

"Our brave hero," Boone says, standing and bowing at me. "Standing in the face of the Cheese. Never backing down." Ah, so this is what they must have been speaking of before I appeared and distracted them. I push Boone back down in the scrub, laughing despite myself.

"It was from a lack of oxygen," I say. "You know. To my brain." I point to my head and we all laugh. "Besides, the Cheese left, right? He didn't steal anything, he didn't take anybody. So, one point to Rae!" I curtsy and then realize what I just said about the Cheese not taking anyone. I flush as Boone finds something very compelling to study in the scrub.

"What is this ruckus?" Aunt Billie comes out onto the porch, lunch sacks in her hands. She hands one to me and one to Temple. "Those fields won't clear themselves."

"Yes, ma'am," Temple says, standing and shaking the dust and bits of scrub from her long skirt. She takes her lunch sack. I put my knife and the little statue back into my apron pocket and grab my lunch. Aunt Billie reaches out and puts her hand under my chin, looking at my face, my hair. She frowns and hands me a small, cloudy plastic container. It fits in my palm. I am meant to inhale the contents inside, straight into my nose, if I have a breathing attack in the field.

I drop the bottle into the pocket of my apron.

"In case of an emergency only. Do your counting first." Aunt Billie's crystal-blue eyes dart to clouds of dust blowing by in the breeze. She clears her throat and turns her face from the wind. The air blows her hair out like a flag.

We're running out of the medicine. She hasn't told

me this, of course, but I know. My attacks have been coming more often and the medicine supply scavenged from the *Origin* is finite. Aunt Billie has been letting me help her cultivate seedlings for plants that might help replace some of the medicines, but so far nothing can tolerate the heat.

The counting sometimes helps me steady my breaths so I don't need to use the drops, but not always. I'm practicing, though. For when the drops run out.

"Too bad the drops do not also foster hair growth," Temple says, and I stick my tongue out at her.

"Meet your papa a bit before midday for lessons, please," Aunt Billie says, ignoring us. "You, too, Boone. I know how you like to feel 'unwell' around lesson time." Aunt Billie gives him a stern look. She takes hold of Boone and peers at the angry web of flesh on the side of his head where his left ear used to be. She says nothing, just looks him over good and then releases him.

Boone hops into his saddle. It slides around on Raj's back, and it takes him a second to steady it with his knees. Boone's horse is growing skinnier every day.

"See you later, brave protector," Boone says to me with the flash of a smile. He salutes me and then kicks at Raj and yells, "Hyah!" They're off in a burst of dust.

Aunt Billie shakes her head. "He's going to wear out that animal, riding him like that in the heat of the morning."

I walk off the porch and over to the side of the house where Heetle is tied up under a sagging awning. I untie her and help Temple into the saddle. Then I hop on in front of her. "We won't be late for lessons," I say, giving Heetle a quick "Hyah!" of my own, but making sure she stays at a respectable trot.

"Rae!" Aunt Billie yells after us, holding her hand up to protect her eyes from the already burning suns. "If your field work is finished early we can practice some poultices and tinctures tonight!" I smile bright. She still likes me well enough to work on healer studies? Maybe she can forgive me for my transgressions after all. One point to short-haired Rae.

"And, Rae!" she continues as Heetle picks up speed. "Keep your sister safe!" I raise my hand to wave at Aunt Billie, and gently squeeze Heetle with my knees so she'll speed up.

It doesn't take that long to get to the field. It's not a large area of land—just a few acres between Boone's homestead and ours. Boone is already over on his end, pushing a huge red rock into the gorge that marks the—abrupt—end of the field. The gorge spreads even farther along the horizon than the looming Red Crescent, an enormous frown that hangs in the sky. On a clear day, we can see the swirling clouds of the planet our people were supposed to reach but never did. So close. But still so far away.

Our shared field is small and it's filled with rocks and boulders churned up by the last electrical storm, making it impossible to plow the gum thing. If we're going to get the seedlings in the ground before high summer, then Temple and Boone and I are going to have to work double time, throwing the boulders in the gorge. Fun times ahead.

Temple leaps off Heetle and walks to the very edge of the gorge, where she sits, clearly leaving all of the hundreds of boulders for me to take care of. Well, that is not going to do. I tie up Heetle under the cracked metal awning hammered onto four posts that serves as her shelter from the suns, and I march over to Temple. The wind snaps the front of the awning up and down onto the tops of the posts, making a noise louder than Papa's sneezes. It is like a drumbeat playing for me as I prepare my angry speech about lazy younger sisters who only want to daydream while their older sisters grow hunchbacked and bedraggled from—

"Can you see that?" Temple asks as I come up behind her. She surprises me and I momentarily forget my speech.

"What?"

She points to the other side of the gorge. "Shine tree."

I pull my dusty gogs up from around my neck and look through them. Yep. Shine tree. "So?"

"So how'd it get over there? Was it there yesterday? I don't think it was."

I shrug. "I don't know, Temple. Shine trees grow anywhere, and they grow fast. They love the suns. They eat the heat."

Temple turns and looks up at me from where she's sitting. She puts her hand up to shade her eyes, even though she's wearing a wide-brimmed hat. She smiles and says, "Rae, you're a poet."

I drop my gogs back around my neck and make a face. "What do you mean?"

13

"'Love the suns,' 'eat the heat,'" Temple laughs. "You're a poet and you don't know it."

"We gotta get to work, Temp."

She turns back to look out over the gorge. "I know it. I just wonder how that tree got there, is all. Papa says the Cheese don't grow shine trees."

"Maybe they stole it from us," I say. "Maybe the wind blew a seed over there and it started growing up on its own."

Temple shakes her head. "Shine trees don't grow from seeds. They only grow from the needles they shoot."

And that's when it hits me. It gum near knocks all the breath out of my body.

Only two people in this settlement have been shot by a shine tree needle. Only two times anyone's ever seen it happen. One time was me, one was Rory. Shine tree is why I only have four fingers on my right hand. I don't know about Rory's hands or arms or legs or head because the Cheese got to her first. They took her just as the poison was making her cry out.

"You think that tree has something to do with Rory?" I whisper. You can hardly hear my voice over the hot gusts whipping by.

Temple nods once. She stands, swiping a tear across her dusty face. "Don't say anything to Boone," she says.

"You know I won't," I say. I lick the salty grit from my bottom lip and then kick a rock over the edge of the field into the gorge. It cracks and snaps as it bounces off ledges

14

and outcroppings on its way to the bottom. "C'mon. We got ten hundred rocks to clear."

I give her a quick one-armed hug. I can't imagine what my life would be like without Temple, even if she is a gum rockhead sometimes. How Boone still breathes and eats and lives without Rory is a mystery I will never solve.

Temple and I both reach into the pockets of our ratty canvas aprons and pull on our gloves made of the same canvas scavenged from the *Origin* back in the early days before we were even born. The pinkie finger in my right glove is tied in a knot so it doesn't get in my way.

"Hey, Temp," I say, staring at my glove. "You ever think about what these gloves were like before they were gloves?"

"Huh?" Temple looks at me like I have night beetles in my hair.

"You know. Our aprons, too. This canvas. It was probably part of some vital mission on the *Origin*."

"Or part of a tablecloth on the *Origin*." Temple wanders over to a giant boulder and gives it a shove. It doesn't move. "How do you think this canvas got up here?" Temple asks. It's a familiar discussion between us. "I mean, how did it really get up here? How did any of the supplies get up here, out of the gorge?"

"Papa says everything comes from the wings of angels," I say, though what he means by that I'm not sure.

"They must be strong angels," Temple says. "And tireless." She shoves the boulder again, and again it doesn't move. It is the biggest, nastiest one of the bunch, for sure, nearly as tall as she is. Even with both of us pushing, we can't budge it.

I go and untie Heetle. It's tricky with the big rocks like this. I pull some grotty old rope out of one of Heetle's saddlebags and tie a big slipknot. Temple helps me pull the circle of rope around the boulder. The knot pulls tight as I yank on the rope and tie it to Heetle's saddle.

This is not something we like to do, but sometimes it's the only choice. Can't plow a boulder. And no seedling is gonna grow on top of one, either. I give Heetle's haunch a pat and she trots forward a few feet, pulling the rope taut. Another couple of trots and the boulder rolls forward a bit. A swarm of prairie spiders comes flying out of the hole and Temple and I both shriek like a dactyl, and leap almost as high as one, too.

Heetle is none too pleased at our antics, and rears up at me, waving her hooves in an impressive display of *You better watch out or I will brain you with my feet just to teach you how big of a rockhead you are.*

I whisper and purr at her, getting her to sidestep closer and closer to the edge of the gorge, so that she's dragging that boulder behind her, kind of diagonally to the drop-off. She is not happy with me. I try to keep my breathing even and steady, so she can see I'm calm, even though I hate doing this to her.

"I don't like this part, either, girl," I say to her as calmly as I can. "But Temple's quick with the knife and the gum rope is trash anyway." Heetle stamps and edges away from

16

where I want her to go. But with a few prods she swings her backside close enough to the gorge that the rock follows and starts to slip off the crumbling edge. Heetle's eyes tell me she feels the weight behind her giving her a tug. My heart lurches as hard as her front legs do as they try to regain purchase.

"Now!" I shout to Temple. "Now! Now!" I'm patting Heetle's neck with one hand, and realize I'm gripping on to her saddle with the other. As if I could pull her to safety with my matchstick arms.

Temple saws away at the rope as the boulder slips farther over the edge. Heetle loses a bit of footing in her hind legs now, slips a foot or so, and lets out a fuss. My heart hammers through my body like a quake.

"What is taking so gum long?" I shout at Temple. I see her sweating back there, sawing through the rope.

"Rope is stronger than you thought, rockhead," Temple shouts back.

Heetle's feet slip some more, kicking up a cloud of dirt and dust that the wind grips and turns into devil spirals that spin off across the field just like the spiders. Heetle, she looks at me—I swear she does—with eyes that say, *Lookit what you done now, Rae,* as her back legs slip closer and closer to the edge.

But then Temple lets out a whoop, the severed rope springs back and whips me across the face, and the loosed boulder crashes into the gorge below.

Heetle takes off at a gallop to go stand under the awning

and shoot me looks of rage, while Temple saunters over, twirling her knife.

"That was exciting, eh?" She grins and flips the knife shut before dropping it back into her pocket.

"Too exciting," I say, reaching up and touching the red welt growing on my cheek. It's as if Heetle herself slapped me good. And deservedly so. "Can you imagine explaining to Papa how we accidentally dropped Heetle over the edge of the gorge?"

Temple's eyes go wide and then we both start laughing. The idea is so terrifying and absurd—and close to the truth—that it's either laugh or cry, I suppose.

We sit in the scrub for a minute, taking sips from our canteens and not saying a word.

"You wanna hear a story, Temp?" I ask, holding my hand out to help her stand. Temple nods and pulls her hat lower over her eyes to protect from the suns that are out full force now. "It's the story about how the Cheese got their name," I say.

Temple smiles, sweaty dirt and grime lining her face like an old lady's. I know she loves this one.

3

"THE SHIP CAN'T MAINTAIN ALTITUDE! EVERY-thing is failing!" I run around the field and flail my arms over my head. Temple laughs. "We're dooooomed!" I cry. "Dooooomed!"

"But why are we doomed?" Temple asks, playing along. We've acted out this part of the story dozens of times. Rory used to tromp behind us and chant "Dooooomed, dooooomed, dooooomed" in a low voice. She'd have us rolling in the dust, we were laughing so hard.

"Those gum fools on Old Earth couldn't program a horse to water!" I shout. "They've mucked us up but good!"

"Whatever shall we dooooo?" Temple says in her fake cry that almost sounds like she's singing. Together we push a boulder into the gorge and wait for one beat, two beats, three beats, and then watch it hit the blackened skeleton of the rear of the *Origin*.

"We shall pray to the gods," I answer, marching to the next big rock. "We shall pray that all five thousand of us and our animals won't be smashed to bits or eaten by monsters or lost completely when this infernal machine plummets to the red moon below."

"Red mooooooon?" Temple singsongs, holding her hand to her forehead just like she did earlier when she was pretending to be me fainting. "But that doesn't sound like the glorious New Earth we were promised in the newsgrams of the Star Farmers Act!" We shove the next boulder into the gorge and then heave some smaller rocks in after it.

"You speak the truth, crusty-nosed maiden!" I say. Temple punches me in the arm and then wipes her nose with the back of her glove. "We have veered terribly off course and kept it a secret from everyone."

She pretends to beat me with the rock in her hand and I pretend to cower in the dust.

"Do me no harm, ugly child!" I shout. "I am your captain! I have sailed you hundreds of light-years into the blackest of space. I have fought star pirates and space narwhals to keep you safe!"

At this, Temple breaks character and doubles over laughing. "Star pirates? Space narwhals? What is a *narwhal*?"

"Pay you no mind!" I say in my deep captain's voice, sweeping my arm out in front of me, thinking of how much Rory would have loved to tell a story about space pirates.

Rae. Don't. Stop thinking about Rory.

"Do not continue beating me with your loathsome, weak hands," I continue, trying to shake the thoughts of Rory from my head. Trying to ignore the shine tree across the gorge.

Temple throws a small rock at me and it bounces off my handbow holster. "Watch it," I say. This time, I'm the one breaking character. "If you break my handbow Papa will whip us both." Temple winces.

"What shall we doooo, Captain?" she says, returning to our story. "Surely we will all diiiiieeee!" We heave another stone into the gorge. It bounces off the growing pile of rocks below.

"Watch over us, gods!" I shout. "The time is nigh!"

This is the part in the story when we run around like lunatics, screaming into the wind and whipping our heads and arms around as we reenact the historic crash of the *Origin*, thirty summers ago, into the smallest moon of KL-5, third planet in the Kepler galaxy.

KL-5 . . . unreachable even as it looms overhead. We call it Red Crescent because of how it hangs in the sky. We call our moon nothing. It was too insignificant to warrant a name when it was discovered. And even though we have inhabited this dusty rock for thirty summers it still remains nameless. I do not know why. Maybe because there is still a shred of hope we might leave it someday. There are people

21

on the Red Crescent. Not humans, but . . . not Cheese. Reenacting their battles with the *Origin* homesteaders is another favorite game of ours.

I always wonder if they will come back, but Papa is sure they will not. "Not after having a taste of our mighty strength," he says, and it makes me think—don't we *want* them to come back? Wasn't the entire reason for the *Origin*'s journey to obtain lands on the Red Crescent? What do we gain by having scared them away? It perplexes me.

By this time, Boone has wandered over from the far side of the field where he was working. He must think we are both suffering from heat madness. He quickly figures out what we're doing, though, and takes a seat on a large rock, pulling his hat low over his eyes, but tilting his head back so he can watch and laugh. He aims his good ear at us.

Temple and I both collapse on the scrub to catch our breath. The suns are really beating down now. I wish I had my hat.

"Hallelujah!" I shout, after I've rested a moment. I sit up. "I did not get burned alive or eaten by monsters after that dreadful crash!"

"Nor did I!" Temple says, sitting and shaking scrub from her hair.

"It appears many of our shipmates have been killed, though," I say. "Woe is me. Also, I think some of them have been eaten. But by what?"

Temple's hand flies to her mouth and she points to the sky. I know this is part of the story, but my heart always jumps when she points. I lift my head and pretend to see a dactyl for the first time.

"Oh, gods! What is this beast? Why does it shimmer pink in the sky? Why must it clack its huge jaws in our direction?!"

"We are breakfast, I fear, Captain! Biscuits for the beast!" Boone laughs at this and Temple shoots him a grin.

"Come then!" I say, remembering that we're supposed to be clearing the field and not just playing. I throw several more rocks into the gorge and Temple follows suit. Boone stays reclined on his rock until we shove him off and then push his boulder over the edge. "We must run away from this beast!" I continue. "Gather the survivors before we are all of us gobbled up!"

Temple grabs Boone's arm and pulls him up and we all run around in circles for a moment before I shout, "Here is where we shall hide! This cave carved in the walls of the deep gash we have crashed into."

"This cave does not seem saaaaafe!" Temple wails.

"Perhaps you would rather be eaten by a flying monster?" I say, gesturing to the sky. I see Temple break character for just a second as her panicked eyes move to the sky. But then she's right back with me.

"I choose the cave!" Temple says, and Boone claps, making us all laugh. We toss a bunch of small rocks into the gorge and the wind carries the crashes they make as they bash into the pile below.

"I shall turn on the lights on the exterior of my helmet,"

I say. "So that we can see inside this mysterious cave."

"I forgot they were wearing space suits," Temple giggles. Then she pretends to turn her helmet lights on, too.

"Oh my!" I shout. "Whatever is this I see?" I kneel by a boulder that was scorched by an electric strike during one of the storms last month. "How can this be?"

"What is it?" Temple says in her high-pitched voice. "A message from the gods?"

"It is . . . ," I say. "It is . . . a drawing of cheese!" I use a small rock to carve a crude drawing in the charred place. "Perhaps a tube of clotted cheese?"

Boone and Temple both bust out laughing. I've altered the story from the usual and I can't help but laugh, too. The story we usually act out—the story told to us by Papa and Aunt Billie that their parents told them—is that the captain and the few survivors saw pictographs in the cave that matched the basic shape of the dactyls that had chased them there. They saw drawings of humanoid figures, too. Then everyone heard a vibrating whistle and a red-moon native said something that sounded like "Chee-hoot." Before anyone could react, he snatched a man right from the opening of the cave and fed him straight to a dactyl that had landed beside the native. From then on, the natives were called Cheese.

Not as funny as my story.

"This drawing of cheese is remarkable!" Temple says, still playing. "The tube looks so realistic." I laugh because my drawing is pretty much the worst thing ever.

"Cheese," Boone says.

"I looooove to squoosh it on biscuits," Temple says, patting the drawing on the rock.

"No," Boone says, pulling on his gogs. The right lens is still smashed from over a moon ago when Raj trampled it during one of our races. "Cheese." He's standing still, staring out over the gorge.

I drop the rock I've been drawing with and snap my gogs over my eyes. Sure enough, there's a Cheese standing across the gorge from us. He's alone, with no dactyl, no obvious weapons. Strange.

"Rae." Temple has her gogs on, too. She grabs my hand.

The Cheese is smaller than the warrior from the other night, thin but muscled. I would guess he is not much older than we are. He's standing by the shine tree, but not too close to it. Smart Cheese. I flick at the side of my gogs and zoom in. He's just standing there, with the dusky brownish-red ropes of his hair whipping in the wind. And he's wearing what? Only underpants? It looks like they're made of dactyl skin. I've only ever seen the Cheese painted and shining, ready for raiding. He looks small and not so fierce, with a pack slung over his shoulder and no sparkling swirls on his skin. He is staring at us.

There's a familiar sizzle that sounds through the air and I turn, seeing Papa's flare become a brief third sun. It's time for studies.

"Come on," I say, still holding Temple's hand. Boone

runs to his side of the field and mounts Raj. I push Temple onto Heetle and climb on. Boone waits for us at the rise to the schoolhouse and we gallop in. Today, it's not a race. Today, we stay together.

4

"OH, DEAR GODS," PAPA SAYS WHEN HE SEES ME.
He does not say it in a funny way or a tired way. He says
it in a drop-down-on-his-knees-and-pray-about-it-right-
gum-now way. "Ramona Darling, what have you done?"
He whispers that part.

I find it hard to meet his eyes. He does not understand
what it is to be a girl-child on this moon. To know you are
hunted.

Papa takes a step closer to me and I shrink back. He
will whip me for sure. The gods say not to hit a girl-
child—unless you are her father and you are teaching
her deference to the gods. I would rather not experience
this particular lesson in front of Boone, though. I lift
my eyes finally to meet Papa's. They are black as mine,

sparking. He works his jaw, but says nothing else.

"I will be safer this way," I whisper.

He reaches out and I flinch, but he doesn't hit me. He just pushes hard on my shoulder and I sit on my stool in a burst of skirts.

We are the only ones in the schoolhouse, so there is no one other than Boone to be bothered by this familial scene. And no one to be bothered as we eat our sack lunches during the first part of lessons. Well, no one to be bothered other than Papa, who is grouchy to say the least. He is not just grouchy with me, though. He is unhappy that the other children have not come—again—and now he protests against our eating here at the school table instead of the field. He wants us to "pay full attention!" And "If I can eat while on duty and take time from my work to teach you, you can respect me by not spilling crumbs on the schoolhouse tables!" As if we would waste any crumbs by dropping them.

"There are too many rocks, Papa," Temple says, between bites of her biscuit. "That storm churned the field up good. There's no time to eat if we are to keep coming to studies *and* clear the whole field before we take the journey to the cooling flats." Temple is good at being reasonable—and at looking up out of deep-blue eyes and smiling in a way that seems to work only on Papa.

Papa grunts, but says nothing. We decided on the ride over not to tell him or Aunt Billie, or Boone's mama, about the lone Cheese or the shine tree. There's nothing any of us can do about either one of those things, except worry and invent stories. And I don't like to worry Aunt Billie and Papa more than necessary. At least on purpose.

Papa sighs deeply and sweeps his long arms across the table, collecting our chalk and slates. He abruptly stands, pulling his satchel out from under his chair and slinging it over his shoulder.

"We're going to Old Settlement today. For just a little while. I have to make sure the scholars are obeying the laws. I thought . . . after everything"—and here he stares at me, hard—"you would all benefit from meeting an . . . acquaintance . . . of mine."

"Old Settlement?" I say, my heart thrumming instantly. "Right now? Does Aunt Billie know you're doing this? Maybe we should find a handbow for Temple—" Papa holds up his hush-your-gum-mouth pinched fingers. I can't help it, though. Old Settlement!

I lean over and whisper "Old Settlement!" to Temple and she shares an eye roll with Boone. I don't know why they're not more excited.

Abandoned ancient homesteads from before the *Origin* crashed!

Mysterious buildings that belonged to people who were not the Cheese!

Drawings and carvings that can't be translated!

This is everything the scholars have studied since before I was born. Maybe keys to the mystery of getting off this godsforsaken rock. Everything I've always wanted to see.

"What changed your mind?" I blurt out. "About taking us to Old Settlement? I thought it was off-limits for anyone who is not a scholar—or the Sheriff Reverend."

Papa rubs his beard, then puts on his sheriff's hat. "Stop asking questions, Rae. Don't ruin it."

I bite my bottom lip and shove my hands into the pockets of my apron. I grip the armless statue next to my knife. Maybe there will be old wires or twine at Old Settlement that I can scavenge to make new arms. The thought makes me nearly forget Papa's coarseness and smile anew.

"Saddle up Heetle, Rae. Boone, is Raj up for the ride?" Boone sucks in his cheeks, then opens his mouth to speak.

"On second thought," Papa says after seeing Boone's hesitation, "Rae, I want you to remove Heetle's armor and have Boone help you put it on Raj. Then saddle them both up."

"What?! But . . . ," I say. "I mean no disrespect to Boone"—and here I toss him a feeble glance that's supposed to be a smile—"but Heetle needs her armor. She's still getting used to it, and if she's not accustomed to it before high summer, well—"

Papa holds up his fingers again. I really hate it when he does that. "Do as I say, Rae. Or we won't be going anywhere."

I bite my bottom lip again and wonder why Papa hates me so much. Then I stomp out to the side of the house, with Boone and Temple right behind me.

I flip the latches under Heetle's belly and up under her throat. I unsnap the casing around her full snout and remove the shades from her eyes. Temple is cooing to her and letting her snuffle her hands while I yank and tug and grumble.

Boone is silent, taking the lightweight pieces of polymer as I hand them to him. Soon he has a stack on his arms nearly up to his gum eyeballs.

Heetle whinnies and stamps her feet in a little dance and I shake my head, trying to stay mad and not smile. "I know, girl, you think you're free of that mess. But you're not. Just for this afternoon." I shoot Boone a look so he knows what I said is true—just for this afternoon. He sees my look and then stares at his dusty boots. They're so worn that his mama has patched them in places with canvas. Then it hits me. Oh, Rae, you're such a rockhead. Of course Raj needs the armor for our trip today. He's nearly as old as Boone's boots—in horse years. And you can't patch a horse with canvas when he gets worn out.

I throw Heetle's saddle onto her back and situate the bridle while Boone and Temple work on getting the armor snapped and strapped to Raj. Raj doesn't seem too happy about it, but once he's running across the open plains, I know the old beast will think differently. I walk over to make sure the armor is secure. It's loose in some places but there's nothing to do about that. Raj is all skin and bones compared with Heetle. There's only so much adjustment the armor plating can take. If he were to wear it all the time I could probably scrounge some metal and wire and fashion up a few new buckles, but he won't be. This is

Heetle's armor. Maybe someday Raj will get his own.

"Clamp on tight with your knees," I say to Boone. "We don't need you sliding off in the middle of the gum plains."

"I'm not a rockhead, Rae," Boone says, his nose twitching up in the briefest of snarls.

I don't say anything, I just hop onto Heetle and pull Temple up with me. A black mood is settling between my eyes and the fact that it's happening on a day when I am about to see Old Settlement makes me feel even blacker.

"Hyah!" I yell, giving Heetle a squeeze, and she bursts out and away from the schoolhouse in a cloud of red dust.

"You best slow her down!" Papa yells after me. He's riding the one-man. It belches its stink into the air, mingling with the dust, and my face crinkles with the gum yuckness of it all. Temple pulls out her handkerchief and ties it around her nose. My handkerchief is in a ball on the floor next to my cot. Blast.

I pull back on the reins and Heetle slows to a trot. Boone and Papa catch up to us, and Papa takes the lead. He lets one hand rest easily on the cage that surrounds the seat, while he steers with the other. It's hard to miss that the hand resting on the cage is the one with his handbow. The plains are common territory for both the homesteaders and the Cheese. We are all supposed to have easy access and safe passage, but that's not how it always works out. It didn't work that way for Aunt Billie's son, Benny, who was taken like Rory.

Benny. The only boy ever taken by the Cheese. A special badge worn by the Darling family. I wonder if Papa told Boone's mama that we were making this trip today. I doubt she'd give permission. But then, it doesn't make sense that he wouldn't ask her first. No one is as straight up and rule-following as Papa. Sheriff Reverend Darling of Origin Township would never in a million years hide anything or lie to anyone. Of course she must know.

Heetle snorts against the stink of the one-man and I steer to the side a bit, hoping to miss the biggest of the belching white clouds coming from the pipe in the back. Boone trots Raj over to the other side and I see that the armor is already turning a very light blue. I feel bad that I was angry about sharing it. Papa was right. Today, Raj obviously needs the armor more than Heetle does. It's good to see it working, cooling him off. A true test for the summer. A true test for *Heetle's* summer. I don't know how Raj will survive.

Papa slows the one-man as we ride over a small rise that then dips into a valley.

And there it is. Old Settlement. It's laid out just as Papa has always described, just as I've seen it when I close my eyes. Homesteads taller than three of our cabins stacked on top of one another—made from something Papa calls "brick." It's an ancient building device we've not had the luxury to use. Papa says it takes too much water and we cannot spare it. The buildings look like they've been made from dust and dirt, as if magically conjured. It's hard to believe it takes water to do this.

There are shorter buildings. And a long one. There are not just whole buildings, but what I think must be ruins, too, and a tall structure that is beyond anything I could have imagined, with stairs and pillars and a frozen clockface set in a triangle holding up what's left of the roof. It's all so fascinating . . . and beautiful. I know Rory would laugh if she could see me, openmouthed, staring at broken-down buildings like they were flowers or sweet cakes, but I can't help it.

"I think your brain is smiling," she'd say, punching my arm. And I'd grab her hand and hold it behind her back while I tickled her neck until she screamed for mercy.

Oh, Rory.

Don't think about Rory.

The buildings are on the right and left of us, but none are in the center. This, I know, was called a road.

In the middle of the road stands a Cheese.

His hands are on his head, his scaled face is painted in the silver and gold swirls I've come to fear. The fat ropes of his hair are tied up on the top of his head to look like a horse's tail. A similar fat rope lies coiled in a box on the mantel above the cooling grate back at the homestead, taken from a Cheese that Papa killed many, many summers ago. It's a talisman now, proof that humans can best even the strongest warriors. Temple and I are not allowed to touch it.

A dactyl flaps its large and scaly wings, but stands other-wise still next to him, two heads taller at least. It snaps its jaws into the wind and looks like it's smiling greedily at us.

Papa slows down the one-man so we can catch up.

"Do not move from this spot," he says in a low voice. "I will come back to fetch you." Then he speeds up the one-man and heads straight for that gum Cheese. Temple turns to look at me with wide eyes, and Boone walks Raj over. Where is the acquaintance Papa wants us to meet? Has the Cheese done something with him? Papa should not approach the enemy on his own—that violates several of the rules he repeats to us every day.

Without a word, Boone and I slip on our handbows and follow slowly behind Papa. Temple squeezes her arms around my waist. We are his deputies today, whether Papa likes it or not.

5

I CANNOT HEAR ONE GUM WORD THEY'RE saying. The wind whips around us, directionless, blowing grit and dust into my face. I pull on my gogs and tap the right side once to zoom. It looks like they're . . . talking. But I know that isn't possible because the Cheese and the homesteaders do not speak the same words. The Cheese's hands stay on his head as Papa seems to talk to him. The dactyl's head clicks from side to side in a way that seems to say, *You are looking mighty tasty, homesteaders.*

Papa turns his face against the wind and shields his eyes against the suns. His other hand—the one with the handbow—flies up to press down on his hat as a gust tries to take it from him. The suns glint off the sheriff's star that is always pinned to the right side of his vest.

When the gust dies down, Papa points to us and says something to the Cheese. Then he reaches into his pocket and pulls out . . . what? It's too small for me to see. The Cheese doesn't move his eyes from Papa, but his lips move and the dactyl suddenly lunges forward.

I hear the creature shriek. Temple looks at me, her eyes huge. We haven't had many lessons on dactyls, but there was one I will never forget. A dactyl lunges with certain speed when it begins eating. And often, a dactyl will begin eating its prey before the prey has been fully killed. Dactyls shriek in pain . . . and in joy.

The dactyl is about to eat Papa.

"Stay with Boone!" I order, dropping Temple to the scrub. I charge Heetle into the valley. I hold my fist out, the holoscope of my handbow bouncing around, trying to compensate for my rapid, lurching movement. My gogs show the dactyl lunging at Papa again, I hear more shrieks, and then a burst of dust blows in front of me. The gum gogs try to focus on the dust and I lose sight of what's happening. I'm blind to the scene now, my gogs having gone staticky; I rip them down around my neck and as Heetle hurtles toward the obscured triangle of the Cheese and Papa and the dactyl, I take aim at the pink, scaly shimmers that break through the dust cloud.

Zip-pew!
Zip-pew!
I let fly with two light arrows.

Papa swings around and waves his arms wildly, and I fear he must be already in his death throes.

Heetle is so fast, I'm through the dust cloud and can hear nothing but my slamming heartbeat and her hooves pounding the scrub. As the wind takes another direction, I hear one more scream from the dactyl. The Cheese's hands are off his head now and he's gesturing at me and at Papa. Probably instructing the dactyl to finish off Papa quickly so it can carry the rest of us off for supper.

Papa goes down on one knee and the dactyl lunges its pointy head at him as it screams again.

Zip-pew!

Zip-pew!

Papa's arm flies up. The dust is everywhere. His mouth is moving, but I can't hear him.

I shoot two more light arrows and this time the dactyl's shriek is different. I've struck my target. I can only hope it was in time to save Papa. The dactyl is now horizontal and the Cheese is down next to it. Papa is hunched over. I'm close enough now that I slow Heetle and jump off, running toward the scene.

"You leave my papa be, you gum rockhead!" I shout. Then, repeating the words Papa says every night when we pray to the gods before we sleep, I yell, "We will not be threatened by the Cheese! We live on the wings of angels! Oh, gods, deliver us from harm!"

I've reached them now, and having also reached the capacity of my lungs, I bend over, elbows on my knees, taking great gasps of dust and hot air from the one-man chugging off to the side. I lift my eyes to the scene. The Cheese's eyes are round with surprise, his arm bleeding and burned. The dactyl is dead, a black hole where its left eye should be. Papa stands and walks to me. Relief floods my body. I was on time. I aimed well. Papa is safe.

I push myself up off my elbows, taking more-measured breaths now. I smile at Papa as he rushes to me. Then my smile shatters as he smacks my face with the strength of ten men.

"What have you done, girl?" he says, spit flying into my face. His eyes look like Heetle's when an electrical storm is coming. "What in the name of the gods have you done?"

There are no words. They've been slapped from my head, sent flying into the scrub along with a mouthful of spit and maybe some blood. I sputter, my face burning not just from the slap, but from confusion, shame. I can't grasp how I have messed this up. I saved Papa from the dactyl. I protected the family from the Cheese. I did not back down. I showed the backbone of a homesteader.

The Cheese stands, his hands dripping with blood. It takes me a minute to realize he is not terribly injured, but has harvested the heart of the dactyl. I remember learning of this custom after the Cheese took Rory but left behind a dactyl corpse, lost in the fight. They had taken its heart but left the rest of the dead creature. We ate stringy dactyl for days.

The Cheese drips slowly up to me, close enough to get

blood on my boots. I see the burn mark on his arm where my light arrow grazed him. The metallic paint on his face shimmers in the light of the suns like nothing I've ever seen. Prettier than a shine tree. But under the pretty paint is a lined and frowning face covered in scales. His upper lip is bony and pointed, almost like a beak. And with his hair piled on top of his scalp, I see the fleshy ovals on the sides of his head, the skin tight as drums. Cheese ears are like lizard ears, Papa has told us during lessons, even though we are not sure what lizards are. This is the first time I have seen a Cheese this close up. He is much less human than I thought.

While he is not human, and I might not speak the Cheese language, his pinched and shaking face very clearly tells me he is angry. He shouts something I can't understand and points a dripping, bloody hand at me. I take two steps back. The Cheese keeps shouting and jabbing his finger at me until Papa steps in front of me and holds out his hands. He says something to the Cheese.

Papa speaks Cheese?

The Cheese grabs me by my hair and forces me to my knees. I cry out, my heart banging in my chest. Why is Papa doing nothing to help me? How can he be so calm? Do his eyes no longer function? Can he not see what the Cheese is doing to me?

Still holding my hair, the Cheese thrusts the dactyl heart so close to my face I can feel its warmth. It smells terrible. I try to turn away, but his grip is tight. He shouts something at me and jerks my hair so that I have to face his bloody hand holding the heart. He leans in so close I can see the details in the creases of the scales on his face. I can see the paint cracking from his angry expression. I want to cry out, but I dare not open my mouth. My heart ricochets through my rib cage, a sandmoth caught in a trap.

The Cheese leans forward, never taking his eyes from mine, and takes a bite of the heart. A fine spray of blood hits my face as the organ bursts between his beaky lips. Blood and viscera drip from the heart, from his hand, onto my skirts. I choke back bile.

"It is Cheese custom." Papa's voice is low and steady. "Each rider shares a special bond with his dactyl, and must eat of its heart when it dies."

I am crying now, my tears and snot mixing with the blood spatter on my face, pink ribbons trickling from my chin. As the Cheese chews slowly I can see so many emotions on his strange face. Or maybe I am just feeling them because he is still so close to me. He's angry and ferocious, but there is such a sadness, too. The sadness seeps into my own heart.

He releases his grip on my hair. I stand and Papa quickly puts his arm around my waist, pulling me away from the Cheese. He holds on to me tightly and I lean into him, pressing my face into his hard chest, ruining his shirt.

The Cheese shakes his head and throws the rest of the bloody heart at Papa's boots.

Papa keeps one eye on the Cheese as he turns his head

41

slightly. "Get on Heetle and go home as fast as you can. Send Boone to his homestead. No more fields today. When I get home, you and Temple better be in the pit, or so help me." His voice is so low that it shakes. It rumbles. It growls like a stormy wind. He puts a hand on my arm, and I feel that it, too, shakes. I turn and run as fast as I ever have. I heave myself onto Heetle and yank Temple into the saddle, roughly, by one arm. She screams at the bloody sight of me, starts to ask questions, but I give her Papa's pinched-finger move.

"Papa says to go home, Boone. No more fields today. Don't leave the homestead."

And then I kick Heetle gently and she's off like the wind.

TEMPLE AND I HAVE BEEN IN THE HIDING PIT
for hours. So much for studying poultices and tinctures.
Aunt Billie and Papa fight in fierce whispers. I don't understand one gum thing that's happened today.

Not.

One.

Gum.

Thing.

My face is still a bloody mess. It still burns from Papa's
slap.

Temple's hand is on my arm, patting out a beat to a
song. I know she's trying to calm me and keep me from
panicking in the dark. Keep my breathing steady. My gogs
are on and set to night sight, but I know I'll have to turn

them off soon. The solar batteries haven't held their charge properly in over a moon, so that now they'll work for barely a few minutes if they aren't in direct sunlight. I've been clicking them on every time I feel the dark crawling up my neck. Then I turn them off again. Then on. *Click, click, click, click.* One, two, three, four. Fight, fight, fight, fight. Every now and then Temple's stomach will growl to add its own beat to our maddening new song.

The metal creaks as Aunt Billie peeks into the hiding pit. "Get on out of there," she says, throwing the metal sheet wide open and holding her hand first to Temple and then to me. We climb out, filthy from the red dirt, the blood, and from the hard riding this afternoon. Papa glowers, his handbows scattered on the table. A glass of spirits sits in front of him.

"The Red Crescent hangs low tonight," he says, his voice sounding like crunching scrub. "Aunt Billie feels it is too dark for an ambush."

I swallow. My throat is dusty and dry. "Papa—" I start, but he holds up his hand.

I pull my thumb to my mouth and chew the nail. It's the same color and shape as the Red Crescent outside.

Papa starts to speak and then stops. He takes a sip of the spirits and grimaces. Then he lifts his eyes to look at me. His hair, matted from sweat and grit, falls across his forehead in a black slash. When his eyes finally meet mine, they're tired and round, not angry slants like this afternoon.

"The Cheese you saw today is named Strength of the

44

Suns—A'alanatka of the Kihuut. I call him Fist. His dactyl is—was—named Hoot. I was feeding Hoot some biscuit crumbs when you shot him through the eye. After, I should add, I tried to stop you."

"Stop me?" The buzzing bewilderment in my head just keeps growing. "You were being eaten!"

Papa flails his arms out to the side, crosses them over his head, and flails them out again. His movements are sloppy with spirits.

"This means 'stop,' child. It means 'whoa.' It means 'wait.' It does not mean 'shoot at me freely until you can shoot no longer.'" Papa's eyes flash, his hands ball into fists.

"I was . . . ," I say, swallowing hard, "I was protecting you. Protecting the family. Being a leader, making quick decisions." I nearly whisper the last part. My face burns as I look at the floor.

"A *leader*?" Papa barks out a laugh that cuts inches off my stature. "In your childish wish to thrum your nose at what girls *ought* to be doing . . . in your fool-headedness, you grazed Fist and gave me that." He sloppily points to his hat hanging on the tackboard by the door. There's a hole burned clear through the front and out the back.

"Fist goes to great lengths to work with me in trying to create a peace between the homesteaders and the Cheese. As I am the Sheriff Reverend of Origin Township, so is he a keeper of peace among his own people. It was difficult for us to forge this union; difficult to build the trust necessary to work together. We have kept the alliance a secret, but with his people becoming more restless and my knowing that at any time something could happen to change this tentative agreement . . . I felt it time to introduce you. Rae, if the Cheese ever come after you or Temple, you are only to shout Fist's name and you will be left alone. At least that was our original bargain. Now, I do not know." He takes another sip of spirits and mutters, "Gods help us all."

My mouth is dry as scrub. Does he not see I was trying to protect him? I didn't know. I didn't—

"Fist has—had—become something of a . . . friend." Papa rubs his hand over his face and sighs. "While our gods do not allow us to walk over the threshold of Old Settlement structures, Fist's people believe in no such gods. He is not just helping me keep the peace, he is helping me discern whether Old Settlement has any usefulness to the township."

At this, Aunt Billie gasps. Papa cannot meet her eyes. I, too, am shocked to hear that not only has Papa made *friends* with a Cheese, he has allowed that Cheese to go against the gods and trespass on sacred ground.

Boone's father used to argue endlessly that Old Settlement was not sacred ground; that we knew of no actual deaths that had occurred there, and that it was abandoned and not eternal sleeping grounds. But Papa said until he had proof that the people left the settlement of their own accord and did not somehow perish there, he would not forsake the gods by stepping foot on their sacred ground, nor would he allow anyone else to do so, either. Boone's father thought this was ridiculous, but he was only a scholar and Papa is the Sheriff Reverend.

Papa holds my gaze, though he cannot hold Aunt Billie's. "I was intent to introduce you to Fist, and show you three that not all the Cheese are to be feared. I was intent to show you that a leader must sometimes make difficult decisions for the good of the township, for the protection of its people. But now—"

"Why teach us this today?" I whisper as I swipe away the chewed thumbnail that has found its way to my lip. Is Papa ill? Will Temple and I be orphaned, only to live with Aunt Billie, who would not smile even if she was dipped in a cold bath? Not that Papa ever smiles, either, but . . . I feel dizzy and sick at the thought.

Papa shakes his head. "Fist was gravely offended today," he says almost to himself. "The Cheese will seek retribution."

"Why today?" I ask again. Aunt Billie hands me a biscuit and a drink.

Papa slams his hand on the table. "You gum child!" he shouts. "Don't you see? Fist is a leader of his people. He makes the rules. Fist has aligned with me so that we can work toward mending fences. But now . . ."

I want to yell, to interrupt, to say, "You're *mending fences* with the people who killed Mama? Who stole Benny? Who took Rory? The Cheese who gave chase the other evening was just playing? Only scaring me for the fun of it? How lovely." But I say nothing. My hand goes to my pocket, squeezes the little statue. I contemplate throwing it against the wall.

There's a *BANG-BANG-BANG* on the front door, the metal vibrating with each strike. We all jump. Papa grabs one of his handbows and lurches at the door, flipping the peephole open. He flips it shut just as quick and swings the door open. The stink of a one-man wafts in, and the stink of something else does, too. Old Man Dan and his rangy son, Pete. Pete is so skinny and slithery he shares the single seat of the one-man as if he were his father's shadow. And he is his father's shadow in so many ways.

Pete wrinkles his nose at my filthy appearance, and winks at Temple. She spits across the room and it lands at his feet.

"Temple!" Aunt Billie shouts. "Oh, gods, what have you done to my nieces today?" She grabs us both by an earlobe and drags us to the bedroom. We can still hear Old Man Dan yelling, though.

"Word in town is that you've wed and bled a Flatface." I can hear the taunt in his voice. "Ain't nobody keen on your bringin' trouble down on us, Zeke."

Aunt Billie winces. We may all be terrified of the Cheese after what happened with Mama and Aunt Billie and then Boone's family, but we're strictly forbidden from calling them Flatfaces. Ever.

"I have an ally, Brother Livingston," Papa says, his voice low. "And you're good to call me Sheriff Reverend Darling, not Zeke." Papa pauses. "You were not at studies today, Pete."

I can only imagine the look of discontent Pete must be flashing.

"Pete was helping me in the fields, Sheriff Reverend Darling," Old Man Dan says, his voice thick and syrupy with contempt. "We *work* at the Livingston homestead during planting season. We don't fancy-foot around, wearing dresses and playing games with the Cheese."

I want to go poke Old Man Dan in the eye. I never fancy-foot around in my dress! I work. Hard. Every day. I only wear the gum skirt because no one will let me wear any pants!

"My ally is willing to span the divide, Brother Livingston," Papa says through gritted teeth. "He is my concern, and mine only. I'm not wed to him. He is not my brother or my kin. He is a . . . great asset for all residents of Origin Township."

"Nice speech," Old Man Dan says. "But everyone in Origin Township knows the Cheese are not to be trusted. You ought not to have meddled with them in the first place. And now—if the rumors are true—"

"And where did you come by these rumors?" Papa interrupts. "To whom may I offer my thanks for opening their wide and industrious mouth?"

The spirits have loosened Papa's tongue.

"Never you mind that, Zeke," Old Man Dan says. "I mean, Sheriff Reverend Darling. I just came by to find out what's true. If we need to warn folks to add extra protection to their homesteads, and you, as Sheriff Reverend, say nothing—"

"Good night, Brother Livingston. I have had a tiring day and do not wish to stand here jawing with you. Unless, of course, you and Pete would care to partake in our nightly worship."

And here, I imagine Old Man Dan sneering just like Pete, but with dirtier teeth.

Papa shuts the door before Old Man Dan can say anything else.

"For the sake of the gods, wash your faces, and then to bed. Both of you," Aunt Billie says. "This house will be silent after prayers."

I hear a belch from Old Man Dan's one-man powering up. Then I hear Pete say loudly, "Don't worry, Pa, Rae will toss her skirts around and protect us all. From our *hats*." Their laughter trails on the wind as they drive off.

My jaw tightens as I look through the bedroom doorway and see, once again, the hole I shot in Papa's hat. I could wallop Pete with one arm behind my back and both eyes sewn shut.

Temple and I scrub ourselves at the basin, the water turning pink and nasty. We put on our sleeping clothes and climb into our cots. Aunt Billie puts a hand on each cot as she kneels between us. Papa comes and kneels beside her. He leads us in our nightly prayers to the gods, asking for our health and safety, thanking the gods for everything bestowed upon the family and the township, and offering sacrifice in the form of daily devotion to the gods' will. He ends as he always does, intoning, "All we need is borne on the wings of angels and for this we are grateful."

I think of these angels, visiting in the night with buckets of water on their wings and scavenged metal slung across their backs. It strikes me suddenly as a ridiculous notion, even though this is what I've been told all my life. How *does* the water appear in the troughs? Why do the angels not strap *us* on their backs and deliver us to the Red Crescent, where we were meant to live? Why do the angels bring us water and supplies only to ultimately leave us on this moon to bake and suffer?

Papa leaves the room as soon as he's done murmuring the prayers. Aunt Billie stands and smooths the apron over her skirt.

"Will we go to the field tomorrow?" Temple asks.

"I don't know," Aunt Billie answers. "We shall see how the night goes." She walks out of the room, leaving us bathed in the deep-red twilight of the Red Crescent. I look out the cloudy plastic window, thinking of how this day could have turned out differently.

"Good night, Rae," Temple whispers, and reaches across her cot to hold my hand. "I like your hair."

7

MY EYES OPEN WIDE. WHAT WOKE ME? WAS IT a dream? A sound? I put my hands to my chest. No tightness. I'm breathing easy—other than the start that woke me. I scan the room. Papa is snoring softly in his bed. Aunt Billie is a smooth mound in hers. Temple is curled in a ball at the end of her cot. The clouded plastic window offers a deep-crimson light from the Red Crescent hanging in the sky. Maybe it was Papa's snoring that woke me. My eyes are heavy again, closing against the night.

A rustle.

My eyes fly open again. What's that noise? I slide my legs over the side of my cot and go to the window. I press my face against the cloudy plastic, trying to make out any shapes in the night. There's a figure standing next to Heetle, patting her mane.

"Heet—" I start to shout, but a hand clamps over my mouth.

"Hush!" Temple whispers. She's on her tiptoes so she can reach my mouth. "You know what he'll do if he sees us? We don't know how many of them are out there." Her hand is sweaty against my face.

I swallow hard. Temple takes her hand away.

The dark figure grabs Heetle's bridle and leads her away. "He's taking Heetle," I whisper. "I have to go stop him." I throw my knee up on the jagged window ledge, my hands pushing on the plastic, but Temple yanks me back.

"You can't go out there, rockhead," she hisses. "Rae. He'll take you, too."

She's right. I know she's right. But my heart is seizing. Heetle is my best companion and a harder worker than I am by a hundred. I can't imagine my days without her.

The figure—and the horse—move silently out of sight, my heart still clanging in my chest. Temple swipes her long, filthy blond hair out of her eyes and says, "Just be happy he didn't try to take us, too. We got lucky tonight, Rae." She really is too smart to have barely nine summers.

"I hope they don't eat her," I say. "Those gum Cheese."

"Well, you did shoot one of their dactyls," Temple whispers.

"I know it," I say. "But it was trying to eat Papa."

"Not actually," Temple says.

Heetle is gone. This is the worst thing that has ever happened, excepting Rory.

Aunt Billie walks to the window, a blanket pulled around her shoulders.

"What's the ruckus?" she asks quietly. Papa is still snoring. He could sleep through the Red Crescent cracking in two and landing in the gorge. Aunt Billie peers out the window.

"A Cheese just took Heetle," I say around the rising lump in my throat. "Just walked right off with her."

Aunt Billie puts a hand on my shoulder. "I'm sorry, Rae. Under the circumstances, though, I think we're very lucky this is all they took."

"Unless they're coming back," Temple says. Aunt Billie shoots her the stink eye and Temple shrugs.

"Back to bed, both of you," Aunt Billie says. Her face is unmoving, un*moved*. I know she must be thinking of when the Cheese took Benny, so many summers ago. Temple was just a babe, and I was barely out of training pants. Mama sacrificed her own life to save us, but Aunt Billie ran to the hiding pit. It is a night I don't remember, but it haunts me even so.

"The morning comes early and the work goes late." Aunt Billie pushes us gently toward our cots.

"But, Aunt Billie!" I say, turning and facing her straight on. "How will we clear the big boulders without Heetle? How will I get to the cooling flats? How will I do anything?" I run my hand through what's left of my hair and feel the grit of the afternoon still clinging to my scalp. Thank the gods it is so short now, so much less stifling in the heat. Papa is still angry that I cut it, I'm sure, but at least now we have bigger problems to fight over.

"Get your rest, Rae," Aunt Billie says. "Take deep breaths. We'll talk about it in the morning."

But I don't want to rest. I don't want to talk about it in the morning. I want my gum horse back. I turn back to the window, clenching my fists at my sides. Aunt Billie sighs. I hear her tucking Temple into her cot, but I don't move. Maybe if I stand here and stare long enough, Heetle will hear my thoughts and escape.

Aunt Billie puts a hand on my shoulder and whispers, "I'm sorry about Heetle, Rae. But *you're* safe, and I'm not sorry for that at all." She puts her hand on the back of my head and then I hear her walk across the room and climb back into her cot. Papa grunts and his snores start back up again. It's funny that Aunt Billie has to pat the back of my head now. She used to pat the top of it, but I guess I'm getting too tall.

The morning comes quickly even though I spent the rest of the night tossing and turning, worrying about Heetle, trying to hold back the anger that bubbled up into my head, making my eyes hot and watery.

Papa says nothing at breakfast when Temple blurts out the story. He just drinks his chicory and shakes his head, staring absently out the window.

55

A bang on the door startles us all. Papa reaches for his handbow as Aunt Billie peers through the peephole. She drops her hand quickly, though, and I see an almost smile play at the corners of her mouth. She swings open the door and Boone is standing there, holding Heetle's armor. It's stacked so high in his arms I can't see his face. He tries to carefully set it all down just inside the doorway, but it falls into a huge pile and he grins sheepishly.

"Sorry about the mess. Mama said I'd better bring it back right away in case Raj breaks it or something since we can't afford to replace . . ." He looks from me to Temple to Papa to Aunt Billie and back to me again. "What? Why are you looking at me like that?"

"The Cheese took Heetle in the night," I say, staring at the scuffed metal tabletop. "Just walked away with her." Temple nods to confirm my story.

"Oh no!" Boone says, putting his hands up in his hair. "Did you give chase?" Then he says to himself, "No, Boone, of course they didn't. That would've been suicide." He absently rubs the place where his ear used to be.

Papa sets down his cup of chicory and tugs his beard. "Boone, take Raj home and come back in your one-man. Think you can get it started?"

Boone looks skeptical. "Maybe, I don't know. It's been a long time since we even tried to start the gum thing up." His eyes flash up to Aunt Billie, but she says nothing about the swearing.

"Well, see to it that you get it working. And quickly.

Then, if you please, bring your mama back here. It'll be a tight fit, but I think your one-man can handle it. Your mama and Aunt Billie will be safer together and must work the fields for the next few days. The rest of us are going to the cooling flats before any other gum thing goes wrong."

The room goes as still as a dune before a storm.

Aunt Billie is the first to break the silence. Her voice is quiet with alarm. "The cooling flats? Now? Is it safe? The township will miss your presence."

Papa shrugs. "At this point, nothing is safe anymore. If we go today, we can hope the Cheese are satisfied with having Heetle as recompense and they'll leave us be. We'll be able to gather what we need and get back in time to hole up in case they return and lay siege." He sighs deeply. "At least it's early enough in the season that we'll be the first to the flats and have our pick of the minerals."

"First of the season?" I pipe up. "It isn't even the season yet. If someone like Old Man Dan sees us out there . . ." I don't even finish because we all know what could happen. Charges filed, fines, penalties, Papa could lose his position as Sheriff Reverend . . .

Papa slams his hand on the table and we all jump. "You have put us in this situation, Rae. *You.*" He points at me in case I've forgotten who I am. "We go now while we're *maybe* safe from the Cheese—*if* they see fit not to raid us two days in a row—or we wait until the law dictates the season and lose all our ears or lives, *or* find the flats blocked by angry Cheese who would just watch us burn to death in the high summer." He pauses, taking several quick breaths, and stares at me, his eyes boring into mine like light arrows. "So what is my choice here, Rae?"

My throat has gone dry. He's right. This is all my fault. "We go today," I choke out, barely above a whisper. I clear my throat, but then say nothing else. Aunt Billie looks at the tabletop. Temple is watching me with soupy, watery eyes. I don't want to see the mix of pity and terror and bravery in those blue, blue eyes. I turn to Boone, who looks like he wishes he could fall in a hole and tunnel his way back home.

"I'll . . . ," Boone says, backing toward the door. "I'll go get the one-man. And Mama."

Papa nods once and follows Boone to the door. He glances down at the pile of armor. "We'll take this with us and sell it in the market. No need for it now." I want to tell him Raj could use it. I could make new buckles so it would fit better. But I don't say anything.

8

IT'S CALLED A ONE-MAN FOR A REASON, I THINK,
as one of my legs hangs off the side of the seat, my skirt
gathered in a lump in my lap to keep it from dragging and tangling in the scrub. It's a struggle not to be
thrown to the rocks as Boone drives us quickly over
the prairie.

"Just imagine a gum night beetle trying to fly a dactyl."
That's what Rory would say, and her laugh would shatter
the heat. Boone would whack her in the head, or try to
race her if she was driving her own one-man. That giggle
of hers . . . it would carry on the wind, infecting all of us,
making us smile and forget why we were out here.

Rae. Stop. No more Rory.

The awful machine belches acrid smoke all around us;

smoke that mingles with the dusty air and clings to the sweat on our skin like a gritty caul.

I should not complain. These tiny vehicles are thirty summers old and survived the crash of the *Origin*. They were not meant for long-term use; their patched and reinforced aluminum frames prove this. They have no doors, no protection from the suns, and hollow, plastic wheels. They were only meant for moving supplies around in the belly of the *Origin*. It's not their fault they had to be retrofitted with awful combustion engines. It is a wonder and a miracle that they have lasted this long.

Even so, I hate them.

Papa and Temple are just ahead. She's small enough still to sit on Papa's lap. Heetle's heat armor is tied to the top of their one-man's frame, offering them coveted shade even as it slaps up and down, fighting against the wind.

"This stink's gonna burn out my gum nose hairs," I yell to Boone over the engine noise.

"Runs on bodily wastes, rockhead. You think it's gonna smell like cakes?"

I guess it doesn't matter if my nose hairs all burn off. After hours of traveling like this I'll be lucky if my whole nose doesn't bounce off altogether.

Papa waves his arm up and down twice, and slows, signaling us to pull up alongside him.

"Gonna stop for lunch," he shouts over the belches and whines of both the idling engines. He points a ways into the distance at an outcropping of rock that's been carved by the wind. Strangest-looking thing—like a horseshoe, standing on its end, sticking up out of the prairie. Might as well be waving a flag to the Cheese. "Hey there! We're eating our biscuits! Want to attack? That'd be mighty fine!"

Papa lurches ahead in his one-man, Temple's shouting laughter at almost being tossed out carries on the thick breeze. Boone kicks our beastly machine into gear and we follow after them, arriving at the outcropping in only a few minutes. While Boone helps set out the canteens and biscuits, I check the small metal cart we've been towing. Just like everything else made on-planet, it was put together with supplies scrounged from the *Origin*.

I don't know what part of the hull the metal pieces were carved from, but I imagine our cart came from the giant exposed belly of the ship. The silvery quality of the lightweight metal is rough and scratched from years of use— but maybe also from the glances and close calls of asteroids and other space debris. It amazes me to think of it.

The jugs and boxes meant to carry back a season's worth of cooling minerals for both my family and Boone and his mama are still tightly bound to the cart, despite the bouncy journey.

"Rae! I will eat this biscuit if you do not get here in one minute!" Temple is in a jolly mood today. She always loves a trip away from the homestead. I usually do, too, but because of the circumstances, and without Heetle, this one feels . . . wrong.

I jog over to the rest of them and sit on a boulder at the foot of the horseshoe-shaped colossus.

"Seems like a funny place for lunch, Papa," I say, squinting at him as the suns sear the sky behind his head. "Not very subtle."

Boone shoots me a look. But I'm not baiting Papa. I'm genuinely curious.

"It's not like we're being very subtle anyway," Papa says, gesturing at the two vehicles parked in front of us. "There's no sneaking around in a one-man." He takes a bite of his biscuit, swiping crumbs out of his beard, but missing a few. "We will partake of what little shade we can find. And no one's out this way yet, so we should be safe." He swallows his biscuit and rubs his forehead with his handkerchief. "Hopefully."

I cast my eyes from one end of the horizon to the next. During the season, this part of the prairie is full of tracks from travelers going back and forth to the flats. You'd think the first homesteaders would have settled closer to the crystals, seeing as how important they are when it comes to surviving the high summer, but no. Papa says our seeds won't grow by the flats, something to do with the chemicals in the soil. I imagine the proximity to dactyl nests didn't help much, either.

Today the prairie is just dirt and scrub. No tracks. No one in sight. No Cheese, either. I want to ask Papa about the Cheese at Old Settlement—Fist. I want to know how they met, how long they've been working together. But

Papa's mood is temperamental at best and if I were to anger him he might just forbid me to come on trips like this ever again—leave me at home to do the wash with Aunt Billie.

It may be Papa's curse and Aunt Billie's fathomless sadness, but it is our greatest blessing, mine and Temple's, that there are no boys in our family. We have freedoms other girls in the township do not have. If you count memorizing poultice recipes, pushing boulders, and bouncing your nose off in a one-man to be great freedoms. Which I do.

My biscuit is gone, though my belly growls still. I pick the crumbs from the front of my blouse and lick them from my dirty fingers.

A loud caw breaks through the whistling wind and all four of our heads jerk to the sky as if some mighty hand has yanked a string. The dactyl swoops low once, twice, and then begins a high circle around us.

Boone and I jump up. Our handbows are in the one-man. But Papa holds his arm out to stop us. He holds a finger to his lips and never takes his eyes from the sky. His head is tilted so far back his hat must be staying on by sheer force of will.

The dactyl is huge, glittering in the sky. Each of its scales must be at least as large as my head. I can feel my breath coming in spikes, my chest tightening. Oh no. Not now. Easy, I think. Keep it calm, Rae. Easy now. The edges of my sight are going dark as I struggle to right my breathing. Temple takes my hands, looks into my eyes. She starts counting in a whisper.

"One. Two. Three. Four." I count with her. We get to twenty-five before the darkness goes away. I try to swallow, but my throat is too dry. I reach down for my canteen, but my shaky hand knocks it from one boulder to the next, making a clattering sound that can probably be heard on the Red Crescent itself.

The dactyl shrieks and dives and we all instinctively flatten ourselves to the scrub. The creature has gotten so close this time I can see that it has no rider. Wild dactyls aren't unheard of, but usually they fly in packs. A lone wild dactyl . . . I turn my head, the scrub scratching at my face, and look at Temple. She gives me a shaky shrug and grabs my hand.

The air-splitting screeches of the creature are fading now and I glance up into the burning pink sky to see it retreating, flying in a direction I've never been—away from both the township and the cooling flats. There must be a nest nearby. Papa will have to ask the scholars to add it to the maps.

"Where's it going?" Boone asks, sitting up and shaking dirt and scrub from his hair, which is longer than mine since I had my way with the shears.

"Away from here," Papa says. "And that's all that matters." He stands and helps Temple to her feet. I scramble up on my own, grabbing my canteen, which has rolled to the ground. No one makes mention of my clumsiness or breathing attack. But they don't have to. I can feel it in the silence around us. I am a liability. I will get us all killed someday if I can't be more careful, if I can't make better decisions. The problem is, I seem to cause dire circumstances by trying to save people, by trying to drink from a canteen. I will get us all killed someday for just being Rae.

Without another word, we set off again toward the cooling flats. We'll have to camp tonight no matter what, but I know Papa wants to get as far as possible the first day. I do, too.

9

I WANT TO DRINK THE AIR. THE COOLING FLATS
gleam in the light of the suns, throwing a blue haze
against the ever-present Red Crescent. I feel like I can
breathe all the way to my toes. Something about the
flats doesn't just cool the air, but quiets the winds, too.
Each lungful of air is equal to ten dusty gasps on the
homestead. If only we could bottle the air of the cooling flats, I wouldn't need any more of the breathing
drops.

Thankfully, even after the excitement of the lone dactyl,
we all got a decent rest last night. Or at least I did. And we
only had to travel a few hours this morning before arriving.
It's nice that we made it without any of us falling out of a
gum one-man or getting eaten by a dactyl or choking on

our own lungs. It makes one's spirit much lighter to be alive after a trip across the prairie.

We have hiked over the first of the flats, where the minerals mingle with the scrub and dust. Papa is right to head straight to the center. We can find the purest crystals there, the ones that will last the longest.

"Quickly," Papa says. "We leave as soon as we can. And don't grab everything from one place. It must look as if we've never been here."

I drop the hitch of the cart and begin untying the boxes and other vessels. My arms burn from having pulled the thing this far, but even though we are technically poaching, we know better than to drive a one-man through the flats. That would be a crime against nature, which I think can sometimes be worse than a crime against humans.

"Look sharp!" I call out to Boone, tossing a box at him. He catches it easily and grins. The waves of coolness are making us giddy. I toss a box to Papa, and even he smiles. My ears are chilled and this makes me grab Temple so I can hold one of them up against her flushed cheek until she squeals. She takes a box, too, and we all head out in separate directions to make our poaching less obvious.

The smaller crystals are easy. I just grab them from the surface and toss them into the box, feeling the metal of the container getting cooler and cooler the fuller it gets. Boone is off in the distance, on his hands and knees working at something. I can hear the clink of his chisel and I hope he's not tearing away at a big one.

"Gentle!" I yell toward him. "They work longer if they haven't been mangled!"

Boone looks up and makes an ugly hand gesture at me, which makes me laugh. Even with a lame ear he still heard me from this distance. There is magic at the cooling flats.

I'm tying down the first wave of full boxes when I hear it. Another dactyl screams. Boone, Papa, Temple, and I are so spread out on the flats now, I can only see the others as specks in the distance in front and to the sides of me. But by the way the specks all stand as still as shadows I can tell they heard the shriek, too.

The Red Crescent is low in the sky now and the clearness of the cool air shows off the swirls and curls of the white clouds on the planet. I think I can even make out some green on the surface. Then, coming over the horizon, blocking out the swirls of the Red Crescent's clouds is a swarm of pink. At first I think it's a dust storm, but there's no wind. Then the swarm gets larger and comes into focus.

More dactyls than I've ever seen in one place. In a formation of some sort. They are coming at us in a V shape, cutting through the air like a blade.

The specks that are Boone, Temple, and Papa all start running toward me and the cart. I grab the hitch of the cart and begin hauling it as fast as I can toward the edge of the flats. Toward the one-man. Toward escape.

We are not fast enough.

The dactyls are upon us before we are even together again.

The first scream I hear is Temple's and my breath lurches in my lungs. I drop the cart and swing around just in time to see her form as it is lifted from the flats and hurled into the sky. She floats free for a moment, like a girl-shaped piece of dust caught in a swirling wind. Then another dactyl catches her with its talons and she screams again.

My breath is coming in jagged bursts. My chest is caving in on itself. Even in the cool air of the flats I can't breathe. Whether it's a breathing attack or from fright, I can't guess. But I know I will pass out if I don't calm down.

The second scream is Papa's. A low yell, full of swearing. He is jerked into the sky, but when the dactyl releases him another does not catch him. I watch in terror and disbelief as he falls to the flats, a black smudge against the blue crystals.

I start running toward the fray now, despite the fact that my handbow is nowhere to be found (where did I leave the gum thing?!) and despite the tightness in my chest and despite those gum stupid stars that flutter before me. The air is filled with shrieks and screams and it's hard for me to tell what is animal and what is human and what is Cheese, because yes. I see them now. Their face paint glitters in the light.

It is a raiding party.

The stars have almost completely taken over my vision. I stop and fumble at my skirts, but realize suddenly I'm not wearing my apron. The bottle of medicine from a few days ago is not with me.

Panic upon panic.

The dactyls are swooping and screaming. The Cheese are also doing that vibrating whistle they do. Temple screams in the distance. I have lost all sight of Boone.

And then.

And then my feet are off the ground. The blue crystals shrink as I blink over and over, trying to understand what's happening.

My shoulders are wet and I don't understand until I see the blood running down my arms, the talons puncturing my shoulder blades and chest. Then, just as quickly as they grabbed me, the talons let go and I am falling. The blue crystals zoom up toward me faster and faster and then I am caught. Not by the ground, but by pink scales, a rough arm.

I'm sliding off the side of a dactyl and I kick out, not knowing if I'm kicking to stay on or kicking to escape. Just instinct. Just lashing out. I am screaming, "Fist is supposed to keep us safe! Fist! Fist! FIST!" The rough arm squeezes my waist. The Cheese screams at me in words I don't understand. His face is furious, painted, sweat dripping from his scaly temples, and as he screams at me drops of sweaty paint fly into the air around his face like golden flecks of light. The oval ear skins on the sides of his head tighten then bulge as he yells. His ropes of hair slash through the wind.

It is no wonder he is not responding to my shouts of "Fist! Fist! Fist!" Because this *is* Fist. Papa's acquaintance. He is angry. So angry.

He wears a necklace of ears.

Fist grips the dactyl with his knees and swivels his torso to grab me with both hands. His nails are long and dark as claws. Maybe they *are* claws. It strikes me—in the middle of everything—how much the Cheese and the dactyls are alike.

I am sprawled on my back, like an overturned beetle, sideways across the back of the beast. I kick and slap Fist's hands away, losing purchase, sliding off the monster. He spits in my face, startling me. This gives him enough time to yank me into a sitting position behind him, scratching my neck in the process. He twists back around and grabs a long stretch of rope that is like a set of reins, but huge. He throws the reins around my waist and his own so we are tied together, and tied to the beast. He makes a noise that I can feel more than hear and kicks the beast, which flies straight up into the sky like a flare.

My eyes roll back in my head and I am fainting not from breathing troubles but from no breath at all. I am afraid the dactyl is flying us straight into space and the Red Crescent beyond.

I can't breathe.

We are so high.

One-two-three-four-five . . .

But that's as far as I get. My head lolls to the side, I catch a glimpse of the half-full cart sitting on the cooling flats like a dead beetle, and then there's nothing.

10

THERE IS YELLING, BUT I CAN'T UNDERSTAND
the words or sounds. Wind is beating my face with such
ferocity I can barely open my eyes. I'm still tethered to
Fist and the dactyl, but Fist has a hand gripping my knee.
He's shouting at me over his shoulder but nothing makes
sense. I can't decipher the vibrating words, but I can hear—
and feel—the urgency behind them. I can see that in his
squinting eyes and rapidly moving mouth he's trying to
impart something important. Maybe he's warning me that
we are about to crash into the Red Crescent, for it looms
so immense in the sky I can see nothing else. The swirl of
clouds on the enormous planet mimics my racing thoughts.

I tear my eyes from the Red Crescent and look down.
Dunes fly by. They're as red as the blood that still flows

freely down my arms and from my chest. The dunes look small enough to be night beetle nests. We are so high. I swallow and tighten my knees against the beast. We cannot be flying to the Red Crescent. That is impossible. I have not had rigorous study, but I do know humans cannot live in space. And I know there is space—however little—between this godsforsaken rock and that massive glittering expanse in the sky.

It is somewhat calming to know we will not race into the vacuum that is surely only meters away. But where *are* we heading? Where is Temple? Is she hurt? And what of Boone? Is Papa dead? How long have we been flying? In what direction? Why can't I see the other dactyls? I hazard another look down and see no homesteads, either. No blue glow of the cooling flats.

I close my eyes against the brutal, slicing wind and for the first time feel the deep aching of my wounds. Or maybe it's something else. Beneath my closed eyes I see Rory's face. I see her pain from the shine tree needle, I see her trying to fight. I see the Cheese dragging her by one leg behind a horse.

No.

No.

No.

Rae. Do not think of Rory.

I whip my eyes open, and water streams from them, but it is only from the howling wind, I tell myself. Only from the wind.

Settling on the easiest of the questions racing through my head, I decide to determine where we are exactly. It would help to know how long I lost consciousness. It would help if I knew anything about the gum moon other than that it is smaller than the Red Crescent and that most lands on it are forbidden to *Origin* homesteaders.

I look back down and only now do I realize why the dunes are so dark red, why the wind is whipping tears from my eyes and streaming them straight across my cheeks and into my ears.

A storm is coming.

No, not coming. A storm is *here*.

It is dangerous to be anywhere outside when an electrical storm hits. Even being inside offers little safety during the worst storms. Being *in the sky* during one is unthinkable.

I feel a tingle scuttle across my arms, see Fist's long hair reach out to the sky, even in the harsh wind, and then the light is blinding. The crash is so gum loud I think it has surely made my ears bleed. The dactyl banks and suddenly the bloodred dunes are to my side instead of below me. My stomach lurches, and even though I can barely wrap my feeble mind around whatever is happening here, I am very thankful—at the moment—to be tethered to both the beast and Fist, who appears to be a very skilled rider.

Fist shouts to me again and I shout back, "I don't understand!" but the wind steals my words and throws them behind me like scrub in a whirling devil spiral. The dactyl rights itself. There's another blinding bolt, another crash. The dactyl screams in protest and Fist screams something to it in return.

Another flash.

Another deafening boom.

I remember that my gogs are hanging around my neck and I struggle to pull them up over my eyes so I can see through the slicing wind. In the distance is the gorge. The gorge! I have a moment of lunacy where I think of leaping from the beast and following the edge of the gorge home. But before I can figure out how to untie myself and survive a fall from the sky, the dactyl banks again and the compass in my gogs spins. We are now heading away from the gorge at a rapid pace.

The creature aims its nose straight into the glow of the Red Crescent, which breaks through the storm clouds, and begins to climb yet higher. We are going *into* the storm, which doesn't seem the wisest move, but I am not an expert on flying scaled creatures through electrical storms. I can only hope that Fist wants to keep himself alive, and thus me alive, as I am tethered to him. And yet, this seems like madness.

Electrical bolts fly in every direction around us, making even the tiniest hairs on my neck stand tall. Wisps of gray clouds scurry past us as if they, too, are trying to escape. I can feel the thunderous booms deep in my chest, which I discover is still bleeding, but not as much as before.

We climb and climb and I wonder if maybe Fist is trying to take us above the clouds. That would be smart, but the storm clouds appear to be endless. The bolts are coming faster and faster, until there is more time spent dodging them than flying straight. Fist must realize the futility of his attempt because he barks an order and kicks the beast and we descend in a dive that I fear will rip my clothes off and send them sailing out behind me into the sky.

We emerge from the middle of the storm, and as the dactyl darts and dives to avoid more bolts I catch a glimpse of the ground beneath us. It is Old Settlement.

Fist shouts orders and thumps the dactyl's flank, not ungently, but with purpose. The creature swerves and darts away from the bolts and finally lands in a skidding plume of dust and scrub. The storm still rages around us, but we are on the ground again, and for that I am grateful.

Fist quickly unties us and yanks me off the back of the beast. The dactyl screams in what sounds like fury and takes back to the sparking, fiery sky. Fist tightens his hand around my arm, so that it feels fairly glued there by sticky blood, and drags me behind a string of attached and abandoned Old Settlement buildings. This is not how I imagined learning about this place—at the hands of a murderous Cheese. I shiver despite the heat. If there are ghosts here, I pray that they are more merciful than Fist.

Just as a bolt lands behind us and a crash rattles my teeth, Fist twists a knob and pushes open a door. He thrusts me inside a building, then follows, wrestling with the open door against the wind and then pushing it shut behind us.

All is dark, except for what I can see illuminated from the flashes of the bolts.

Oh, gods.

I am trespassing on sacred ground. I am bleeding. I have been taken by the Cheese. But what I see before me is worse than all of those gum things put together.

11

IT IS A HAT, LYING UPSIDE DOWN ON A FLOOR coated with inches of dust. Light flashes in from the windows and confirms my terror.

It is not just a hat. It is Temple's hat. It is torn. It is bloody. There is long blond hair stuck to part of it like a grotesque horsetail. Temple's hat. Temple's hair.

Temple's blood.

I lean over and heave my meager lunch of biscuits all over Fist's feet. Then, with no mind to what I'm doing, I strike him. A fist for a Fist. I haul off again and pound him in the throbbing oval on the side of his head, and as he takes a step back I slam him in the stomach. I run at him, full tilt, and knock into his scaled chin, feeling the sharpness of his skull bruise the crown of my head. He reels back and crashes into something I can't see. I reach for my knife in my pocket and once again realize I am not wearing my apron. Gum stupid girl!

The electrical flashes are coming less often now and we are plunged into almost full dark. The windows are so crusted over with dirt and dust only the brightest light can seep through.

Fist is only on the defensive for a moment. Soon he has regained his balance and lunges at me, twisting me around and throwing me up against a wall. There's a crunching sound and at first I don't know if it's me or the wall. Then pain shatters through my body. Doesn't he know you're not supposed to hit girls? He's not my father.

Fist wrenches both my arms behind me and somehow—do the Cheese have three hands?—binds my wrists together. He whirls me around to face him.

I spit at his smeared silver and gold paint.

He smashes his fist into the side of my face and time slows. Stars explode into my vision, pain explodes even brighter. I fall to my knees, blood seeping from my mouth and dripping in long ribbons onto the shadowed floor.

"You don't. Hit. Girls," I say, spitting blood at his feet.

With flicks and trills of his tongue Fist shouts at me, grabs me by the hair, and yanks my head back so that I'm looking into his face. He pulls my hair tighter until I cry out, and he keeps shouting, his black eyes reflecting the bolt flashes, though I would not be surprised if they flashed on their own. The necklace of shriveled ears shudders at his collarbone, and I wonder if one of them belongs to Boone. I close my eyes before I am sick again.

He releases my hair and my head sinks back down. I spit more blood and maybe part of a tooth into the dust. Another flash reveals Temple's hat not three hands from me. The hair is not so much as I first thought. Neither the blood. Perhaps she is still okay. Wounded, yes, but alive.

Fist grabs my hair again and this time pulls me to my feet. He shouts at me some more, then clamps a hand on my arm and yanks me forward through the darkness. The air is so close and stifling it is like walking through a room of secrets that have somehow taken solid form.

The storm has all but stopped now and we are drenched in darkness. I hear a crack and then an orange glow lights up Fist's sweating and scaled face as he turns to me. His voice is lower, but still seems angry. Words I can't understand come vibrating at me like shards of metal. Why is he mad at me? Didn't he expect me to fight back? I would just as soon have been left to my own devices at the cooling flats. I did not ask for this. Not on purpose, at least.

Fist waves the light in front of my face and I recognize it as a kind of glowing flare, but without fire. A chemical reaction, Aunt Billie told us years ago when we had several of the things. They had been brought up from the *Origin* on the wings of angels. It looks like the Cheese have found a use for them, too. I wonder if they also use angels for goods deliveries.

He is saying something to me in his rough voice and

gesturing with the fireless flare. I stare at him dumbly, for I'm not concerned with what he's trying to say. I am struck by my surroundings. With the eerie orange light showing me only small glimpses here and there of the room we're in, I am still numbed by what lies before me. An expanse of tables, much smaller than our table at home. Chairs knocked over on the floor, or stacked in the corners. A long, tall table-type thing spans one whole side of the room, with tall chairs bolted to the floor in front of it. Behind the long, tall table is a wall of shattered glass, and along this wall of glass are shelves, some broken, some not. On the unbroken shelves are bottles filled with liquids of varying colors.

Fist stops trying to talk to me and goes behind the long, tall table. He takes one of the bottles off an unbroken shelf and brings it around to me. He pushes me into a chair and it is only then that I realize how tired and weak I truly feel. I am warm, too, which is not unusual, and yet this sweaty warmth is bothersome, and itchy panic rises within me. Am I feverish? Nothing good comes of fevers. If I have learned anything from Aunt Billie working as the township's physician, it's that fevers are a sign of infection, and infection is a sign of bad gum news when the only true medicine you have is ancient and limited.

Fist grabs me by the hair again, but gentler this time. With his other hand he rips the remains of my tattered shirt off, leaving me in only my bloodied, sleeveless shift. My wounds are fully exposed now, as I feel the rest of me is, too. Even more heat rises to my face.

He releases my hair and squats in front of me. He holds up the bottle and tilts his head to the side. His eyes close and then open, staring at me intently. He says, "You. This. Hurt." His mouth stumbles over the words, but I understand them. I open my mouth to respond, but before I can he's standing as fast as an electrical bolt, one hand grasping my hair at the scalp, the other pouring the liquid from the bottle across my shoulders. It is like the suns themselves have set fire to my flesh. I cry out and struggle to leap from the chair, but Fist holds me fast by the hair, with a knee across my legs. He pours most of the contents of the bottle over my wounds as I shout and hiss at the pain.

Surely, we are in an evil apothecary shop.

He then wrests my head back and pours a slosh across my split lip and into my mouth. The liquid slips down my throat even though I resist, and I splutter and cough as it burns a path into my belly.

I feel a quick heaviness in my arms and legs, a cloudiness in my brain, and I wonder why Fist would have risked so much to drag me into an Old Settlement building only to poison me in the end. When he is satisfied that I am tortured enough, he takes a large gulp from the remnants of the bottle and sighs deeply. Not poison, then. But what is it?

And then I realize. Spirits. Like Papa drinks in the evenings of the nights he snores louder than usual. "For the constitution," he often says. I guess whoever abandoned these buildings had many constitutions to build, for there's enough of a supply of spirits to last a thousand summers.

Fist now inspects each of my wounds with one hand, while still clamping on to my hair with the other. Grunting a sound that I hope means I won't die from my wounds, he pulls me to my feet. I am dizzy from the spirits, or from the blood loss, I don't know, but I have no choice but to follow the Cheese as he pulls me roughly behind him, the orange fireless flare leading us out of this room.

The next room is empty but for a pile of . . . something . . . in a corner. Fabric of some sort, I cannot tell. Fist walks to the pile, and, yes, it is a bunch of stained and ripped shirts and pants. There are also discarded vials and needles, empty medicine packets stamped with the Star Farmers seal. But how can that be? Homesteaders have never been allowed in these buildings.

Fist pushes and kicks at the pile until I see that underneath is a hatch, just like the hiding pit at home. I wonder if he means to take us into a pit to hide from the storm. It seems to be over, but they are known to flare back up and last for days.

Fist lifts the trapdoor and descends a rickety set of metal stairs, pulling me in behind him. The stairs go some distance. This is no mere pit. By the time we hit soft dirt my heart is stopping and stuttering from the exertion and from the feeling of darkness closing in on me. Just when I'm afraid I will cry out from the dark, Fist holds the glowing orange stick in front of my face and gestures for me to stay. He then begins climbing back up the stairs.

What?

Is he going to leave me down here? Alone? With no light?

I scramble for my gogs, knowing the night sight will only last seconds. They can barely hold a charge on normal days, and today the suns were blocked by those awful storm clouds.

I click on the gogs and see Fist climbing the stairs. I zoom in, watching his lean bronze back covered in silver and gold spirals as he ascends. His clothes are a shirt and pants combined into one piece. The back and front of the shirt part are open, showing the paint. And the material fits him tightly, almost like a stocking for his body. It's made of a material I do not know. Perhaps dactyl skin.

Fist reaches the top of the stairs and pushes his head and torso up through the trapdoor.

"You gum Cheese!" I yell. "You can't just leave me here!"

I can't see what he's doing, but he's not climbing all the way out. The muscles in his back contort. He's pulling something. And then the trapdoor closes and he begins climbing back down the stairs.

He was covering the trapdoor, I think. Just like at home. He's not leaving me. I am awash with relief. It makes me want to laugh in a terrible way, to be relieved to still hold company with the Cheese who has wreaked such havoc upon me and my own.

My gogs fail and I slide them back down around my neck. I can hear Fist's footfalls clanking down the stairs, chasing away the crawling darkness. The faint orange glow shows his feet, clad in strange shoes that mold to his toes, showing each digit individually, as if he is wearing no shoes at all. In sharp contrast to the rest of his brutally elegant appearance, his shoes are so ugly they are almost indecent. But practical, I guess. Not nearly as heavy or sweaty as boots, and still offering protection from the blistering sands.

Fist appears at my side and takes my arm. He leads me a few meters ahead and the walls begin to close tightly around us. We are in a tunnel.

There is no end in sight.

12

FIST HAS PUSHED ME AHEAD OF HIM TO LEAD the way, I guess so I don't try to turn around and run the other direction. He has given me the fireless flare to hold. It only lights a small distance in front of my feet, so I move slow. Plus, I am weak from my injuries and from the spirits, so I'm not sure I could move fast if I wanted to.

I walk, trudging ahead. The tunnel has widened around us. It's big enough for me to ride Heetle through, and only have to barely duck my head. I wonder if, wherever we're going, I will see Heetle again. And Temple and Boone. Maybe even Benny, whom I don't remember at all.

And Rory. Of course, Rory.

"That gum tunnel!" Rory might say, laughing and shaking her head. "Tromp, tromp, tromp for a million days and nights. You'd think they were taking us to meet the gods themselves!"

Something flutters along the footpath and I think it's a sandmoth drawn to the light, but no. It is a small, ripped piece of canvas. My breath catches in my throat. I pretend to stumble and I grab at the canvas. Fist squeezes my arm with his rough hand and pulls me to my feet. He says something that I don't understand, but probably means "Watch it." Or "Be careful." That's what his tone says.

I hold the canvas in my pocket and take a quick chance to look at it. Though the glow from the flameless flare makes everything look orange, I can see the smudges on the canvas that are red from the dirt. My heart quickens and I know it's crazy, but I also know Temple is a smart kid.

Sure enough, a little farther down the footpath I see another piece of smudged canvas. She's ripping up her apron, or her gloves, to leave a trail. She must be! I start walking faster. Maybe we can catch up to her and her Cheese. I need to know she's okay.

We walk for a long time, and always, just when I'm about to give up, I find another shred of Temple's canvas and it gives a kind of magical power to my legs and feet to just keep moving, even though I want to collapse.

Fist has started to chant, low and rumbling. I wish I could understand his words. Is he asking for forgiveness? Is he offering a blessing before he kills me? After a time, the chanting becomes more like a low, vibrating singing. It's like a night beetle calling in the darkness, and even though right now I hate this man, this Cheese, more than anything, it strikes me how beautiful his low singing is. It's mournful with melodies I've never heard. I don't realize I've stopped to listen to him until he gently pushes my arm and I turn around to walk again.

We've been in the tunnel so long now I wonder if we're going to stop and sleep in it at some point, or just keep walking until I pass out on my feet. My thoughts drift to Papa's lifeless form clumped upon the cooling flats. Aunt Billie isn't even missing us yet, as we aren't due home for a few days. If someone like Old Man Dan finds Papa out there it won't matter if he's dead or alive, he will seek retribution for our violating the cooling crystal harvesting season.

Up ahead there is a faint glow of dark-red light. Nighttime. I've no idea where the tunnel leads, but I'm thrilled at the prospect of fresh air and catching up with Temple. Fist stops singing when he notices the light. He pulls at my arm and we change places, him in front and me behind him.

It is not long before we emerge from the mouth of the tunnel into the night. The storm clouds have passed, leaving a clear night sky, the Red Crescent hanging low, a frown judging us all.

We are at the *Origin* wreckage, in the middle of the gorge. I have only seen this from such a far distance above I had no idea of the magnitude of the ship—or what's left of the ship. Its burned-out bulk is like a monstrous skeleton, reaching dozens of hands above me and almost as far as I can see in front of me. I can see where pieces of the ship have been scavenged, where people have cut holes and entered the carcass.

Fist walks through a crack in the wreckage and I follow, awed by the presence of the broken beast that brought my infant parents and long-gone grandparents to this rock. I think of the noises and the smells of the crash. Of the screaming and dying. I see scorch marks on the wreckage and wonder if they are from the crash or from the fighting with the Cheese after the crash. Am I really standing on the same ground where the Origin Massacre took place? I shiver.

It takes many minutes to make our way cautiously through the weathered destruction. When we finally emerge on the other side I see that a small campsite has been set up. Several dactyls graze on something gruesome; there are blankets on the ground, a pile of rocks to the side, having been cleared, I imagine, to make lying down more comfortable. There is a Cheese sitting on one of the blankets, and a figure next to him.

Even though she is facing away from me, I know it's Temple.

"Temple!" I run to her, ignoring the shouts from Fist, and kneel in front of her. Her head leans heavily against the Cheese's arm, leaving a faint but bloody streak. Her eyes have a woozy look, but she smiles when she sees me.

"Did you get my messages?" she asks. Her voice is soft, quiet, like she's half asleep.

I nod and take her hand. It's cold and damp. "Your little sandmoths led me to you." My muddled brain wants to offer a reassuring smile, but my face will not comply. "Thank you for letting me know you're okay."

She coughs out a laugh and grimaces. "Well, I don't know if I'm okay, but I'm alive and I was sure hoping you were, too, Rae." She swallows and her eyes focus a little better. "May we never be tossed in the air by dactyls again." She puts her hand to her head and winces. I put my hand gently on her wound, inspecting it to see how deeply it goes. It seems to be a scratch, really, not nearly as bad as I thought. Even so . . . Temple is bleeding and I did not stop it from happening.

"He did this to you," I say. It is not a question. I stand, ready to leap on the Cheese who is next to her; the Cheese who is eyeing me with what appears to be amusement playing at his bony upper lip. He is smaller than Fist, but thicker. I think I am surely faster than he is and for a brief moment I debate grabbing Temple and making a run for it through the gorge.

Temple puts a hand on my arm. "My injuries are from the dactyl, Rae. The Cheese . . . she has been only kind to me."

"She?" I say. I look at the stout warrior in front of me, all muscle and scales and ferocity. "How do you know?"

"Darker lips, wider hips." Temple says. She shrugs. "You do not pay attention during lessons, Rae."

I am not sure I believe her. This raider is a girl? The idea that something of this sort is possible makes my aching head ache more. The gods forbid women to do so many things. But then, I remind myself, the Cheese do not worship the same gods we do. Or possibly any gods at all. See? I do remember lessons.

Now it is Temple's turn to inspect my injuries. I try not to jerk back as she runs her hand over my cheekbone and nose.

"This is not from a dactyl, then?" she says in a low voice, her eyes sparking in the light of the Red Crescent.

"Fist and I have had some differences of opinion," I say.

"This should all be a dream, Rae," Temple says, putting her face in her hands. "But it's not all a dream, is it? It's not all just a terrible dream?"

I lean forward and put my arms around her even though it hurts us both. "It's going to be okay, Temple. We'll make it okay."

"How?"

Her question cuts almost as deep as the dactyl's talons. Because she's right. How do I know things will be okay? "I don't know," I answer, and she buries her face in my searing shoulder.

The woman Cheese sitting next to Temple stands up and goes off with Fist a few steps away, where they talk in a low buzz.

"Do you think Papa is okay?" Temple whispers. "Have you seen anything of Boone?"

I don't know how to answer her. Did she see Papa

crumpled up like that? I don't want to ask her. I don't want to think about it.

The woman Cheese walks back over and hands us each a small, rough bag. She puts her hand to her mouth a few times to indicate "eat." She even seems to smile, showing off rows of sharpened teeth. Temple smiles back, but I do not.

Inside the bag are something like a biscuit, a few pinches of scrub tied with twine, and some small brown balls that do not look appetizing at all. I take out the scrub and frown. "This is food?"

Temple shrugs. The girl Cheese makes an "eat" hand motion again. I am starved, but not inclined to eat scrub. I put it back in the bag and take out the biscuit. It is hard and nearly tasteless—much like the biscuits we cook. I swallow it in three bites. My stomach is far from full but I am loath to eat scrub or to taste the foul-looking brown balls. I see Temple peering into her bag and sighing. If Rory were here she would have eaten everything from all of our bags by now. She was not picky, that one.

I take out a brown ball, and thinking of Rory, close my eyes and toss the whole thing into my mouth. I am expecting something foul, but instead my mouth is coated in smooth sweetness. The ball has melted onto my tongue. I don't even need to chew. The sweetness glides down my throat and into my belly, and I don't know if it's the sheer hunger I feel, or the actuality of the food, but it is the best gum thing I have ever tasted.

I open my eyes to see Temple staring at me intently.

"Temple," I say, licking my fingers and then reaching into my bag for another ball. "You have never tasted such a wonder." I put the second ball in my mouth and it is just as wonderful as the first.

Temple gasps and then smiles huge, the melted brown smeared across her teeth. "Rae, what *is* this?"

"I don't know, Temp," I say, eating the last of mine. "But now I know why Rory and Benny haven't come home."

As soon as it's out of my mouth, I regret it. Now is not the time for the blackest of humor. But the food and the sweetness have relaxed my charged-up nerves. I feel calmer, more energized, but less angry. I wonder if it's something in the food making me feel this way. An herb maybe? My studies with Aunt Billie have only just begun. It is difficult to tell all the roots and herbs apart. She would know, though. Aunt Billie seems to know everything.

Temple begins to chew on her parcel of scrub. She makes a face and I smile. "Not a magical new dinner accompaniment, your scrub?" I ask. Temple grimaces and swallows.

"It's not so bad," she says, picking tiny dried leaves from her teeth. "Though I'm not sure I can find the nutritional merit." She laughs quietly.

I take small crunches of my own scrub, wondering why the Cheese would eat such a thing, and then a wave of exhaustion hits me and the world turns on its side. Of course. The bitter taste on the back of my tongue gently shakes my memory. Sleeping root. The Cheese have drugged us. Such gum stupid children.

As my eyes close I see that Temple is already asleep—it is alarming how quickly her laughter was snuffed out.

13

I AWAKE AND IT IS STILL NIGHT.

Temple is sleeping at my side; Fist is sleeping at the entrance to the tunnel, which I see is now concealed with wreckage, blending seamlessly into the *Origin* tableau. The woman Cheese is sprawled out not too far from Fist, her snores echoing over to us.

Standing, I shake my head, clearing the clouds from the sleeping root. My wounds are sore, but feeling better. Perhaps there was a healing herb mixed in with the sleeping root. I roll my shoulders and neck, touch the sore spots on my face, my lip. I would not make a pretty sight for anyone looking at me, that is the truth.

I expect the Cheese thought I'd be unconscious much longer than this, but having suffered from so many illnesses as a child, and having had to be sedated to be treated, I have developed quite a tolerance for sleeping root. One point for the weakling Rae.

It is not worth trying for escape. I feel like the worst kind of fool not to even try, with our captors sleeping at some distance from us, but my lessons have taught me that the gorge spans the whole moon. Its walls are so high I cannot see over them. Somewhere up there, the homestead leans in the wind. If only I had the wings of angels to bring me home.

I glance at the dactyl nest in the distance. There is only one dactyl now, curled up, asleep. Too bad those wings won't do. I imagine it chasing me and Temple as we try for escape, potentially playing tossing games with us in the air once again. It is just not worth the risk to Temple or to myself. So rather than plot and scheme an inevitable failure of an escape, I instead walk softly to the side of the destruction that was once the *Origin*.

Temple and I—and Boone and Rory, and all of the children of Origin Township—have been told stories of the *Origin* since before we could talk ourselves. Tales of bravery and sacrifice, stories of horror turned into myths of how unstoppable mankind can be when faced with adversity. I am standing in front of both school lessons and bedtime stories. I put my hand on the metal, surprised at the coolness it holds on such a sweltering night. This is the blackened, hollowed-out history of my people on this moon.

I step through a hole in the hull and into the ship. The

many numbered floors above me have collapsed to rubble at my feet, leaving a mess that is thirty summers old and unrecognizable. The dirt and dust that seeps into everything blows in drifts at my feet, and sprinkles down from the jagged holes that tower above me. I try to imagine the ship as it flew through space, holding my grandparents, who were young, with babes in arms; holding other young families; holding hope for the human species; holding pioneers who had been promised distant lands through the Star Farmers Act.

Faded and peeling paint shows the way to exits that no longer exist. Walls are stripped of the shelving and whatever equipment survived the crash. The glow from the Red Crescent eerily reflects off the weathered interior and I wonder if this was what it was like just before the crash—a dark-red emergency glow.

A hand on my shoulder stills my blood. I swallow, turn slowly, and it is Temple's Cheese. Her throat rumbles, vibrating like a bug. She opens her mouth, her bony, beaklike upper lip showing a row of sharpened teeth. The vibrating in her throat increases in line with the rate of my heartbeat. Her hand does not grip me like Fist's did, but sits gently, and I am surprised by this.

"You," she manages to say in a low, guttural voice. "This." Her eyes look toward the sky that breaks through the holes in the ceiling. "Not . . . sssssafe." She motions for me to follow her out of the wreck, but I am frozen.

"You speak my language?" I say stupidly. "But how?"

"I have old," she says slowly, chewing the words. "I learn much."

"Did you learn from someone?" I ask, the hairs standing up along my neck. "A girl? Younger than me? A girl named—"

She holds out a hand. "Come now. Not sssssafe."

"But . . . ," I say, and she, apparently having had enough of me not listening, grabs my hand and pulls me hard, my shoulder throwing lightning bolts of pain down my arm. She is very strong and I lose my footing, toppling onto her. We roll out of the *Origin* and onto the scrub. There is a deafening crash. A boulder has fallen into the wreck, collapsing more of the ceiling onto where I just stood.

I lie on top of the Cheese, on the scrub, smelling her sweat, feeling her scaly arms under me. She smiles and rolls me off of her. She points to the *Origin*.

"I have telling you this," she says, with a smirk.

"What?" I say. "Did you just say 'I told you so'?" She nods and tries to stifle a laugh. I have never heard a Cheese laugh before. It is a snuffling snicker almost like Heetle when she sees a sweetroot cube.

"What is your name?" I ask the woman Cheese. "I am Ramona Darling but everyone calls me Rae. My sister is Temple." I look to my feet, feeling a burning behind my eyes that is embarrassing. "Thank you . . . for not hurting her." I look up and she is regarding me with her shiny black eyes, her head barely tilted to one side, the red ropes of her hair fanning out in the predawn breeze.

"Where are you taking us?" I whisper. "My papa and Aunt Billie will be beside themselves with grief."

Her eyes roll up to the sky again, and I realize she's thinking—trying to find the right words.

"I am . . ."—and she smiles—"One Who Talk Too Many Word." Then she says something that sounds like, "Jo-keel-i-kern-hall."

"Can I call you Jo?" I ask. "That sounds better to me than 'cornhole.'"

She looks to the sky again, and smiles, showing off those terrifying, sharpened warrior teeth. "Jo." She pats her chest. "Is nice. Jo Who Talk Too Many Word."

I smile back, feeling my lip split anew at the movement. "I, too, talk too many words."

"Rae Too Too," Jo says, smiling.

"No," I say, "just Rae. Not Too Too—"

"Rae Tootie." Jo nods.

"No—"

A growl behind me interrupts us. I turn and Fist is there, face narrowed and pinched, disapproving. He says something to Jo, and Jo responds in stiff words like when Aunt Billie tells Papa not to discuss the lack of merits in her biscuits.

"He say," Jo says to me, looking to the sky once more, then back to my face. "He say your name should be She Who Cry the Most and Never Think Before She Act." Then she says it in Cheese language and it is full of trilling tongue noises and something like a cough at the end.

"That's a very long name," I say, raising my bleeding lip in a snarl, "for someone who has known me but one cycle of the suns."

"He's got you pegged like a hat on the wall, Rae," Temple says from a few hands away where she is sitting up on the blanket.

"He and Papa share some characteristics, then," I mutter.

Jo goes off a distance while Fist stands, feet apart, arms crossed over his chest, and watches me. Jo returns with handfuls of . . . something. It looks like a combination of small seeds and prairie beetle droppings. She offers some to Temple, who holds her hand out.

"Temple!" I shout. "No! What if they're trying to drug us again?" Temple licks her lips hungrily, but retracts her hand. Jo regards me, eyes squinting. Then, in one quick stride she is upon me, her claws squeezing my cheeks open. I struggle to escape, but this only causes her claws to scratch my already bruised and sore face.

She pushes a handful of the something into my mouth and I spit it back in her face. She clacks her beaky jaws and squeezes my cheeks harder. I cry out and Temple yells, "Rae!"

Jo smashes another handful into my mouth and presses my jaw shut, forcing me to chew. Instead of tasting like death or sleeping root, the flavor is a combination that is sweet and sturdy. There is no bitterness on my tongue at all. I shoot her a look that I hope can cause physical pain as I reluctantly begin to chew on my own.

I can feel strength coming from whatever this is, and I know that I won't have to eat much of it to feel full. I cannot believe that beetle droppings would be sweet and chewy and flavorful, but I don't know what else this could be.

Jo releases my face and makes a snuffling noise like, *See? It's just food. Good gods, you gum child.* She offers some to Temple. Temple looks at me and I nod, feeling foolish. She takes a handful and nearly inhales it. Jo offers me more, which I gladly take in my hand instead of smashed into my mouth.

I hold up a dark lump. "What is this?" I ask Jo.

"Is . . . ah . . . fruits from hashava plant."

I don't know what this is, but that's okay. I am not eating bug leavings or being drugged and so my morning has brightened considerably.

Jo rolls up the blankets and lashes them to the side of a dactyl that has been quietly snapping its jaws off to the side of our camp. "Is long journey," Jo shouts over her shoulder. "We take . . . ah . . . I know not your word. *Kwihuutsuu.*"

"*Kwihuutsuu?*" I repeat, and point to the dactyl. "You mean dactyls?"

"Dak-teels?" Jo says, and scrunches up her face. "No pretty word for such pretty . . . ah . . . beast."

Fist stamps his foot, shouts, and claps his hands together. He is getting impatient with us. Jo suddenly grabs Temple hard along the waist and holds her easily as Temple, wide eyed and frightened, struggles to free herself. I don't understand what is happening. We were all just talking, and now . . . now what is Jo doing?

I run to her, yelling, "Let Temple be!" and pull my arm back, hoping to strike Jo hard enough to get her to drop the squirming girl. In an almost lazy move, Jo reaches out a hand and pushes me into the dirt. I land on my behind in a puff of dust. As I scramble to my feet, intent on putting up a bigger fight, Jo ignores me, taking a handful of dirt, spitting into it several times and then rubbing it throughout Temple's long hair. Temple shouts and ducks and tries to get away from the Cheese, but Jo continues to hold her tight as she works. I realize she is not hurting Temple. She is disguising her. When Jo is done, Temple's blond hair is matted and red and can almost pass for Cheese hair. Jo eyes me. Fist says something and then shrugs.

"He say nothing to do with you." She points her finger to the first sun rising above the gorge. "It is up to Oonatka to make"—she motions long hair, then holds out her hair and drops it back down to below her shoulders—"for you. We can wait only."

I am not sure why this long-hair business is so gum important to all living creatures but me, but I don't ask. Fist is glowering and the ovals on the sides of his head are throbbing. I feel I should not encourage conversation at this moment.

Jo, too, sees Fist's unrest and lifts Temple onto the back of the dactyl. Temple doesn't laugh and smile like she does when I toss her onto Heetle, but she doesn't look terrified anymore. She is holding some strands of red, matted hair in her hand and turning them over and over. She has a spark in her eye that I recognize—she is curious. And yet, I know she cannot have forgotten about Papa and Boone so soon. She cannot be . . . *liking* . . . these animal Cheese.

There is a cry and a cloud of dust and another dactyl lands by us. How do they know to come? I turn and see that Fist has blown into a silent whistle that hangs on a string around his neck.

Fist pushes at me in the small of my back and mutters something. I climb onto the beast—the *Kwihuutsuu*—and Fist climbs on in front of me. He repeats his movements of yesterday, tying us together on the back of the creature, then with a shout and a squeeze of his knees my stomach is left swirling in the scrub as the dactyl flies straight up and out of the gorge.

The hulk of the *Origin* grows smaller as we climb higher. I pull on my gogs and the compass tells me we are moving to the south. I throw a glance behind me and tap my gogs to zoom in. We are already too far up and away to catch even a glimpse of the homestead. We are heading to the lands never settled, or even explored, by humans. The lands past the gorge. The lands we could never reach.

Temple's *Kwihuutsuu* is no more than ten hands from us now. Her newly red hair flies out behind her in the swirling wind. She could be a child of the Cheese from this angle. No one would see the difference.

14

JO WAS RIGHT. IT IS A LONG JOURNEY. A DAY, A night, and another day on the backs of our dactyls. It has been quite a trick trying to relieve myself while flying thousands of hands above the moon. My skirt will need to be burned.

Fist seems practiced in such riding. He has barely eaten, has not relieved himself one time, and does not seem fatigued at all. The *Kwihuutsuu*, as well, seems full of boundless energy, like it is of the wind itself.

At points during the journey, the two *Kwihuutsuu* would slow so that Fist and Jo could speak, shouting over the wind. I would ask Temple if she was okay, and she would seem exhilarated by the ride. I can say with surety, though, that if I am needing food and drink at this point, Temple must be barely conscious.

I tap Fist on the shoulder for the hundredth time. He turns for the first time.

"Drink!" I shout. "Food!" I point to my mouth, my stomach. I make a face like I am dead to show him that he is starving me. He says something that is garbled by the wind, but that I wouldn't have understood anyway.

Below us, I see what I think he was talking about. In the near distance, smoke rises on the wind and caves are nestled into rock walls that reach high into the sky, but not quite as high as we are. And far, far ahead of us, there is something strange. A darkness looms on the horizon, vast mounds of land.

"What is that?" I shout, pointing past Fist's face, at the darkness.

His head turns slightly, and he smiles. It is not a mean smile or a scary smile, it reaches all the way to his eyes, making creases in his scaly face I have not yet seen. It is a smile of relief, of happiness.

"Ebibi," he shouts back, smiling broadly now. "EBIBI!" He touches his chest and briefly closes his eyes. He gives the *Kwihuutsuu* a quick kick and we fly fast and low, landing with grace in front of a fire pit in the middle of the ring of caves. Just behind us land Jo and Temple.

Fist unties me from the back of the *Kwihuutsuu* and I fairly fall off, landing in the scrub, leaving an embarrassing streak of filth down the side of the creature as I fall. I lie in the scrub, trying to catch my breath, wondering if I'm having a breathing attack or if it's from hunger, or anticipation.

106

I close my eyes and start to count, low, under my breath.

A foot nudges at my rib cage and I open my eyes. What I see startles me so much, I scurry backward a few hands as if I am an insect, turned over on its back. Hundreds of black eyes peer down at me. Hundreds of Cheese with their beaky, bony upper lips, chattering in low vibrations. Hundreds of throbbing ear skins as they listen to my groans and to the winds and to the loud *Kwihuutsuu* as the beasts caw and chirp at treats they are given.

Hands reach down and pat me all over, tugging at my shift, poking at me. There are snuffling giggles directed at my skirt, and hands patting my hair, my face, rubbing and pulling on my ears. They are murmuring something that sounds like, "*Lolobee, lolobee, lolobee,*" over and over again. It is all very indecent seeming. And then, there are so many hands on my ears, pulling, hurting, that I clap my own hands over my ears and start shaking my head with my elbows pointed out, to make some space for myself. The Cheese will pull me apart!

The hands lift me now and a few of the Cheese jump back, their hands covering their noses and mouths. Yes. I stink. Amid the scuffle of hands and noise of incomprehensible chattering I see another clot of Cheese surrounding what must be Temple. Their noises are more joyful than the disgusted noises of my crowd. Or maybe I am just hearing it wrong.

The hands turn me by my shoulders and I am face-to-face—well, face to chest—with an extraordinarily tall, thin Cheese, with fingers long as shine tree needles. This Cheese has wider hips and dark lips like Jo, but is not stout and fierce. She is lithe and graceful, her turtle nose is upturned in an almost elegant way. She smiles at me even as she wrinkles her nose in disgust. Her hair ropes fall down her chest to almost her waist, and are decorated with bits of metal that seem to match the metal of the *Origin*. Her eyes are big, her skin scaly, but smooth. She has very high cheekbones and looks like an ancient image we studied once with one of the scholars. It was an image I could never forget because of the woman's profile and the strong eye staring at me from the drawing on the scholar's slate. Like that eye knew something about me. Like it knew the world.

The new woman Cheese walks alongside me as another Cheese pushes me out of the crowd toward a cave. I dig in my heels. "Temple," I say. "My sister. Can I see her?" But as I turn I see that Temple is on Jo's shoulders and Jo is running through the crowd with her while other Cheese pat Temple's knees and she giggles, holding Jo's hair like reins.

"*Kala omma*," the tall Cheese says, and I am sure to my bones that she means, "Your sister is fine."

We walk into a cave that is lit by small fires contained in stone vessels. There are rugs on the floor and some on the walls, though mostly the walls are bare red rock. There is an area to the side that has been carved out of the stone wall and I see bowls stacked and rough fabric bags. There is a low-burning fire near the entrance, the smoke escaping through the doorway. This must be their kitchen. The woman Cheese pushes me farther and farther back into the cave and I am surprised it goes so far. The air cools around us and dampens and at my feet there is a lapping pool of water. I lean down and let my fingers skim the surface.

"Ha!" I shout with glee, before realizing I have done so. The Cheese tilts her head at me, her eyes going soft. She walks into the pool, which appears to be as deep as her waist, which is nearly neck high for me, and she motions for me to come to her. I do not have to be asked twice. I would not care if this pool held ten hundred Rae-eating monsters, it would be worth being eaten to feel the coolness over my whole body.

Still, I have never seen water pooled in such a way before. Our tanks at home are filled from the wings of angels, Papa always says, assuring me that miracles are a daily fact in our blessed Origin Township. I wonder if there must be pools like this somewhere near the township, though. Surely it is more reasonable to believe in hidden pools of water rather than angels. But no one ever told me about any pools—or told anyone that I know about any such thing.

I feel a pang of betrayal as I step into the water.

The Cheese points to my boots.

"*Ottan*," she says.

"Off?" I say. "Take them off?"

She nods. "Owfffff."

I lean down and unlace my boots, placing them on the dusty floor just out of reach of the water. The coolness between my toes makes me gasp out loud and the Cheese laughs. It sounds a lot like Jo laughing, an animal-like snuffling that is so filled with comfort that I both ache for Heetle and ache for the ability to make a noise like that myself.

I would like to take off my skirt and shift, too, and throw myself naked into the coolness, but I feel too modest with this woman Cheese, even if she is not a human. I pull my gogs from around my neck and place them by my boots. Then I walk farther into the water, feeling my skirt grow heavy and feeling the tickle of bubbles rising up my legs. Soon I am within arm's length of the Cheese and she reaches out, snatching me by the elbow and then pushing me completely underwater.

My arms fly out instinctively, my lungs fill with liquid as I struggle. She pulls my head out of the water and I cough, splutter, and choke out streams of water. Then, with a mighty strength, she pulls off my clothes and flings them from the pool. They land with a loud *thwap* on the floor of the cave.

Naked and shivering, I feel my joy at the cool water running cold in my veins as her abnormally long fingers grip me around my belly. She produces a rag from gods only know where and begins scrubbing at my hair, my face, my back, my arms. The water is soon tinted pink because the blood from my wounds is running freely again from the roughness of her scrubbing. I cry out a few times, but try to remain silent. She does not seem to be hurting me on purpose, though I can't help but struggle and fight against the pain. She is terribly strong and not gentle, but she moves with purpose, scrubbing off days of muck and gunk and grit and dirt.

When she is done, she releases me and I scramble out of the water. I am gasping for breath, shivering, naked and terrified. She climbs out of the water after me. I flinch at her closeness but she brushes by, disappearing farther into the cave. For a moment I think she's left me by myself, but she returns with a folded stack of fabric. She drops it by my shoes, motions that I am meant to cover myself with what apparently is a towel.

I do as instructed, even as she stares, feeling cold and vulnerable in my nakedness. I quickly wrap the towel around me. The Cheese woman kneels in front of me, grabbing my hands, roughly pulling me, trying to get me closer to her. I do not want to be closer to her. I ache from the journey, I ache from my wounds, I ache from her rough cleaning. I just want to be left alone.

I twist my body, jerk my arms, resist her pulling, and the flat of her hand meets my cheek in a stinging slap. Gulping air, trying not to cry, trying not to look weak, I resist for another moment but she is too strong.

She pulls me close and begins plastering my wounds with a poultice. It smells of mint and roots that so fiercely remind me of Aunt Billie I know the stinging in my eyes is not just from the pain of the herbs, but from one that goes deeper. The Cheese binds the poultice into my shoulders with rough fabric that she ties off in knots, and then she hands me a shirt made of dactyl skin that has no sleeves and seems invented to show off my weakling arms and bandages. It is against the word of the gods for women and girls to show their arms in a polite setting of both men and women, and so I balk at the shirt. She hits me again, though her eyes seem strangely calm as she does so. She does not show the fire and spark that Papa does when he strikes me. She thrusts the shirt at me. I spit on it. She grabs me around the waist with one arm and as I struggle with the last bit of energy I have, she forces the shirt onto me. She is so very strong.

Next she holds out a small strip of fabric that is apparently supposed to serve as diaper-looking pants, but I would rather eat actual beetle droppings than put it on, so I take the pants and fling them into the pool. She blows air from her mouth, grabs my face with a clawed hand. I feel the sharpness of her nails digging into both cheeks as she squeezes my face, forces me to look at her. She shouts something I do not understand. I shout back, "I will not wear your gum ugly indecent pants!" and for a moment we have a standoff. By now I do not care if she hits me again. My body is going numb from so much pain already.

After another moment of staring and shouting, she roughly releases my cheeks and stalks off into the distance. She returns with a wad of coarse fabric and throws it into my chest. Pants. I put them on and she kneels in front of me, tying a piece of twine around my waist to keep the pants up. She pulls tightly at the twine, making me gasp. If she were human, I would swear she clucked her tongue at my stubbornness, or maybe about how skinny I am. But she is not human.

The Cheese pushes me back to the front of the cave, where there is a boy near my age, maybe older, it's hard to tell because his Cheese features are so different from mine. He is sitting on the floor, restringing a handbow that looks to be older than us both combined.

The Cheese woman says something to him, her voice sharp, commanding. She nudges his foot, clad in the ridiculous Cheese shoes that hug every toe. He slowly lifts his head and his gaze meets mine. He looks me up and down twice, leans back on one elbow, and does the snickering, snuffling Cheese laugh for so long that the woman Cheese rolls her eyes, says a few more sharp words, and pushes me out of the mouth of the cave.

It is near evening now. Cheese walk through the village carrying animal hides and baskets, talking to one another in small clumps. A group appears to be gathering in the center of the village common area around the fire pit. I look for Temple, but do not see her. I think of Boone and wonder what has happened to him, not daring to go to the dark places my mind suggests.

I hear a laugh on the breeze and my heart stops. Can it be? But no. It's just a higher-pitched Cheese snuffle. Not Rory. How could it be Rory? I look at my right hand, my missing finger. Rory took her shine tree needle full in her flank. There's no way she survived. No way.

"You don't know anything," she'd say to me if she were here. Laughing, swiping her hair from her eyes. "So serious all the time, Rae. Like the Red Crescent is just sitting on your shoulders all gum day." She'd snatch me up in a hug if no one was looking. A quick hug. A tight hug.

More Cheese begin filing out of the caves, congregating around the fire that is now sputtering to life. Some of them are wearing clothes like I have never seen. A woman has cooling crystals woven into her hair, blue paint cascading down her arms in intricate circles. A man is painted black as night with yellow spots dotting his face and body and even hair. Another Cheese is wearing dactyl skin colored yellow—bright yellow, like the suns. And then there is a child, covered in red, laughing and running with other children. Thin ropes trail for several hands behind the child, tied to the child's ankles. At the ends of the ropes are knobs of rock that spark and flash as they hit the stones littering the scrub under our feet. It is the most magnificent display I have ever seen.

I look again for Temple, but do not see her.

Firm hands press on my shoulders and I sit on a rock bench that is one of many that encircle the fire. I look to see who has made me sit, expecting the elegant, fierce woman cheese, or even Fist or Jo, but it is someone new. A Cheese with startling blue eyes that remind me of Temple's. He smiles and puts a hand on my arm.

114

This Cheese is no Cheese at all. He is a human man. He does not have the claw nails or the scales or the bony upper lip. His hair is similar to theirs, but when I stare I see it is caked in dirt much like Temple's was after Jo had finished with it. This man has grown his fingernails to points and when he smiles I see that he has sharpened some of his teeth as well.

"They tell me you are Mayrikafsa . . . She Who Cry the Most." His language is rusty and bears the trills and grunts of the Cheese.

"My name is Ramona Darling," I say.

The blue-eyed man-Cheese's eyebrows raise sky high. "Did you say 'Darling'?"

I nod. He shakes his head and looks to the sky, sighing. "It has been a long time since I heard that name." He looks down and stares hard at me, his face expressionless. "You are Ramona Darling no more, my little cousin. Not after this night."

I am readying to speak, feeling affronted, just realizing he has said the word "cousin," when the music begins. It is low, like insects on the prairie, but builds quickly into a frenzy that reminds me of a swarm, the music flying through my ears and making my chest thump. It is a combination of humming, whistling, and a beat drummed with sticks on the stones themselves.

The woman with cooling crystals dances to the center of the ring of benches, in front of the fire. The suns have gone low now and the Red Crescent looms, lending a dark-red hue to the sky with its glowing frown.

Her arms reach into the air and back down again, her legs bending at the knees and propelling her gracefully into leaps around the fire.

"This dancer represents Mara," the blue-eyed Cheese whispers in my ear. "The god of wind."

The woman playing Mara gracefully leaps and reaches until she is moving so quickly she is nearly a blur. The yellow-dressed Cheese cries out and runs through the fire. Right gum through it. I gasp and the blue-eyed Cheese laughs. As the man leaps from the fire, his costume smoking but not burning, he lifts Mara over his head and carries her in a circle.

"This is Oonatka," the man whispers to me. "God of the first of the suns. He steals Mara, the wind."

I want to ask questions, but find that I am loath to miss any part of this production. Oonatka and Mara dance-fight around the fire until a woman in yellow I did not see before appears. She, too, runs right through the fire, and then is dancing alongside the man in yellow as they leap and twirl, giving dance-chase to Mara.

"And this is Oonan, goddess of the second sun. She is Oonatka's sister. They must decide to share the wind between them." I can sense he is looking at my face, measuring my reaction to the scene before me. I cannot hide my awe or surprise at the spectacle, even though I want to be obstinate. Who are these Cheese to steal me away from my family, my home, injure me, embarrass me, and then show me beautiful things?

The two sun gods are now throwing something into the fire that makes it spark and burn red. The Cheese on the rock benches watch as raptly as I do, some of them eating seeds from small fabric pouches and whispering and laughing. Parents do not shush the children, but let them run and play and shout, as long as they stay out of the scene playing before them. A mother hands a child a handful of the sweet, brown hashava fruit and it is then that I realize how hungry I am.

As if he can sense my thoughts, the human Cheese pulls out a fabric bag of his own and offers it to me. I intend to devour the entire contents of this bag.

The man painted in black leaps from behind the benches and the Cheese let out a unanimous yelp and then quick snickers. He runs to the fire, throwing handfuls of dust into it until it turns blazing blue.

"Now we have Ebibi," the human Cheese whispers through the seeds in his mouth. He touches his chest and closes his eyes. "Ebibi, the god of darkness, wants Mara as well."

Ebibi dramatically pulls at Mara's arms and the suns release the wind to him, but still give chase for some reason. The dance is around the fire, but also through the audience. There are shrieks and gasps, and the faces of the Cheese are distorted by the flashing blue flames. I am feeling dizzy and disoriented after the dreamlike quality of this night. I close my eyes to steady myself. When I open them, the dance-chase is slowing as the music becomes a quiet twinkle. There is a child's giggle as the adult dancers begin to slow their movements exaggeratedly. The child appears, chasing fast circles around the slower adult gods, kicking up sparks from the stones tied to his ankles.

"A'akow," whispers the blue-eyed Cheese. "Child god of fire, representative of A'akowitoa, this blazing-hot moon we live on. Oonatka and Oonan, Ebibi, too, are so enamored with the beauty of the fire child they stop fighting, just to watch her. But the fire child does not love them. She only loves Mara, the wind, because Mara can carry her through the air."

The woman playing Mara has broken away from the other dancers and is chasing A'akow, careful of the sparks trailing from the child's feet. The child slows, turns, and is lifted into the air by this woman in blue. The child laughs out loud and I realize, This is no Cheese. This is Temple! Painted, running as if she is one with them!

I stand, spilling the bag of seeds, and start to shout, "Temp—," but the blue-eyed Cheese pulls me back down.

"Ebibi, who is the god of darkness, remember, and the sun gods agree to share watch over the fire child and the wind, to make sure they are safe and protected. The fire child and the wind cannot escape, but they are protected and loved. And they love each other as well." I struggle to stand, to go to Temple, but the man-Cheese holds tightly to my arm. Ignoring my protestations, he looks at me. His mouth is smiling, but his eyes are not. "It is beautiful, no? There is another part, dealing with Hosani, god of the

Red Crescent, but I have not seen it, myself. It is before my time, and has not been spoken of since the people of Hosani grew very ill and stopped all trade with A'akowitoa and the Kihuut."

He is speaking in so many strange words, I am having trouble understanding what he says. Temple is fully part of the ceremony now, and my brain struggles to make sense of what is happening with her, and of what he's saying. It is too much information at once.

"The Red Crescent?" I sputter finally. "Hosani? What illness? I have only heard stories of homesteaders fighting a series of quickly won but violent battles."

"Of course," he says. "The Origin Massacre."

"No," I say, shaking my head. "The Origin Massacre was when the Cheese killed so many of the survivors of the crash."

The man-Cheese tilts his head to the side and purses his lips. "That's not exactly what happened."

I watch as Temple laughs and runs around the fire. Is she not frightened, as I am? Is she not bewildered by this place, these people?

I put my head in my hands for a moment, then look up. "That *is* exactly what happened. The *Origin* crashed. The Cheese killed many survivors. The people of the Red Crescent joined with the Cheese to battle the *Origin* home-steaders and then there was the Miracle of the Gorge when the homesteaders prevailed."

The blue-eyed Cheese shrugs. "Perhaps I remember my

lessons incorrectly. It has been a long time after all."

The ceremony has continued throughout our conversation. I have so many more questions, but I see the blue woman carrying Temple off into a cave, and I lose my thoughts. The other dancers follow them into the cave as the Cheese build the song into another swarm of sound. Then everything is quiet.

"This is the history of our moon," the man-Cheese whispers. "A history of love and compromise."

Love and compromise? *This* moon? If I weren't so stunned from what I've just seen and heard, I'd laugh.

Fist walks to the center of the circle and begins to chant. He holds his hands above his head and the man-Cheese pulls me to my feet. "Now we enjoy the story of beast versus beast. A celebration of our moon as it is today." He smiles at me, his eyes not quite matching his upturned lips, and it stills my heart. He drags me to Fist even though I dig my heels in, a very bad feeling crawling up my neck. We go past the boy who was in the cave with the pool earlier. The boy stands on one side of the circle, a sneer on his face, his arms crossed over his chest. He watches intently as the man-Cheese pushes me toward Fist. Fist shouts something to the crowd and is answered with a series of cheers and hollers.

The man-Cheese backs away, whispering, "Good luck."

Good luck? My stomach is filled with sandmoths and I regret the heaps of hashava I just ate. My bad feeling grows by leaps and bounds.

Before I even know what's happening, the boy Cheese charges me, his bony head smashing into my chest and knocking me off my feet. My wounds from the dactyl claws burn, chunks of poultice falling from the bindings.

I lie on the dusty ground, stunned, and the boy kicks me in my belly. Entire universes of pain explode through my ribs, my breath dissolving into a series of gasps. Why is he doing this?

The ringing in my ears is loud, but I can still make out the sounds of the crowd. They are cheering. They are cheering for him to beat on me! My face burns as hot as the high-summer suns when the realization hits. They think I am nothing but a gum weakling. A poor, scrawny human girl.

The boy Cheese's foot rears back, but this time I am ready. Despite my exhaustion and the pain in my arms and chest, I grab his foot and pull, knocking him off balance. He falls next to me, his bottom crunching in the dirt. The crowd is on their feet now, shouting, whooping, snickering, yelling words I don't understand. Everything echoes off the surrounding stones, creating such a noise it feels almost electric in the air.

I am still holding the boy's foot as he kicks out, trying to free himself. My grip is tight and strong, despite my missing finger. I have years of tending to a gruff Heetle to thank for this grip.

The boy uses his other foot to smash my fingers, causing me to yell in pain and release his foot. He scrambles to his feet as I scramble to mine. We circle each other like animals while the crowd magnifies its noise. I hope to the gods they do not also make Temple fight like this. Surely even heathens respect that she is too young.

Exhaustion makes my arms and legs heavy. Sweat drips into my eyes, stings the cuts all over my face. My initial burst of frightened energy is waning quickly. I do not want to be fighting. I do not want to be here. I want to fall to my knees and weep. I want to go home.

The boy must see the energy leave my face because he laughs into the sky and charges at me.

Well.

I may be tired, but I am still Ramona Darling and this monster will not win as easily as that. I hold out my arm, stiff, and ram the heel of my hand into his nose. Blood bursts forth as the crowd's noises turn from yells to sympathetic groans.

The boy screams and grabs my arm, pins it behind my back, pushing me to my knees. My vision is clouding at the sides, the pain intolerable. I do the only thing I can think to do, I reach my face around and bite the other hand that grips my shoulder.

He hollers but does not let go. I sink my teeth in deeper, tasting the tang of Cheese blood. My jaw bites so hard that even when his fingers reflexively let go of my shoulder, my mouth holds his hand in place. He is screaming freely now, attempting to shake me off of him, but I hold on tight. I will never let go. I will never let these heathens believe a human can be beaten so easily. Even an injured human, even a scared and bleeding girl-child can best one of these monsters. If Papa can kill a Cheese warrior and save a rope of hair in a box, I can win a fight and save a shred of self-respect in my heart.

I breathe hard as I bite, feeling more animal than I have ever felt before. His screams drown out the screams of the crowd.

There are hands on my shoulders now, a third hand smashing into my face, wrenching my jaw from the boy's hand. I am on my back in the dust, blood everywhere. My blood? His blood? I do not know.

The boy is also on the ground, tears streaming down his face, his hand cradled against his chest. The tall woman is with him now, looking at me with what I can only guess is surprise. Fist stands over me, pulls me to my feet. His dark claws clap me on the back as the crowd cheers wildly. He shouts words I do not understand and the crowd is ebullient, cheering and laughing.

I cannot help but to smile, just a little, as people swarm me, patting me on the back, nodding, approving of my horrific violence. I can only imagine how I look, hair in disarray, dust and dirt and blood everywhere. A human girl-child pushed to the brink of madness.

From nowhere, the man-Cheese is at my side.

"My gods, Mayrikafsa, that was quite a show." The

crowd parts as he leads me close to the fire pit, where Fist and the tall woman are now standing together. The boy sits behind them, an old Cheese tending to his hand.

"I thought I was to watch the *Kwihuutsuu* feast on a weak and terrified girl-child, but you have surprised me. You have surprised us all."

"They were going to feed me to the dactyls if I lost?" My voice is hoarse, I can feel the sticky drying blood cracking on my chin as my mouth moves.

The man-Cheese says nothing as he gently pushes me onto my knees and puts the crook of his elbow around my neck, holding me in place.

"It goes numb fast enough," he says quietly in my ear. My eyes go wide and wild as I see they've brought Temple out, too. I struggle against his arm. "No! No! She cannot fight! She is too young! She . . ." I shout my protests as she is made to kneel next to me, still painted in deep red, her white teeth standing out like stars. Another Cheese holds her in the same way I am being held and she stops smiling.

"Rae?" she says. "Your face. What did you do to that boy? What's . . ."

But she doesn't have time to finish. Fist pulls two long sticks from the flames, sticks of metal that are glowing red at the end. Chanting loudly now, with other chants from the hundreds of Cheese filling in the spaces where he takes a breath, he nods once. The two Cheese holding me and Temple push our heads forward into the dirt.

"Do not struggle," the man-Cheese says in a low voice. "Whatever you do, do not struggle."

I don't know why I listen to him, but I do. My body goes limp. And then there's a searing, fiery pain across the back of my neck as one of the red-hot metal sticks brands my skin. I cry out at the same time Temple does, our screams filling the night air, echoing through the ring of caves.

And then there is such a jubilant cry from the crowd that even as I lie in agonizing pain in the scrub, gasping, choking, my hands held behind my back, I feel the jubilation lifting me up—or, no, hands are lifting me. Temple and I are being carefully carried above the heads of the crowd until we are deposited at the mouth of the cave with the pool. The tall woman is there, the ovals on the sides of her head beating in and out, in and out. The metal in her hair shines in the bloodred light of the Red Crescent. She lifts her silver-and-gold-painted face to the night sky and trills a noise that comes from somewhere that is not shared with humans. Jo appears at her side and translates, pausing as she searches for the right words:

"Now we, Klarakova, *krasnoakafsa* of Kihuut, and A'alanatka, partner and *tontakafsa* to chieftess, watch over you as the gods watch over us. Mayrikafsa, She Who Cry the Most, and Kalashava, She of Sweet Scrub, you are . . . now one with Kihuut, with people of A'akowitoa. You have third eye to watch for blessings and curses. You are us. We . . . you."

The woman walks to us, Fist at her side. They both hold

out their hands, and together, in voices somehow both melodious and made of quakes, they say, "*Lo'a Lia.*"

"Welcome," Jo translates. "Welcome home."

And she places our hands in theirs.

15

THE MORNING COMES EARLY AND THE WORK goes late for the Cheese, too. But in different ways than with the settlers. I am in an open space of dirt and large boulders. We are here earlier than yesterday; the morning suns have not yet reached their full height. Jo is with me, carrying a large woven bag of mysteries, just has she has done every day for weeks now. Yesterday, it contained a broken handbow, a spear, a broken light rifle, and a rock. The day before, it contained nothing but handfuls of what she called "knife dust." The day before that it was full of pebbles.

"Remember you mouth?" Jo clacks her jaws and snuffle-laughs. "Anything can be weapon," she says. My cuts and bruises—and growing swiftness at avoiding more cuts and bruises—are proving her right.

Temple is not here. She is never here. I have seen her twice since the fire ceremony, and both those times only for an instant as she ran by in a clump of Cheese children laughing and chasing a plini. They bounced rocks off its hard shell as its fast little legs carried it away in a cloud of dust. It appears the Cheese do indeed respect that she is still a little girl, and, even though I hate them, I am grateful for this allowance.

Jo tosses the bag on the ground and smiles. "What in this bag?" she asks me. *"Neh plitoka?"*

"Neh plitoka?" I repeat, feeling my tongue trip over the words. "In the bag?" I kick it. "There's nothing in the bag."

"Naa," Jo says, shaking her head. "You are wrong. There is not nothing in this bag. *Mara* in this bag."

"The wind?" I say, confused.

Jo nods, smiling wide, showing off her sharpened teeth. "Today we practice running like the wind, Tootie."

"Tootie?" I say. "It's just Rae. Or Ramona. Not Tootie. 'Tootie' means 'to stink.'" I hold my nose to indicate its meaning.

"Ah, then this name work on *maa kali*—many level—yes? Now, run, Tootie."

Jo whistles and a *Kwihuutsuu*—a small nasty-looking one, with extra-sharp teeth and deeply pink scales—plummets to the ground as if the Red Crescent has spit her at us.

"Go, Kwihuu, sweet baby beast. Find your lunch."

"Lunch?!" I yell, starting to run and tripping over my

boots, thankful that at least I no longer wear heavy, cumbersome skirts. The baby *Kwihuutsuu* throws her head to the sky, screeches out a deafening caw, and flies right at me.

"Use third eye, Tootie," Jo calls after me, touching the back of her neck to indicate the raw scar on mine. "If Klara think you worthy to be warrior, then *be* warrior."

"Aaaaah!" I scream, and take off as fast as I can as the creature darts and dives and pecks at me. I did not ask for a searing-hot stick of metal to brand my skin. I did not ask for this third eye. I do not ask to be a warrior. And yet . . . here I am.

"Run as the wind, Tootie. You pray to Mara today." Jo snuffles out a long laugh. "Hopefully you will also learn to watch close. Be strong. Be faster." She laughs again.

I curse her and run, sweating, around the entirety of the open space, which, to me, feels like circling the suns and back again.

I round the far corner of the space and as I do, I pass the man-Cheese with blue eyes, the one I have learned is called Ben-ton, my long-lost cousin Benny, whom I only knew as a babe and don't remember at all. He brings canteens and supplies to the clutch of boys who also come to the practice grounds every day. He has been watching me these many days, as I shoot or run or fall, and I do not like how his eyes narrow and roam when he sees me. Each time I see him, I find it harder to see the nice things I saw about him on the night of the ceremony. Perhaps I mistook cunning interest for niceties.

"What is your lesson today, cousin?" he calls to me as I stop briefly to catch my breath.

"Mara," I pant. "Dactyls. Running. Not dying."

Ben-ton laughs. "Jo likes teaching lessons about harnessing the air as a weapon. She remembers the old days."

The baby dactyl is so high in the sky now, I can barely see her. It's nice to have a minute to breathe. "I don't understand what you mean," I say.

Ben-ton steps closer, his voice low. "Jo remembers the plague. She was a child then, you know, when the *Origin* crashed. When, after the fighting, suddenly sickness raged and the humans were blamed. The air brought death. She has been obsessed ever since."

"Tootie!" Jo yells from the other side of the open space. "Is not resting time!" She blows a silent whistle hanging around her neck and the baby dactyl is upon me like a bolt of electricity. I am running before I have a chance to ask any more questions.

Ben-ton laughs as I fly by, then calls out, "Natka!" He throws a canteen. The boy I fought the first night—the son of Klara and Fist—catches it with ease and drains it. He and a group of his friends are in the same place they were yesterday and the day before and the day before that and so on. They are like prairie spiders hiding and waiting to jump. They practice throwing small rocks tied to long ropes in loops above my head. I flinch as I pass and they begin to laugh.

"*La gowa hee ta!*" one of them shouts at me. It is a

rough translation but I think he has just yelled "She pees now!" at me.

"*Mayrikafsa looa'a kakee!*" another shouts. Again, I am not sure what this means, but think it has something to do with a suckling baby.

"*Pitar!*" Natka yells. This is something he calls me all the time. No one will translate, but Klara hates it. She will flick him on the head with her long claws every time she hears him say it. "*Mayrikafsa pitar!*" he yells, and the boys laugh and laugh. Ben-ton looks like he's trying to stifle a grin. Either that or he needs to visit the latrine. Kwihuu dives at my head, scraping my scalp with her beak, and I can't respond to Natka, though I would ask him how his hand is feeling. I can see it seeping through its bandage. I am only slightly surprised at how *not* guilty I feel about his lingering wound.

I run now faster than I ever have before, feeling as though my heart and my anger will explode any second and shoot me into the sky like the *Origin* reborn.

It has been long enough for the suns to begin their descent in the sky and yet, I am still running from the gum baby dactyl. Even she seems to be tiring; her pecking at my head is no longer strong enough to draw blood.

I stumble twice, fearing that at any moment I will be struggling for breath and seeing stars. I am shocked that I haven't seen them already. There must be something about this village that helps me keep my breath about me. Maybe

131

it is that the heat and dust are less here among the caves and canyon walls than out by the gorge and the homesteads. It is perplexing.

Finally, Jo holds her hand up, swishing her claws together, signaling we are done for the day. I fall to the ground at her feet and roll onto my back, puffing for air, sweating puddles into the dirt. She empties a canteen onto my face and I relish the coolness, slurping what I can from the falling water.

"Rae!" I hear Temple's familiar shout and for a moment I am lost, not remembering where we are or what has happened. I feel as though I am back in the field, resting, and Temple is coming to tell me of Aunt Billie's flare or of Boone's insistence that it is time for supper. How I long to hear Boone tell me how bossy I am, to hear him crooning at Raj, to be able to fuss at him for those busted gogs.

I sit up, shaking water from my face and hair, and see her plummeting toward me, a comet trailing red, as her hair is continually caked and matted with red dirt now. She is upon me in no time, knocking me back down, hugging me, rolling in the dirt. I am laughing at her girlish kisses to my forehead. She is laughing, too, having adopted a few snickers that sound like the Cheese's. As she laughs, I see one of her teeth has been sharpened.

"Temple!" I push her from my lap and onto the dirt, making her face me. I grab her cheeks, squeezing them between my thumb and forefinger so that her lips splay open and I can see the tooth better. "What happened to your tooth?"

"I got my first kill," she says with triumph, her eyes sparkling. "That's what I was coming to tell you. Tootie." She winks and snort-laughs as she rummages through the woven pack on her back. She pulls out a shell that is about as long as her forearm. "One of the plini. I got it with this." She puts the shell down at my feet and pulls an old hand-bow from the sack. It is obviously broken, the laser generator smashed.

"Don't call me Tootie," I say. "I am still Rae." I pick up the shell and turn it over in my hands. It has been cleaned of all traces of living animal. "How did you kill it? Did you smack it on the head with a broken handbow?" I smile at her, mouth closed, not showing my own unsharpened teeth, not wanting to think of her tooth and what Papa would say.

"No, silly," Temple says. "I used one of these." She pulls a long piece of metal out of the bag. "It's like a light arrow, but made of metal. Very effective."

I take the stick from her and inspect the deadly point. Ah. I see now. The Cheese have fitted the broken handbow to shoot these sharpened pieces of metal. It is genius, really. It requires no charging in the suns and appears to be very effective indeed. I pluck at the strings. The spring action reminds me of the clapping hands on my stone statue so many moons ago. A melancholy feeling settles over me as

I hand the metal stick and the handbow back to Temple.

"They sharpen a tooth for each of your first kills," Temple says, grinning. "I am one of the youngest and quickest of our whole clan." Her face, beneath the dirt and sweat, is glowing.

"It is not our clan," I say to Temple in a low voice.

Her smile falls. "You are not glad for me?"

"Of course I'm glad for you, Temple, it's just . . ." I don't know what to say. It's only been a few weeks and already she is so much like them. "Don't you want to see Aunt Billie and Papa again? Don't you want to find out what happened to Boone?"

"Can't I do all of these things, Mayri—Rae?" she asks, her lips tightening into a line. "Can't I miss Aunt Billie *and* mourn Papa *and* dream of Boone while at the same time accomplishing brave and mighty feats that our township does not think worthy of a girl-child?" She is near whispering now, her eyes growing bright in the light of the waning suns.

"I will always believe you are brave and mighty, Temple. You have *always* been so." I put my hand on hers. "But I do not believe Papa is dead," I say, not at all sure of this conviction—only that I feel like my bones would know if Papa were gone to the gods. "And I do believe we will find a way home."

Temple stands and shakes her head. "I am sorry you are not happy for me." She puts her things back into the bag and starts to walk away.

I jump to my feet. "Temple. Wait! I did not say I'm not happy for you. I only meant, don't forget where we come from."

"I've heard some Cheese say we are the children of humans, the children of people who came here and murdered innocent Kihuut in order to steal their land," Temple says, her voice taking on an eerie Cheese accent.

"We *are* children of humans, Temple, I don't think there's any way around that. . . ." She makes Papa's hush-your-gum-mouth pinched-finger move and it surprises me so much I am momentarily mute.

"They speak of our people murdering those from Hosani, too. That the Origin Massacre was really one where the homesteaders unleashed a magic, invisible weapon. They say we are children of people who doomed humans to never escape this moon."

She is scaring me with this talk. She sounds like Benton. "Temple," I say. "Come on. You *know* where we come from. This is—"

"But really, our ancestors gave us a gift," she says, interrupting. "Did you know that, Mayrikafsa? A gift. We are not the children of humans, not really." Temple's mouth is in a tight line, more serious than I've seen in a long time. She looks me dead in the eyes. "We are the children of Oonatka, Oonan, Mara, and Ebibi." She touches her chest and closes her eyes. When she opens them she says, "We are born of this moon just like the Cheese. Why would you think anything else?"

"Because we come from the other gods, Temple," I say, my voice rising. "Our own gods."

Temple shakes her head. "The gods that say girls must stay quiet and covered and work to make the boys happy and healthy? We were born on this moon. *Of* this moon. Those wrongheaded human gods had nothing to do with it."

I can only stand and gape as she walks away. Her colored hair has grown longer, wilder. It sways in the breeze and blends with the surroundings.

My thoughts cloud over as I watch her go. What is making her speak like this? *Think* like this?

"Temple!" I shout after her. "I love you!" She holds her hand up in a wave, but doesn't turn around.

It has only taken a few weeks and she has forsaken our gods for beautiful stories. My hands go to my hair, my eyes close. Papa will not abide this. I have failed him again.

I am losing Temple.

16

NATKA WILL NOT PASS THE HASHAVA FRUIT.

"Hashava," I say again, in my best Cheese accent, feeling color rise to my cheeks, tension building in my jaw as my teeth grind.

Natka says he can't understand me. He calls me a *pitar* and Klara flicks him with her nails, making him wince. Fist shoots him a glowering look. By now I have guessed what *pitar* must mean, and it matches well with the nickname Tootie, which I can't seem to shake, thanks to Jo.

I don't know why he won't pass the hashava fruit. It is dinner. It is meant for us all. He is just being obstinate. He holds no fondness for me and for that I am grateful. I will feel less guilt when I pound his face with my fists.

Fist growls a few words, Klara nods. Natka's ear

membranes throb and his beaky front lip comes down against his teeth twice as he looks at me.

"Shall I create a poultice for your hand?" I say it with a menacing sweetness. "I'm sure I could remember the correct roots. Then perhaps your fingers would work better and you would *pass*. The. *Gum*. Hash*ava*." I smack the floor with every other syllable. He waves his hand at me, smiles with no mirth, and then pushes the bowl toward me with more force than necessary. Finally I have the hashava.

Natka pounds his fist once on the stone floor where we are eating together (gods do I miss civilized tables and chairs), stands, and storms off toward the pool in the back of the cave. Klara blows air through her mouth and looks at me, tilting her head to the side. For a moment I worry she will strike me. But she looks away.

Fist puts his bowl down and stands, wiping crumbs from the dactyl-skin vest he wears over his bare chest. He follows after Natka and soon I hear them yelling. At one point I swear to the gods I hear Natka yell "Rory-ton!" and my heart begins a gallop.

"Rory?" I say to Klara, who is quietly finishing the hashava fruit. She looks up sharply.

"Was she here? Rory?"

Klara's eyes seem brighter. Wet, almost.

"*Ro-ri-ta*," she says after a moment. She blinks several times, clearing the brightness from her eyes, then she crosses them and sticks out her tongue, making a little singing noise. I am shocked speechless by this sudden ridiculous display. "*Ro-ri-ta*," she says again, and again the silly display.

"Crazy?" I ask. "Stupid? *Ro-ri-ta* means something like that?"

"Cray-zee. Stoo-peed," she says, and nods.

"Oh." I would dearly love to know where Rory is, or if these Cheese know anything about her. But it appears they do not. Just as they do not know what has happened to Boone. Fist questioned the Cheese who rode the dactyl that scooped up Boone but would tell me only that Boone is not in the village. The Cheese don't need boys. This does not settle me.

Natka comes storming back, using his foot to push me into the wall as he goes by. My back hits a shelf, knocking over a small figure. Klara is by my side in an instant. She drags me to my feet, yelling at me in Cheese, "*Naa loma Kailia!*"

I think she is saying "Don't touch Kailia," but I don't know what that means. Then she yells after Natka, "*NAA LOMA KAILIA!*" She is gripping me hard by the front of my shirt, air blowing from her nose in short, hot bursts.

This amount of sudden anger from Klara, who is usually so calm, frightens me. I don't understand it. We were just having dinner. We . . . I wriggle away from her grip, flatten myself against the wall next to the shelf, and stammer, "Wh-what is Kailia?"

As the word comes from my mouth Klara strikes me hard on the cheek. Natka is quickly by her side, his hand

139

on her arm, murmuring something to her. She blows air at me once more, snaps her jaws, then lowers her head and walks away. I am left against the wall, my breath coming fast and my cheek on fire.

"Kailia her sister," Natka says to me, his voice as fiery as my cheek feels. "Killed by hyoo-mans." He grabs my throat with his clawed hand and squeezes until I am gasping. He stares into my eyes, shakes his head, and lets go abruptly.

My hands go to my throat instinctively as I suck in large amounts of air. I no longer find the roughness with girls shocking, though it is still unsettling. The Cheese seem to see no differences between boys and girls whether they be warriors or clothes washers, and I admit, I like this freedom even though it means bruises and split lips. It also means I, too, can hit back, and sometimes that is lovely.

But I don't get the chance to hit Natka back. He goes out into the night as Klara returns. Fist returns to the room as well. He speaks quietly with Klara. She sighs but then nods. He, too, leaves.

I give Klara plenty of space as she huffs around the room. I have so many questions for her, but even if we shared enough language, I have sense enough to know this isn't the right time.

The limited words I have learned so far are about shooting and running and the Cheese gods. Not words I would ask her, like "Please help me find my family before my sister becomes a Cheese forever." Or "I'm afraid my friend was shot by a shine tree and kidnapped by your people and you won't tell me what you know." Or "Why did you think me worthy of having a warrior's third eye branded on my neck, and how can I get the scar to stop itching?" Or "Please tell me about your sister." I don't have these words. And so, with Fist and Natka gone, Klara, having calmed down, begins her nightly job of allowing two Cheese at a time into the cave, working with them to settle disputes. My job is to clear the dishes and rinse them in the pool. But first I find the small totem of Kailia on the floor and put her carefully back on the shelf.

They have been arguing for what feels like an entire cycle of the suns. Natka and I sit in the dark cave, the cooking fire providing the only light, as Klara and Fist shout in their sleeping chamber.

Natka and Fist returned not too long after leaving, and there has been shouting ever since. Natka pulls burning pieces of scrub from the fire and flicks them at me. I am too tired and too irritated to flinch. In fact . . .

I stand and walk out of the cave. There is no reason I have to tolerate this. Natka shouts something after me that I don't understand, but I don't turn around. I am tired of him. Yes. He no longer makes me angry. He makes me tired. I am a human. A *ke'ekutaat*. An invader. Not only have I taken land on his moon, I have beaten him in a public fight and taken space in his home. Surely, if I were Natka, I would hate me, too.

I wish I had a knife, a stone, some wire. My fingers are

restless, as is my mind. I could placate them both by working on a carving. But the Cheese do not trust me with my own knife. For this I do not blame them. I lean against the outside wall of the cave and slide into a sitting position, staring into the distance.

There is a bustle of activity in the village center this night. I hear a commotion from the area where the *Kwihuutsuu* nests are, and shouts from the Cheese and a hoot of laughter. There is a charged feeling in the night air that I would have to be *ro-ri-ta* to miss. The Cheese are preparing for something. But what?

I feel a shadow fall over me. It is oily, blue-eyed Ben-ton. My long-lost cousin. Or perhaps he is not oily. I only know that my belly tightens when I see him, this Cheese who is not a Cheese. I feel danger roll off him like heat from a rock.

Ben-ton sits next to me and clucks his tongue against the roof of his mouth.

"What?" I say, not feeling guilt over the lack of politeness in my tone. The day has been long, I have much to ponder. I miss Boone, who was always good to help me ponder things. I miss Aunt Billie, who would let me talk and offer no comment. I miss Rory. Gods, I miss her. These thoughts cause such a feeling of longing that I almost gasp, as if I've been punched in the stomach; punched in a place that is sore from being punched over and over again.

"It gets easier," Ben-ton says in his voice that shares a Cheese and human accent. I look at him and wrinkle my nose. I do not want to hear sympathies from him—this man who looks at me with such scorn while Jo works me to death every day. He waggles his fingers and with a flourish produces a crystalline rock from behind my ear. Handing it to me, he smiles.

"You should smile more, Tootie. You're prettier when you smile."

I contemplate punching him in the ear. But instead I say, "Can I ask you a question?" I gaze into the distance. The Red Crescent glows.

"Of course," he says, his back straightening.

"Why don't you have a Cheese name? Ben-ton does not sound like Cheese to me. Why am I not Rae-ton? Or Temple, Temple-ton?"

He clears his throat twice and there is such a pause I think he will not answer. "It is because I did not pass a test," he says. There is another long pause. "*Ton* means 'fail.'"

"What test?" Now I turn to look at him, but it is he who is gazing into the distance.

"I am not a girl." Half of his mouth turns up in a smile even though his eyes close slowly. "My long blond hair as a ten-year-old boy did me no favors."

I know this is not funny. It is terrible. A terrible thing happened to young Benny. And, even so, I cannot help but to laugh. Just a little.

"Were they very surprised when they found out?" I ask, trying to temper my smile.

Ben-ton shakes his head, a small smile playing at his

lips. "You should have seen their faces." He pretends to clack his upper lip like a Cheese, and waves his hands over his head.

This is too much and I burst out laughing, quickly clapping my hands over my mouth to stifle the noise.

"I'm sorry," I say. "It's just . . . oh, Ben-ton, what a thing to have happened."

"They stole me for vengeance, you know. After the death of Kailia."

"Klara's sister?"

Ben-ton nods. "She was the last female Kihuut born in the village. A fierce warrior. Killed during a raid out on the plains years and years ago."

A falling sensation fills my belly. "Out on the plains?"

Ben-ton turns to face me. "Coincidentally where your father killed a Cheese, if I am not mistaken. Does he still keep the box on the cooling-grate mantel?"

I nod, having momentarily lost my words. The Cheese Papa was always so proud to have killed . . . could that have been Klara's sister?

"The Kihuut were very angry about this murder, so they returned and killed a woman in retribution. An eye for an eye. Then they took me to replace Kailia and, well, surprise."

My mother was killed as an act of vengeance?

"My gods, Ben-ton." These are the only words I can muster.

He shrugs. "They were to feed me to the *Kwihuutsuu*,

but I promised I could learn; I could be helpful. And yet, from there, I failed other tests, too."

"Like what?" I ask.

"The third eye. I flinched. I showed weakness. I proved I would not make a warrior. And now not only do I pay every day for not being female, I pay every day for being weak."

"Pay for it? How?" I ask. He always seems busy to me, has people he talks to and laughs with, seems not to want for anything, seems, in fact, to pretty much own his way in the village.

He turns to me, eyes flashing. "I am not a warrior. Did you not hear me? I am relegated to serving and staying at camp. I will never, ever escape." Ben-ton stands. "Keep passing the tests, Rae, and you never know. You might be *krasnoakafsa* one day. Beautiful warrior. Chieftess. Though Natka begins his final warrior test in the morning, Kihuut law says he can never actually lead the Kihuut. He is not female. Many of these people have accepted you wholly. You were born of this moon, just as they were."

Ben-ton takes my hands, reminding me of Papa. His hands do not offer strength, though. I feel his sweaty palms and it makes my skin crawl. He squeezes my fingers and when he pulls away there's a piece of canvas in my hand. Written on it, in a childlike scrawl, are the words "Let me help you."

He smiles as his eyes narrow. "Your path continues to be written, Rae. Tootie. Mayrikafsa. It is up to you to choose

145

who you shall be. Don't let wagging tongues dismay you."

"What wagging tongues?" I am still holding the scrap of canvas. I do not know where to put it. I do not want it.

"While you are accepted by many, not every Kihuut is in love with the angry *ke'ekutaat* girl-child. Some would see a male Kihuut become leader rather than a female invader. Though if this angry *ke'ekutaat* had a knowledgeable adviser . . ."

My voice lowers, my jaw clenched. "No one wants me to be a leader, Ben-ton. Right now I'm just trying to stay alive."

Ben-ton looks me up and down. "Why do you think Jo trains you so hard? Why do you think you live with Klarakova and A'alantka? You fought hard that first night, Rae, and now you find yourself conveniently in a place of prominence. They have been trying to find someone worthy of replacing Kailia for years."

The crass tone and absurdities of this conversation cause my stomach to roil. "You think I want to be where I am? That I invited the Cheese to puncture my shoulders and fling me into this world?"

I stand and drop the canvas scrap at his feet. It blows against his *nantola*-clad foot.

Ben-ton shrugs. He begins to stroll away but then stops, turning, his face glowing red in the evening light. "Do you know the word for 'Kihuut warrior,' Rae?"

I shake my head.

"It is *Kihuut*kafsa."

I say nothing.

"Do you know the word for 'chieftess'? It's *krasnoa*kafsa. The word for the chieftess's warrior adviser? *Tonta*kafsa. Now think. Use that human brain of yours." He taps his head with one finger, his eyes flashing. "Mayri*kafsa* does not mean 'she who cries a lot,' Rae. Not even close."

He continues walking away, the breeze blowing his long hair, the light of the Red Crescent gleaming off the jagged scar that runs from the middle of his neck, down the back of his left shoulder blade.

"What does it mean?" I call after him, but he doesn't answer.

What does *any* of it mean? I shiver and walk back to the cave. I don't want to be a warrior or a leader or a replacement. I want to go home.

17

I SCRATCH AT THE BACK OF MY NECK. THE SCAR over my third eye itches fiercely, like a ghost tickling my neck with dried scrub.

"*Ho laa!*" Fist shouts at me, and by now I know he means, "Pay attention!"

Usually, it is Jo who gives me these lessons, but today Fist is the one who brought me to the practice grounds. I do not know where Jo has gone.

Klarakova offered me the usual seeds and chicory drink this morning, and when Fist came storming out of his sleeping chamber, he was dressed in his raiding outfit, wearing his necklace of ears, but not painted with the gold and silver swirls that indicate a raid. He was gruff as always, and he shoved my shoulder into the wall, causing me to spill some of my drink at my feet. "*Tokonata. Hee ta,*" he said in a growl. Practice. Now.

Klara gave him the look she does, and clicked her beaked lip against her bottom teeth. This is the only thing I have ever seen that chagrins Fist enough to quiet a building rage. He blew air through his nose like an angry horse and stomped from the cave.

I do not know what sours Fist's mood. I am still not always sure of the Cheese and their feelings and intentions. Not like I can still read Temple, even as she grows longer hair and adds sharpened teeth by the week. I think maybe he is upset because Natka has not returned home after four days out with his *Kwihuutsuu*. This is Natka's final challenge for becoming a man—to go on a raiding party and come back successful. I shiver to think what "successful" means.

For me, it has been nice with Natka away. I have had a respite from worrying whether I will be drowned in my sleep or strangled on my way to the latrine. Training has been better, too, with the boys minding their own business as their self-proclaimed leader is off punishing humans. Even Ben-ton has only eyed me from afar, sensing perhaps that if he speaks to me again I might practice some newly learned violence on him.

"*HO! LAA!*" Fist shouts again, and throws a rock at me. Two weeks ago I might have had a bruise on my cheek from that rock, but now I catch it and immediately hurl it toward his head.

He darts to the side, the rock barely missing him.

I can't help but smile. He does not smile back, just beats the fabric pillow he is holding to his chest.

"You want me to *shoot* at you?" I yell to him. "I have real arrows." I point to the retrofitted broken handbow. "Very dangerous! I almost just killed you with that rock. Imagine what I could do with sharpened metal."

He marches to me, the pillow bouncing against his chest. Before a word comes from his mouth his foot sweeps my legs, knocking me to the ground. He kneels, a knee to my chest. It's all happened so quickly my eyes are having trouble focusing on his face, which is now inches from mine.

"Ho. Laa." He says it slowly, his Cheese mouth chewing the words, his eyes narrowed, the sides of his head throbbing. His necklace of shriveled ears dangles in my face, making my stomach roil.

"Why do you do that?" I say, my voice low. Sometimes I forget that I hate Fist. Sometimes I forget that I hate what the Cheese have done. This is not one of those times. "The ears." I spit the words into his face. "Why do you take them and wear them? It's horrible."

"Lolobee!" he shouts, his face spreading into a slow, menacing grin. He removes his knee from my chest and grabs my hand, pulling me into a sitting position. He squats next to me, holds up the necklace, and counts the ears. *"Lolobee, lolobee, lolobee, lolobee . . . lolobee."*

"Yes. I can see you have a bunch." I swallow my rising bile. "It is terribly foul."

150

Fist puts a hand up to the throbbing membrane on one side of his head. *"Naa lolobee,"* he says. Then he holds up the necklace again. *"Maa lolobee!"* He smiles.

"You take ears because you have no ears? Or you take ears to make humans look more like Kihuut?"

"Ja!" he shouts. Yes! Which doesn't really answer my question. He stands and walks back across the training field. He smacks the fabric again and motions for me to shoot.

"This seems like a bad idea," I shout to him.

He grins and nods his head and even though just a moment earlier I remembered how much I hate him, that feeling begins to fade again, replaced by a strange kind of affection. The constant flip-flopping of emotions wears at me. These Cheese. I do not know how to feel.

While Fist is an ear-stealer who is often violent with me and is far from kind, he has kept me fed and alive and is making sure I am taught the ways of the Cheese. He even protects me from his own true-blooded child. As far as Fist is concerned Temple and I are Cheese now, no longer human. I truly do not know what to make of it. It is very confusing.

"I don't want to hurt you," I yell at him. This is mostly true.

At this, he laughs. We have been picking up more and more pieces of each other's language over the past several weeks. The idea that Mayrikafsa could hurt A'alanatka is hilarious to him. I whip the handbow up as fast as lightning and shoot while he is still laughing. Fist darts to the side almost as if he is dancing. The arrow sails into the stone behind him with a zing and a crack.

Fist points at me and smiles. "Ja!" he says.

It is perhaps the first compliment I've ever received from an adult of any species. I can't help but smile and look at my feet.

There is yelling in the distance. Fist and I both turn to see what it is. Jo is running to us, waving her arms. She speaks quickly and I don't understand any of the Cheese language except Natka's name, *Kwihuutsuu*, and *owa'a*, which I've learned (by uneasy means) is the word for "hurt." Fist and Jo take off running, away from the practice grounds and back toward the center of the village.

"Wait for me!" I yell, and chase after them. I actually catch up, which is a miracle. My legs can pump faster now, my breath comes stronger, my arms are tighter, my stomach harder. I do not know if it is the Cheese food, or the sunsup-to-sunsdown activities that are making me this way. Maybe a combination of the two. Usually, if I run like this, I have a breathing attack, but I have not had one since coming to the Cheese so many weeks ago.

We enter the village center, breathing hard from the sprint. I am covered in a fine layer of sweat and dust, but the Cheese clothes I'm wearing seem to wick away the dampness so that I stay cool, even in the blasting heat of the midmorning suns. My feet are heavy, sweaty, and hot, though, because I still wear my own boots. No matter what Klara says, no matter how many times Fist yells and slaps my legs, I will not wear those ridiculous Cheese shoes. I will not.

Klara pushes through a crowd of Cheese surrounding Suu, Natka's cawing *Kwihuutsuu*. She cries out—the noises from her throat rising above the nervous chatter of the other Cheese. They move away from Klara as Fist approaches, his face set, grim. Natka is on the ground and even from a distance I can see he is covered in a shiny sweat, his eyes closed.

Shine tree has its name for two reasons. One, the leaves sparkle in the suns, so beautiful, attracting prey from great distances. Two, when struck by a shine tree needle you break out into such an impressive fever, your body shines with sweat. But, often, by the time the shine sweat has set in, it is too late.

Klara and Fist carry Natka to a cave at the edge of the village; a place I have not been before. Jo and I follow at a distance. I show her my hand with the four fingers.

"I have wondered about this . . . hand," Jo says.

"They got to it in time," I say. "Saved me from the shine tree poison. My aunt Billie is a great healer."

Jo's eyes widen a little. "You aunt is healer?"

I nod. "She is the physician for our whole township. I had just started learning little tinctures and things when . . . when . . ."

Jo regards me and I see that she looks at me differently now. Does she hold respect for me because of my aunt, because of what the future could have held for me? Or

153

because I suffered the tragedy of having a finger chopped from my body?

"There was someone else," I say in a low voice. I stop walking. Jo stops, too, and stares at me intently. "Another girl. Hurt by the shine tree. Taken by Cheese—by Kihuut."

Jo swallows and looks away for a moment, then back to my face.

"Rory," I whisper. "My friend."

There is a scream from inside the cave where they took Natka. The poison is taking hold. Jo and I run to the mouth of the cave. Inside, a very old Cheese is leaning over a writhing Natka, who is on a table made of stone. Fist, looking grimmer than usual, holds Klara, who is openly weeping, back from the table. It was she who screamed. I know because she does it again.

Jo tries to restrain me, but I break her grip and go into the cave. I hold up my hand so the old Cheese can see.

"Shine tree," I say loudly, over the wails of Natka and the moans of Klara. "Where was Natka struck? You will have to remove that part of his body."

The old woman is smoothing back Natka's hair from his sweaty face. She is muttering a chant over his left hand, which has swollen to an almost unrecognizable state.

"Has that worked before?" I ask. "The chanting? I don't mean to sound like I am smarter than you, but I have experience with the shine tree." I have learned in my weeks here to defer to the older Cheese in the village. Apologize at will and maybe they will listen to you or offer you what you want. If you show respect you will gain respect. Sometimes. Fist is a different matter entirely.

Jo whispers to me, "This is rare here, injury from *Ebilil* plant. I do not know how he found such tree. Ebibi has called Natka to his kingdom. Is very sad, but full of honor." She touches her chest and closes her eyes.

"But he doesn't have to go," I say. "He doesn't have to *die*, Jo. I know how to save him. Or at least how to try to save him. They will have to take his hand."

Jo's ear ovals throb in and out quickly.

"Will you ask them for me? If they're willing to try it?"

"Tear apart body created by love of the gods? I think not, Tootie."

"Just ask. Please."

Jo translates for me and the old Cheese scowls. She grabs my hand and inspects the area where my finger used to be.

I make a chopping motion with my other hand. "You'll have to take his hand." I look at Fist and Klara. "I'm sorry, but it is the only way. And it might be too late." Natka is moaning softly now, writhing slower. He is still shiny with sweat, sliding on the rock tabletop. His hand has darkened, and ribbons of blackness crawl up his arm.

I point to the ribbons. "This is the poison. It will go to his heart. It will kill him."

The old Cheese says something to Fist and Klara, who both look at me.

"We can save him," I say to them, my voice rising,

pleading. "He does not have to go live with Ebibi. He can stay with us." I hold up my hand. "I did not go to Ebibi."

Jo pulls my hand down. "What you say goes against the gods, Mayrikafsa. Ebibi has made choice. Is time to say good-bye."

"I do not accept that," I say, surprised to feel tears burning my eyes. "Natka and I are far from friends, but he does not deserve this pain." I go to Fist and Klara. "No *owa'a*," I say. "We can stop the *owa'a*. Well, it'll hurt worse at first, but then be all better. Hopefully."

Natka cries out. Klara chokes out a sob. No one is moving. No one is doing anything. The air is so hot and stifling it is as if it has solidified and trapped us all in a net. I push through the heat and silence and grab a knife hanging along the wall. I hold it in the fire that is burning low in the cooking pit. I have watched Aunt Billie take limbs. Not from shine tree poisoning but from injury and infection. Your knife must be clean and sharp. Your movement must be swift.

Jo says, "Do not do it."

"I have to, Jo. I can't just let him die."

"Ebibi wills it." She touches her chest and closes her eyes.

"Ebibi can't have him! He is only a boy! He is a pain in my hind end, and he hates me, but I will not stand by when there is something I can do to help." I pull the red-hot knife from the flame and pray to my own gods that it is sharp enough to do the job I've cast upon it. I am going

156

against the word of an entire culture. Is that right? Is it right to let a boy die when there is a way to save him? My heart—and my sweating hand—have an answer.

I scream all the air from my lungs, startling everyone in the room, except Natka, who continues to writhe. I quickly see where the ribbons of black have reached, and aim for the spot just above the blackness. I grasp the knife with both hands, and with one long arc I land the knife in the middle of Natka's arm between his elbow and his wrist.

We are lucky.

The knife is sharp.

My movement has strength.

The lower arm separates from the upper arm. I have removed Ebibi from Natka's body. Blood is everywhere. Screaming follows. It is chaos. The old Cheese works furiously to bind the wound. Klara is shrieking and on her knees. Jo is trying to hold Fist back; they are both shouting. But Fist is stronger. The last thing I see is the cold blackness of his eyes, then I feel a sharp sting across my cheek as he makes sure to scratch me with his claws as he hits my face.

I see stars and then blackness.

It reminds me of home.

18

NATKA WILL NOT SPEAK. FIST WILL NOT SPEAK, either—at least not to me. He has plenty to say to Jo and to Klarakova. I roll over on my blanket outside the mouth of the cave. Fist will not let me inside. It has been three nights.

During the day Temple comes to sit with me. The people she lives with—her family, she calls them—told her what happened. As the hours pass we watch clusters of Cheese walk by, whispering. We see Ben-ton talking with older women in the village, heads shaking, eyes narrowed as they stare at us. I wonder if he is pleased that I am in such trouble. Clearly any Cheese who thought I might be a warrior or a leader one day would not think that anymore. I don't blame them. I don't want it. I never have.

Temple does not agree with my actions, either. No one seems to. Again, Rae thought she was saving a life, only to be thwarted by her good intentions.

Temple understands the situation, though. She, too, remembers seeing the Cheese boy standing by the lone shine tree. We both wonder if this was Natka, and if that tree marks a grave.

Even though it is night and the sky bleeds a deep red, I walk to the practice grounds. The wind is hot and fast and I wonder if there will be an electrical storm. There has not been one since before my arrival at the village. With the abundant pools of water, lack of electrical storms, and ability to quell my breathing attacks, this village makes me wonder if the Cheese truly are protected by their gods.

I run laps around the practice grounds, my heart pounding. It feels good to have my blood run through my veins so quickly, to feel it thumping in my ears. It is easy to think of nothing else, to feel nothing else, as my feet pound the dirt and sweat pours down my face. My hair tickles my neck, black branches grown longer over the months. I reach into my pocket and pull out a bit of fabric. I tie my hair up into a horsetail as I run, my neck instantly cooling, my third eye tingling as I rub it.

Why won't Natka speak? We know he broke from the raiding party for one full day and night. Jo went to search for him and found him on his *Kwihuutsuu* trying to make it back to the village. His only words at the time were "*Ro-ri-ta Ebilil*"—"Stupid shine tree."

"*Ro-ri-ta E-bi-lil,*" I say to myself as I run. It has a nice pattern to it. "*Ro-ri-ta E-bi-lil. Ro-ri-ta E-bi-lil.*" The running filters everything from my brain except those two words.

What if he wasn't saying "*ro-ri-ta,*" though? What if it was "Rory-ton," like I thought I heard when he fought with Fist? Was Rory a failure? Could Natka have known her? I stop running and lean my elbows on my knees as I catch my breath.

I must know. I will not stand for this any longer. I have already offended Ebibi along with everyone else in the village. I have nothing left to lose.

The Red Crescent frowns at me as I walk briskly back to the cave. The night is so clear, I see the wisps of clouds on the surface of the planet. What must it be like to live there? Ben-ton has spoken of a time when the people of Hosani came to trade with the Kihuut. Why do they no longer come? Why do the Cheese never speak of it? They have gods for the suns, for the darkness, for wind, for fire, but say nothing of the one thing that takes up almost the whole sky. It is strange.

At the mouth of the cave I stand straight and take a breath. I walk inside, hoping Fist and Klara are sleeping. They are, but at Natka's bedside. How will I wake him and speak with him if they, too, will then wake?

My inelegant boots solve this problem for me. Natka's eyes open when I clomp closer to him. The two adults stay sleeping. I doubt they have slept much over the past few days. I point to Natka and then I point out of the cave. His face has no expression, but his ear membranes throb. He carefully moves his legs to the side of the bed. His arm is bandaged tightly to his chest, held over his heart as the wound heals. I follow him from the room.

Once outside, he accosts me with a series of Cheese words and sentences I don't understand. His eyes seem only half open, but his gestures are pointed, his voice low and sharp. He appears to be hostile, but also frightened.

"I don't understand you," I say. "You know I don't." I slow my voice down and speak quietly. "Please . . . talk . . . slower. . . ."

He looks away from me, runs his good hand through his long hair. It's funny to me how many gestures between the Cheese and the humans are similar.

"You disgrace Ebibi," he says slowly, not looking at me, touching his chest and closing his eyes.

"I know," I say. "I'm sorry. I just . . . you were dying. Do you understand these words? Dying. I didn't want you to die."

"But you not like me," Natka says. His voice is clear, his human accent very impressive. He has apparently been hiding from me that he does indeed understand a lot of my words.

"You're right," I say. "I don't like you. You don't like me. But I still would not see you dead."

"This is not the way," Natka says, turning to look at me. His eyes pierce mine.

161

"It is not your way, but it is my way. If it is possible to heal someone or something, it's always worth a try. My aunt Billie taught me that. We do not give way to our gods, without first showing our strength and love and protection of this worldly life." Oh, gods, I sound like Papa.

Natka regards me for a moment, his eyes searching my face. "I like this," he says, finally. "Show bravery to gods. Learn more. Grow stronger."

"Yes," I say. "This is what I wanted for you. No one seems to understand that."

"They have old," he says. "They own too many rules." He lightly rubs his good hand over the bandaged stump held tightly to his chest. "Thank you," he says in a voice I can barely hear over Mara's sighs. "Thank you, Mayrikafsa. For saving my life."

I am surprised at his words, but loath to show it. I nod once and swallow hard. "You are welcome, Natka." We both shuffle our feet and work hard to keep our eyes from meeting. "How did you come by the shine tree?" I ask after a moment.

Natka sits in the dirt, with his back to the outer wall of the cave. "There is single *Ebilil* tree by *Maasakota*. Gorge." He pauses as I sit next to him, then he turns to look at me. "I like to visit sometimes."

I nod, my heart beginning to thrum a faster beat. "Does that tree mark anything significant? I know the shine tree does not usually grow this side of the gorge. Or so I have been taught."

"This is true," Natka says. "We have no *Ebilil* trees, except to mark resting place of someone injured by one."

"What injured person lies beneath that shine tree?" I ask in a whisper, around a growing rock in my throat.

After a torturous pause worse than any punch or kick, Natka says, "Rory-ton," in a strangled whisper. "My sister. My friend." A tear escapes one eye and he swallows hard.

"We think," he says, swallowing hard again, trying to calm his breaking voice. "We think she was *flotaka*."

"*Flotaka*," I say, my eyes searching the sky for the meaning of the word. "Miracle?"

Natka nods. "We think she was untouched by *Ebilil* poison." He rubs his hand over his face. "She came to village very ill, signs of Ebibi taking her was growing through her. . . ." He pats his side. I nod. "But then, the blackness go away. The . . ." He snaps his fingers and says the word for "knife," then shakes his head.

"The needle?" I say. "From the tree?"

He nods. "Yes. This. It was never found. Wantosakaal say she must only have scratch. She got better. We trained together all days."

I close my eyes, I imagine Rory taking the place Kailia would have held in the family. The place that would have been Ben-ton's had he been a girl. The place that is now mine. I imagine her shooting metal arrows and being chased by baby dactyls. I imagine her sleeping on the same pallet in the cave as I do. I imagine her running her laps, laughing with Natka.

"We train, and then, *ha'at* moons later she fail *Kwihuutsuu* test. Flying test. She very angry, say her eyes not work right. Everyone think she lying. She disappoint. Her name taken away, changed to Rory-ton."

"What was her name before?" I ask, running my palms over the dirt, smoothing it out.

"Kamino." Natka pauses, his mouth clasped tightly, his eyes searching my face. "She Who Laugh."

My eyes burn and brim. She Who Laughs. "Of course," I say. "Of course that would be her name."

"Then, only few cycles of suns later she no remember any name. Not hers, not mine, not her other brother who she talked about all times."

Her other brother. "Boone," I say. It makes my heart ache to utter his name.

Natka nods. "And then Ebibi took her." He touches his chest and closes his eyes. "The blackness came over whole body. Wantosakaal thought it was terrible sickness and order body to be taken far from village. And then *Ebilil* tree grow and we understand."

"She was so strong," I say. "She fought the poison for two summers."

Natka looks at me, his eyes bright as I know mine are. "I went back to tell her of you. How I hate you. Hate how you not her." Natka strangles out a laugh. "And she shoot me. She must not like what I say."

I laugh, too. "Always has the last laugh, that Rory. That Kamino."

Natka smiles and I see both Fist and Klarakova in his face. He swipes a tear that has escaped. I, too, have a wet face.

"Thank you for telling me," I say.

"Thank you for saving me," he says.

I stand and help him to his feet.

"We are brother and sister, now," he says. "As Kamino and I were brother and sister."

"Are we?" I ask.

He nods, smiles, and then shoves me. "But I am always bigger and stronger."

We turn to go back in the cave and Klara is standing there, quietly swiping away her tears as she smiles at us both.

19

"PITAR!" I YELL. *"RO-RI-TA, KWIHUUTSUU!"*

Jo is laughing so hard, her snuffle-snickers echo off the rock walls of the small canyon we're in. "Do not fight the *Kwihuutsuu*, Tootie," Jo shouts up at me through her laughter.

"Do not call me Tootie!" I shout back, my hands scrambling over the pink scales of the baby *Kwihuutsuu*'s neck. She is actually not such a baby anymore. Her wingspan is so wide that if you are standing anywhere within ten hands of her, you would be good to step out of the way when she unfurls her wings or else prepare yourself for a mighty smack in the face. And she is not even full grown, yet.

The *Kwihuutsuu* streaks up to the sky like a light arrow, and it's lucky the reins are knotted to one of my hands, otherwise I would have just tumbled to my death. As it is, I am hanging on by one painfully dangling arm as I smack the beast with my other hand and yell things like, "AAACK!" and "Slow down!" and "Whoa!"

"She must understand you is the *barka*, Tootie," Jo yells to me. I can barely hear her over the wind and the pounding of my heart.

"*Barka?*" I yell back, trying to remember the meaning of the word. "Boss, you mean?" I would laugh if my throat weren't filled with terror-induced bile.

"She must trust in you," Jo says as the *Kwihuutsuu* changes course and begins a deadly dive straight into the canyon. "Teach sweet Kwihuu the trust she needs."

Sweet Kwihuu? Right. Now the strap around my hand is saving my life as I fly behind the beast like a spark at the end of A'akow's ankle ropes. She flattens out her dive just a bit and I am able to scrabble onto her back, holding on tightly with my knees. She must feel my knees squeezing her because she whips her head around and tries to bite off my left foot, jaws snapping, eyes narrowed.

"Whoa!" I yell, yanking my foot back. "Did you see that, Jo? She's trying to eat my feet." We skim over Jo's head as I yell to her. She waves up at me.

"If you wear the *nantolas* she not do this thing," Jo says.

"*Naa!*" I shout down at her. "Those are gum ugly shoes, Jo. They are indecent."

Kwihuu decides to show off now, and twists her body in a full spiral, throwing me through the air like a seed blowing in the wind. I hold tightly to the reins, closing my eyes and wishing for this lesson to end.

"*Ho laa!*" Jo yells to me. "You *naa* pay attention to what Kwihuu telling you. She plays now. You must tell her is learning time."

How am I supposed to tell this fierce beast it is not playing time? I think of Papa rapping our knuckles with his slate when we didn't pay attention during lessons. I do not think *Kwihuutsuu* have knuckles.

"Hey!" I yell at her. "Stop this, you beast! We are to be learning now, you and I. I will be disgraced if we cannot get this right."

In response, Kwihuu bucks wildly, trying to throw me off her back. I hold tightly, but bang my face against the saddle several times, feeling blood flow freely from my nose.

"You gum *pitar ro-ri-ta* awful beast!" I scream, letting my anger get the better of me. "Why must you be so difficult?"

At this, Jo erupts into laughter yet again, and my rage grows and slithers toward her, too.

"And you, you Cheese!" I yell at Jo. "You are just trying to kill me. You are not helping at all, just standing there and laughing!" I swipe at the blood, feeling it smear across my cheek, cooling my face in the hot wind.

Jo smiles up at me. "If you not careful, Tootie, I will change your name to Kwihuu the Second—the only other beast in village who matches your . . ."—she waves her hand, thinking of the word—"*plinot*."

I scrunch up my bleeding nose. "*Plini?*" What is she saying? That I am like the shelled beast Temple is so good at hunting?

"*Plinot! Plinot!*" Jo says. "This word you use with Natka!"

I have regained my precarious position on Kwihuu's back, again squeezing her gently with my knees. It is hard enough concentrating on not dying up here, without Jo yelling language lessons at me.

I shout down to her. "Stubborn? Is that what you're trying to say? *Plinot* is 'stubborn'?"

"*Ja!*" Jo says with a smile. "You too stubborn, Tootie. You and Kwihuu share this. Is why we matched you."

"Oh *that's* why," I say, trying as best I can to keep my heavy boots from pushing too hard against Kwihuu's scales. "I thought it was because you and Fist and Klara are conspiring to KILL ME."

Jo snickers as Kwihuu and I swoop down and skim over her head. Then Kwihuu decides it would be fun to try to fly high enough to puncture the Red Crescent.

"Oh, gods," I mutter, the wind catching my words and throwing them away like scrub dust. Reins in both hands now, I give a sharp tug and see Kwihuu's head pull back slightly. She clearly doesn't like this, as she jerks her head forward with a fierce snarl and starts another dive into the canyon. This time, though, I don't give in and scream and panic. I pull on the reins again, with more force, but not ungently. Again, she fights me.

169

Jo has gone silent as she watches us struggle for dominance, high—and then low and then upside down and then high again—in the sky. If I fail this test I will lose my Cheese name and be Mayrikafsa no more.

It is also a struggle within myself, I know. I should not want a Cheese name. Weeks ago, I should have fought and stabbed my way out of the village to try to go back home again even if it meant getting lost on the prairie and dying from the suns. And, yet, I do not wish to do these things. Neither do I want to lose my Cheese name and be relegated to the same status as Ben-ton. I feel that my future is unknowable. There is only now. And *right* now I need to master this beast.

I pull the reins again and again as Kwihuu slowly begins to let me guide her.

"Thank you, girl," I say, happy to be right side up again. "Sweet Kwihuu. We are friends now, yes?"

She sails up and out of the canyon, slow enough that my eyes are open and my breath is calm and for the first time since I came to the village I truly see the expanse of the prairie laid out below me.

What if I were to lead Kwihuu away from the village now? Out above the prairie and over the dunes? I would have to find Temple first, of course, and then we could fly off together. Would we be able to find the homestead? Would Kwihuu be able to find her way back here without us?

I think of Aunt Billie, surely having mourned our deaths by now. I think of Papa and wonder if he is alive or dead.

And what of Boone? What of his mother? I think of the terrible high summer that should be upon the homestead by now and wonder why it is not so deadly hot here with the Cheese. I think of eating sweet cakes at the table, telling stories with Aunt Billie. I think of mending Papa's pants by the cooling grate and practicing the pronunciation of herbs and seedlings.

I think of the fields, probably still full of boulders and unseeded because no one has been there to work them. I wonder if any cooling crystals ever made it back to Aunt Billie and Boone's mama. I swallow hard and wonder if they could survive with their cooling grates empty. Would the other homesteaders find the mercy to help them? Has Old Man Dan taken over the position of Sheriff Reverend? What would Papa think if he saw me like this, sleeveless, muscled, riding a beast? At least my hair is longer now.

I squeeze my knees around Kwihuu's middle and she responds with a playful nip at my boot, but then follows the movements of the reins as I guide her back down into the canyon and we land at Jo's feet. I allow one thought of Heetle and her ease with the reins, and how Klara told me Heetle was offered up to Ebibi shortly after she was taken. Then I shake my head. No more thoughts like these. I have mastered a *Kwihuutsuu* today. I will celebrate this.

Jo's smile is huge, and she throws her pointy, scaly Cheese face up at the Red Crescent and laughs her delight. She claps me on the back as I step onto the rocky scrub of the canyon floor, my knees shaking. I pat Kwihuu's head, but not close enough to her giant teeth that she might playfully take a finger by accident.

"You have done well, Tootie," Jo says, putting her hand under my chin and inspecting the bloody damage inflicted on my face by repeatedly slamming into Kwihuu's saddle. "Klara and A'alanatka—Fist—will be pleased."

I can't help but smile. I like that Jo is learning from me just as I am learning from her. And hearing that Klara and Fist will be pleased fills my heart. I rub my hand over the scar of my third eye, feeling it tingle as my neck and face flush with happiness.

It hits me then, like a blow.

I would never take Kwihuu to run away and risk getting lost on the prairie.

Never.

I do not actually want to leave the Cheese. Not anymore.

Despite all of the pain and torment, they want me to succeed as much as I want to succeed. Here, I am not a weakling. I am an equal among the tribe.

I am part of the Kihuut.

I . . . like it here.

20

TEMPLE CHATTERS WITH THE OTHER CHILDREN
around the fire. She speaks Cheese with them so naturally
that you would never guess it's not her native language.
Her hair has started to take on a more natural red look, I
don't know how. Maybe it is absorbing the mud and dirt
her Cheese people keep caked on her head.

"Tootie!" she yells, running to me in a whirl of hair and
wind. Her dress is made from dactyl skin—it is a beautiful
yellow that makes her blue eyes appear startlingly bright. I
still wear the fabric pants from my first day. They are growing short on me and are so threadbare and grotty they will
probably be ripped off my body with the next strong gust
from Mara.

Temple hugs me tightly. We do not see each other

often, but tonight the whole village is gathering for a feast. This happens every so often. I think it is like a town meeting. The Cheese give updates on projects they're working on, air their grievances, that kind of thing. There is always plentiful food, and Temple and I have an evening to speak of our days and how we are doing.

She grins up at me and I see yet another sharpened tooth. "You haven't moved on to people yet, have you?" I ask her.

Her head tilts, mimicking the movement of many of the Cheese when they do not understand what I'm trying to say.

"*Naa owa'a . . .* uh"—I point to myself—"*ke'ekutaat.*" Invaders. Temple pretends again that she can't understand me. We have been together only two minutes and I am already irritated with her.

"Temple," I say. "Stop this. You understand my words. Explain your tooth." I tap gently on her mouth. "Four sharpened teeth?"

Temple rolls her eyes and I fill with relief. There she is. There is my sister. "My name is Kalashava. Or you can call me Kaye as my people do."

I feel less relief now.

"I am quite good with the bow, Tootie," Temple continues with a grin. "I have advanced past all the children my age. My people say I shall be a fine warrior. Even a raider if I want."

I choke on the seeds I'm eating. "A raider? Temple.

You can't be serious. You are not even ten summers."

Her mouth forms a thin line. "Why wouldn't I be serious about that, Rae?" She shakes her head and scowls. "I mean, Mayrikafsa," she says. I have flustered her with my anger. Good.

"*Tootie.*" She draws out the "Tootie," as if she is Natka, taunting me. "Why shall I be a young warrior? A *Kihuutkafsa*? Because I am a strong fighter. I have the best aim of anyone in this village. I will not just go on raids one day. I will lead them." She lifts her upper lip in a Cheese snarl, showing off two of her sharpened teeth. In that moment—in the evening light of the Red Crescent—she looks vicious. I barely recognize her. Who is this small, boastful girl, speaking in such a thick Cheese accent, her human language coming in stops and starts?

"And I have not been killing *people*, Tootie," she says, stepping back from me, putting her hands on her hips. "Not yet, anyway." She smiles again and runs off to where the other children her age are playing.

My heart stills in my chest. Surely she was joking—giving me a difficult time for still acting as her protector when she is growing so strong. Surely.

I am shaken by the encounter throughout the entire evening, paying no attention to what the Cheese are saying. Klara leads the Kihuut in chants and songs and reenactments of raids. She renders justice upon those who need it. There is even a moment when Klara breaks up a fight between two of the men, but I miss what the fight is about.

Natka sits next to me on the rock bench and offers a handful of hashava fruit. I take it from him and mutter a quick thanks.

"Your head is in the clouds tonight, Tootie," he says. "You offer no insult to me? This make me *gagagaga* like a *kakee*." He pretends to cry like a baby, then shoves me hard in the shoulder. It is a joke that reminds me of Rory. Kamino. I offer him a half smile and he seems pleased with this, taking a few of the hashava fruit from my hand and popping them into his mouth one by one as if it is a game.

Natka's stump is bandaged lightly, and no longer bound to his chest. I have seen him walking to the healer woman's cave often. Her poultices must be very effective, because he seems healthier than he has ever been—he is still impressively strong, even with only one good arm.

"The arm is doing well?" I ask after a moment. He tilts his head in that Cheese way and I look to the sky, trying to find the right words. "*Lomtar*," I say, pointing to the bandage. "*Ooma?* Okay?"

Natka nods. "*Ja.* My *lomtar* is oh-kaye." He smiles. I notice for the first time that he has the same number of sharpened teeth that Temple does.

"When will they let you ride again?" I ask, my eyes on my battered boots. "Suu must miss you."

Natka's voice lowers. "This thing that happen. This thing you cause"—and here he shoves my thigh with one of his pointed claw-nails, scratching me lightly—"it never happen before. *Kaykani* . . . they all *loota*."

I scrunch up my forehead, not understanding his words. "The breakfast biscuits are bathing," I say. "Of course."

Natka snuffles out a laugh. "Not *kayKI lootAR*, you *ro-ri-ta* gum human. *KayKANI looTA*."

It is my turn to laugh. "You said 'gum'! Ha ha! I shall slowly conquer the Cheese with my human swearing!"

Natka scratches at the bandage. "They not know what to do," he says, his voice growing serious.

"New rules," I say. "*Loota kaykani.* That's what you were saying. They are having to make new rules because of what has happened?"

Natka sighs and looks to the stars. "Is because I did not fail test, but also did not succeed. I defied Ebibi," he says, giving me a sharp look, and quickly touching his chest and closing his eyes. He opens them and stares hard at me. "But was not my fault."

"Do they seek to punish me?" I ask. Other than the sharp hit to my face that knocked me out, Fist has not come to me with any punishment. I was allowed back in the cave several days after the incident and no one has spoken of it since. This continues to surprise me, but certainly I will not seek out punishment. I am not that much of a gum *ro-ri-ta* human.

Natka shakes his head. "They decide Ebibi willed it. Is . . . out of their control."

I nod, happy for the confirmation that I will not be

dragged from my bed and fed to the *Kwihuutsuu* as punishment for being a vile rule breaker.

"I know what they think, though," Natka says, pulling tight at his horsetail with his good hand, his mouth going rigid. "They think I never be warrior. Never *Kihuutkafsa*."

A wave of guilt strikes me nearly as hard as Fist's open hand. By saving Natka's life I may well have ruined it. Will he be relegated to work with dregs like the scheming Benton? Surely not. But what *will* he do? If Temple has already four teeth sharpened, she will overtake him when her age allows.

I run my tongue over my smooth teeth, wondering about all the training I've had, and how I have never once shot an arrow at anything other than a rock, or at Fist—but only when he forced me. They are training me to be skilled, to have stamina, to fight, but not to kill. They have given me a name that ends with *kafsa*, but why? And what does *Mayri* mean? I have been too afraid to ask.

I push these questions from my mind. I will worry about them later. Now I must do something to help Natka. His life must not be ruined because of a classic Rae mistake. A thought strikes me. It is crazy. And it, too, might be another trouble-causing, Rae-tries-to-solve-a-problem-by-creating-worse-problems idea. But it gnaws at me, climbing through my head, branching out into my brain like shine tree poison. I do not hear what Natka says, as this poison of an idea invades every thought.

"Natka!" I say, jumping up. "Let us make up their minds for them."

He looks at me as if I have a prairie beetle climbing from my nose.

"I need materials," I say. "Metals, wire, cutters, fabric. Do you have these things somewhere in the village?"

Natka squints, working out my words. "Come with me," he says. I follow him away from the fire and to the edge of the village. The other Cheese are eating and merrymaking as Klara speaks and no one misses us as we move away from the crowds. After several minutes of walking, we stand in front of the healer woman's cave.

I shake my head. "I am not looking for poultices, Natka."

"*Naa*," he says, rattling the beaded curtain that hangs over the cave entrance—a curtain that looks to be made of night beetle carapaces. "Wantosakaal will have these . . . things . . . you need."

She appears then, poking her face through the beads, a puff of smoke around her head. She says something to Natka in a low scratchy voice that I do not understand. He shakes his head, points to me, and says something back. She nods once and holds the curtains aside for us.

I follow Natka into the cave. It looks different from the last time I was here. Bigger, and yet filled with more mysteries; details I missed in my panic of that night that seems so long ago. There are pots boiling over a fire in the front of the cave, the smoke stretching its fingers through the opening and stinging my eyes. Variations of scrub hang upside down, drying over the fire, and also in other places around the cave. Aunt Billie would feel very at home in this cave. I realize with a start, I feel very comfortable, too.

Clay jars fill almost every space on several tables and the large stone table is still in the center, scrubbed clean, showing no trace of Natka's blood, which flowed so freely several weeks ago.

"Show her," Natka says, indicating I should use my hands. "She will try to find what you need."

So I do. I run through a list of all the things I'm looking for and the tools I think I will need. I pantomime, and say the few Cheese words I know to describe them. The healer woman nods or shakes her head each time, and leads me to a small alcove in the back of the cave. She rummages through piles and boxes, producing the objects I've asked for one by one.

As my eyes grow wider, Natka laughs. "Wantosakaal has many, many, many summers, Tootie. She knows all and has all."

Wantosakaal chatters in her prairie beetle voice and Natka laughs, throwing his head back, his snickers climbing all the way to the ceiling and down again.

"What?" I say.

"She say everyone think Klarakova is leader of Kihuut peoples, but really it is Wantosakaal."

I smile. It is just like home. That causes a pang deep inside me and I try to shake it off. Everyone in Origin

Township knew that Papa was the Sheriff Reverend, but they also knew if someone was sick or injured or needed a tincture for some ailment or other, or even a special seed for a difficult-to-grow plant, Aunt Billie would have it, or make it, or do her best to find it. She would be grouchy about it, but she would have it, even old medicines scavenged from the *Origin*. Papa keeps the township safe and blessed, but Aunt Billie keeps it alive.

I swallow hard, and gather the supplies in my arms. I lay them out on the table and study them. This is not going to be easy, but I remember Aunt Billie teaching guest lessons at the schoolhouse. She told us of Old Earth and the almost magical answers they had for the maladies of their people. She said we could not replicate these answers because so much had been destroyed on the *Origin*. But we still have books and stories and maybe one day we will be able to make our own similar technology.

I gently pull Natka down to sit beside me, and place his stump on the table. I measure and trace and then when he retreats back to the shadows to watch I begin to cut and sew and saw and burn and I work through the night, sweating in the damp heat of the cave, everything dropping away as my vision comes to life before me.

My eyes are gritty with exhaustion when I wake Natka. He is slumped against the wall, a blanket over him. The suns are not yet up, but I know they will be soon. Wantosakaal left to tell Klara and Fist where we were and she did not return. They must have offered her dinner and a pallet. She is old and no doubt the walk from the edge of the village exhausted her. I feel bad about this.

Natka wakes and sits up straighter. "Tootie," he says, a smile growing on his face. "What is this?"

I smile and kneel down next to him. "Give me your arm," I say. He holds up his stump and I lash on the new lower arm and hand I have built. With metals and fabric and skin from *Kwihuutsuu*, it is a somewhat successful replica of a lower arm, hand, and five fingers. I pull fine strings of metal up Natka's arm and show him how they tie around his shoulder, padded with fabric.

"If you move just so," I say, moving his arm back and forth and side to side, "you will be able to move some of the fingers." He tries on his own, his eyes growing wider and wider.

"Of course, it is not the same as your own . . . *lomtar*," I say, chewing my bottom lip and making a few adjustments. "But it is as good as I can do. I think with practice— *tokonata*—you will be able to fly Suu again."

I show him how he can lock the fingers in a grasping position and then unlock them. "You can use this hand to hold the reins while you shoot . . . or scratch your *pitar* with your other." I smile.

"You . . . this . . ." It is the first time I have seen Natka struck dumb. He clacks the fingers together, slowly moving his new arm and hand back and forth in front of his eyes.

He grabs me in a tight hug and I can smell that we

both have not bathed in too long. Then he pushes me back, looks me in the eyes, and playfully shoves me.

"*Flotaka*," he whispers, putting his new hand on my shoulder. "It is . . . miracle."

"Well, I don't know about that," I say, feeling delight in his delight. "But maybe it will help Klara and Fist decide that you can ride again. Someone needs to take Suu to the skies before she eats us all."

Natka lets out a whoop and runs from the cave, leaving me to clean up the whole gum mess by myself.

It is still dark outside, but I'm sure Natka's whooping is waking the whole village. I can only hope I have not violated some ancient law of the Cheese by doing this. My luck tends to lean that way, and yet, even if I am once again subjected to Fist's wrath, I do not care. There is light again in Natka's eyes. Light that was removed partly because of me.

I have given him back the hand I took. As best I can, anyway.

I look around the cave once more before I leave, peeking into the jars, stirring the pots. It is a nice place even if it is hot and smells like a *Kwihuutsuu* nest.

There is shouting now, coming from the center of the village. That I can hear it all the way out here is either very good, or very bad. I pull my hair tighter in its horsetail and walk from the cave, back straight, chin high.

Whatever judgment awaits, I am ready.

21

"*NAA OWA'A*," KLARA SAYS. IT WON'T HURT. BUT she's leaning over me with a jagged piece of metal so I do not trust her assessment of the situation. She motions for me to open my mouth.

I lick my lips and take a deep breath. Then I open up. My head is in her lap. There is a ceremonial bowl of water on the floor next to us. She begins to hum in that Cheese way . . . the insectlike buzzing sound that is both unsettling and beautiful. As she hums and chants, she files away at my right incisor.

Fist and Natka sit across from us, both uncharacteristically silent. They, too, begin to hum and chant, closing their eyes. The *scritch-scritch-scritch* of the metal on my tooth is maddening, but I lie still.

Klara dips a piece of rough fabric into the water and wipes it over my tooth. Then she smiles and pats my head. All done. I sit up and run my tongue over the sharpened tooth. I hope I do not slice open my lip while chewing hashava fruit. That would not be very warrior-like.

I smile at Klara and then ask the question that has bothered me since she told me the ceremony was to occur. "Why did you do this? I have killed nothing."

"*Paha'a haikonta* is not just for killing," Natka answers for her. "Is for bravery, for good thinking, as well."

"You think good," Klara says in her halting grasp of human language. I smile at her and she hugs me roughly, squeezing tight.

Natka clacks his fake fingers. "Not as *ro-ri-ta* as we all thought," he says. Fist gives a warning flick to the side of Natka's head, but smiles.

I rub my tongue over the tooth again. Smart? This is what they think? Well, I do not know if they are right, but I will take it.

Fist stands and then returns with a plate of dried plini meat and several bowls of seeds and hashava. Now it is feasting time. Celebration. I shall try not to gash open my mouth while we celebrate my smartness.

"Mayrikafsa." Fist's voice is low as he shakes my shoulder. I roll over and open one eye. My piles of blankets have been especially soft and comfortable lately, after weeks of intense running drills and knife practice and learning how to fly

Kwihuu in complicated maneuvers and in formations with other *Kwihuutsuu* and their riders. Yesterday was no exception. Natka and Suu chased me from one sun to another, so that by the time the suns went down both Kwihuu and I could barely move from exhaustion.

I sit up on my pallet of blankets, rubbing the dreams from my eyes. Racing horses with Boone. Aunt Billie mixing tinctures. Temple before her red hair and sharpened teeth. Old Man Dan with flames in his eyes. Papa, pale, bent the wrong way on the cooling flats, his mouth moving with no sound. It is the same dream I have over and over. Though I am tired, I'm happy to see Fist's face leaning into mine. It is much nicer to be awake.

Natka stands along the cave wall, attaching his hand, pulling the ties tight with his teeth. His hair stands on end, proving he has just been woken as well. While I'm glad to no longer suffer my haunted dreams I do not know why we are awake before the suns.

Klara goes to Natka, fussing over him, making those vibrating Cheese noises that I've learned to listen to for comfort. He mutters to her to please let him be, so she offers him a biscuit and then offers one to me and Fist as well.

As he does most every morning, Fist puts out a pair of *nantolas* for me, and as I do on these mornings I refuse to even look at the gum ugly shoes. Fist is more insistent than usual this morning, giving me a light smack and pointing at the shoes. When I shake my head again he gives me another smack, this time a little harder.

"*Naa*," I say, regretting that "no" is the first word out of my mouth for the day.

"Is not choice today, Mayrikafsa," Fist growls. He throws the shoes on my lap. "Do not bring *tonton* upon this house."

"*Tonton*?" I say.

"Failure," Natka says through the crumbs in his mouth. "He not want you to bring disgrace on us. Though I know this might be . . . difficult . . . for you." He walks over and slugs me in the shoulder with his fake hand.

"You cannot hit me with the hand I made for you," I say, frowning and shaking my finger at Natka.

He shakes his finger back, mimicking me. "You took my real hand, Tootie. I hit you all I want." He slugs me once more, smiles, then picks up my boots from where they lie at the foot of my pallet.

"Hey! Give those back!"

Natka walks to the fire pit.

"No, no no! Okay. Wait. I'll wear the *ro-ri-ta nantolas* today. Just please don't burn my boots."

"Boots," Fist says. It's as if he has just said a word for excrement. He shakes his head, but holds his hand up indicating that Natka should put the boots down. Klara takes them from him and disappears with them.

I tighten the twine on my pants when Fist shakes his head again. "*Naa*, Mayrikafsa. Only *peltan* this day."

What is this? No boots. No pants. "Only *peltan*?" I whine. "But I will be mostly naked."

"You will be like . . . Kihuut," Natka says. Fist nods once.

Klara returns and hands me the *peltan*—it is one piece of clothing that is made from *Kwihuutsuu* skin and serves as both shirt and pants, but the pants are very short, showing off nearly the whole length of my newly muscled legs. I disappear to the back of the cave and change. Oh, gods, am I really to spend my day nearly naked, *and* wearing indecent shoes? What makes this day any different from other days?

I come back to the front room and Klara nods her approval. I tug at the short part, which barely covers my bottom, trying to get it lower. Seeing myself out of the baggy fabric pants and shirt, I realize that while I am growing taller and my muscles look more like boys' muscles than girls', my form is also slightly more ladylike now. Well, as ladylike as a form can be that is flat as a washboard, with a skinny waist, skinny bottom, and long matted black hair that is as wild as the winds.

Fist goes to the carved-out kitchen area and returns to us holding a small pot. He hands it to Natka and Natka begins to paint Fist's face with the golden and silver swirls that still my blood.

We are going on a raid. Now I understand. My heart shoots into my throat like a light arrow. A raid. Is this what comes of the success I've earned from creating Natka's new hand? Is this an order from Klara? If we come back "successful," I will be a warrior in the eyes of the Kihuut. But I do not know what "successful" entails. I cannot go against my own people.

But are they my people still? My dreams say yes. My life says no.

Natka has finished with Fist's face and hands him the bowl. Fist slowly continues to paint thin spirals down his arms and across his chest. He uses the tips of his claw-nails to create a filigree across his abdomen. It is somehow both beautiful and menacing, like the Kihuut themselves.

When Fist finishes with his body paint, he motions for Natka and me to stand next to each other. I've grown taller since coming to the village, as I am nearly the same height as Natka now. My white skin has become browner as I've spent so many days under the suns. My hair is so long that even pulled up in a horsetail it tickles the base of my neck. I am still scrawny compared with my Cheese brother, but not as much so.

Fist begins to hum—starting low with a buzzing coming deep from his throat. He alternates, painting part of Natka's face, then part of mine, back and forth until he's done. Fist spins his hand, motioning for us to turn. I feel his hand pull back my horsetail and the coolness of the paint covers my third-eye scar. He paints Natka's third eye, then turns us back around.

Klara has been standing to the side, watching; now she comes to us. "Mara be with you this day, my *kakono*," she says to Natka, her mouth set in a line, stern, but with bright eyes. She turns her bright eyes to me, and says, "Mara be with you this day, my *kakoni*." She kisses the tops of our heads, then steps back from us. Fist motions that we should leave the cave.

"What is *kakoni*?" I whisper to Natka.

He puts a hand on my shoulder. "It means 'daughter.'"

Daughter.

The word echoes through my skull and lands in my pounding heart.

"May Mara bless all the *Kihuutkafsa* today," Klara calls after us with a buzz in her throat.

I turn and see her standing in the opening of the cave, so tall, so regal. Her face is set, her mouth proud. But her eyes give her away. I see the worry there. I feel it, too.

The whole village has turned out to see us off. It is me, Natka, Fist, Jo, and a few others who make up the raiding party. Ben-ton stands off to the side. He flicks his wrist, magically producing a bunch of scrub flowers tied with twine. He holds the bundle out to me, his lips smiling but his eyes dark.

"For the young warrior," he says, "wearing the future on her shoulders."

I work hard to ignore him.

"For luck, then," he shouts after me, tossing the scrub into the air. My instincts cause me to catch it without thinking.

I walk briskly to the *Kwihuutsuu*, saddled and waiting for us by the always-burning fire in the center of the village.

I look to Ben-ton, who continues to stare at me with . . . what . . . in his eyes. Curiosity? Cunning? Jealousy? Could it be hatred?

I hold up the flowers and he smiles.

Then I feed the bundle to Kwihuu, twine and all.

She is laden with provisions. Bags attached to the saddle are full of biscuits, old but sturdy handbows, canteens of water; there is even a blanket carefully folded and tied to the back of the saddle.

The village does not cheer as we take to the skies. They remain silent, praying to Mara for our safety and success. It is an eerie business seeing so many Cheese and only hearing the howl of the wind and the crackle of the flames.

As the village becomes smaller and we fly higher, I glance at Natka. His face is set, his eyes clear, his bony upper lip clasped tightly over his lower lip. He favors Klara remarkably this morning. His new hand grasps the reins well, as it has through our many practices. He has a handbow tightened around his other hand. He does not look as shaky and bile-filled as I feel. Not even close.

I hug Kwihuu with my knees and she turns to nip at my *nantola*-clad foot. I must admit, the gum ugly shoes feel nice around my toes. It is like not wearing shoes at all. My feet are as light as the wind.

Our journey is on its second day when Fist signals for us to fly in formation. Most of his words catch in the wind and I miss them, but I do recognize his hand gestures. When we get to the township, Natka is to be part of the landing party. I am to stay on Kwihuu and protect the *Kihuutkafsa* from the air. I can do this. I can do this.

Our formation breaks and I see homesteads below us. We crossed Maasakota, but not at the point where the *Origin* crashed, so these homesteads are not part of Origin Township. That is strange, because I know of no other townships on this moon. But as the *Kwihuutsuu* dip and play in the skies I see that these homesteads are abandoned, nearly lost to the winds and dust.

"Who lived here?" I shout over to Natka. He is tossing bits of dried plini flesh through the sky to Suu, who is snapping her jaws over her shoulder and eating them as if they are the last food on the moon.

Natka shrugs. "Is before my time. Father will not speak of it. Old Kihuut talk stories of traders coming from Hosani. Of *soka'a* caves."

"Ghost caves," I say, feeling a shiver run down my arms.

Natka shrugs again. "Is just stories." He flies ahead to catch up with the group.

I linger back, looking down at the ruined structures. If the rumors are true, then who were these people? If people came from Hosani, they would have had to be able to leave again. That means working spaceships.

I urge Kwihuu to fly faster. I want to get past these ghost houses. My chest tightens as we speed up and it strikes me how much hotter the air has become since leaving the village. Dustier, too, even this high up. I do my best to point my face into the wind and take deep breaths. Perhaps I am just nervous. Or scared. Or both.

It is another half day of flying until I see movement below.

A homestead.

People running.

And then we are past them, still flying fast and high.

Fist leads his dactyl into a dive and the rest of us follow in the formation we've practiced so many times.

My heart tries to leap from my chest, my mouth is dry. Kwihuu screams as she dives. We come through a cloud of dust and as I cough the debris from my lungs I break formation as I've been taught, flying a pattern around the perimeter of our group. That's when my eyes clear from the dust and focus and I fully comprehend where we are. Now I know why there are so many of us in this raiding party.

We are above the center of Origin Township, not just a mere homestead. The suns are low in the sky so it is high summer market time. The homesteaders have ventured from the safety of their cooling grates and are conducting business as quickly as they can, buying and trading for food and livestock, goods and supplies.

Even from above I can see what a haggard bunch they are, skinny from not enough food, sweating through their clothes. It is so gum hot, I feel my skin drying and frying in the suns. It is so much hotter on this part of the moon. I cannot wait to get home.

The homesteaders have scattered, screaming, as we fly the *Kwihuutsuu* in slashes and dives over their heads. Parcels of food and supplies lie spilled across the scrub as people leap for cover.

If necessary, I am to make Kwihuu dive and scream and scare the people away from the older *Kihuutkafsa*, who will be doing whatever it is they need to do. I am to fight only to protect myself or the other *Kihuutkafsa*.

Fist, Jo, and Natka have landed and are running through the market. They seem to be taking things indiscriminately, and stuffing them into small sacks. I do not understand what the people of Origin Township have that the Cheese do not already have in their village.

Natka grabs a woman by the hair and throws her out of his way as he storms a booth filled with empty canteens. The metal canteens go everywhere, rattling and crashing on the rocks that litter the ground. The woman screams and screams, her hands in her hair. She is on her knees in the scrub and she won't stop screaming.

Natka throws a canteen at her, but still she continues. I nudge Kwihuu to go lower so I can better see what's happening. Do I know this woman? My blood runs cold watching the scene. It is Virginia. Old Man Dan's wife. I haven't seen her in nearly an entire summer's time as she was with child and under orders from Aunt Billie to stay resting in bed.

Three men come running for Natka, but I skim their

heads with Kwihuu, keeping them back. One of them shoots at me from his handbow, but misses. The woman continues to scream. Natka runs to her, swiping at her head with his knife. There is a spray of blood and he calls out, "*Lolobee!*"

I taste bile and feel dizziness sweep through me—Mara behind my eyes. Natka has taken Virginia's ear. She is silent now, slumped in the dirt, blood pooling around her head. Natka puts the ear in a sack and marches back into the booth.

Kwihuu swoops down as I guide her. "Natka!" I yell. "*Sonako hee ta!*" Stop now! The other raiders are busy with their own battles and no one seems to notice what is happening over here. I cannot be part of this. I cannot do this.

I nudge Kwihuu and she grazes the top of the booth, screeching.

"Natka!"

He emerges from the booth, his eyes shining, and he shrieks into the wind.

He holds up his prize.

It is a baby.

"*Naa! Naa kakee!*" I am screaming "No baby!" as loudly as I can as Kwihuu circles and dives over him, protecting him from the Origin Township citizens who are now coming after him. Someone shoots a laser rifle at him, grazing his fake arm. He laughs at his luck.

Why are they shooting? Gum *ro-ri-ta* men. They could hit the baby.

Natka is trying to make his way back to Suu, through the rifle shots and light arrows, but is not gaining much ground.

I continue yelling at him, but he either doesn't hear me, or doesn't care to listen. We cannot take Old Man Dan's baby. We cannot.

Horses are approaching now, and the men on them engage Fist and Jo and the others in a fierce battle to get closer to Natka. The Cheese warriors are very skilled and not so beaten down from weeks of heat. They easily overcome the humans, and signal Natka that it is time for this raid to be over. He still has his hands full with several armed homesteaders, though, and with me as I try both to protect him and to prevent him from leaving with the baby.

A belching one-man bounces into the market, careening into the melee. Old Man Dan leaps from the vehicle, red faced, sweating. Something glints from his vest. He is wearing Papa's sheriff's star. Papa is dead, then. Or was discovered on the flats and disgraced for violating the harvest season laws. It is too much to think about right now. It's all too much.

Old Man Dan yells, "You keep your hands off my daughter, you evil stinking Flatfaces!" Jo jumps on him, but Old Man Dan shoots her in the shoulder with a light rifle. Jo screams and falls into the scrub. Another Cheese pulls her away and lashes her to a dactyl and then runs back to the fight.

There is enough confusion on the ground that Natka has made it back to Suu and has the baby in a sack on his back.

I fly over to him, hovering on Kwihuu and screaming down, "You cannot take this baby. She is not yours!" Natka says nothing, only lightly kicks Suu and she flaps her wings, readying to take to the sky.

Twisting the reins, I position Kwihuu barely above the ground in front of Suu. "Natka!" I shout, my beast facing his, their jaws snapping at each other. "Listen to me!" But he is not listening. He is waving his arms wildly at me. I turn in time to see a large piece of metal swinging at my head. I duck, feeling a scrape across my shoulder blades. Kwihuu cries out, her blood dripping onto my leg as a gash opens along her side.

I see only white as I leap from Kwihuu and rage toward the person responsible for hurting her. I tackle the man, wrenching the metal from him and hitting him across the face with it. He is unconscious only, I hope, and not dead, but he is bleeding very much. What have I done? I drop the metal, my hands slick with sweat and blood, yet gritty from all the dust.

"Mayrikafsa!" Fist yells. He points at Kwihuu. *"Kwihuu, hee ta!"* He is telling me it's time to leave . . . now.

My breath is tight, strangled. The chaos upon us has slowed before my eyes, the slashing of knives and flashes of light moving in deliberate arcs before me. Even the screams seem to have slowed. I can pick out the Cheese from the men. The men are angry, hurting. The Cheese are dominant, prideful. My chest grows tighter and tighter. Is it the breathing sickness back again? Someone grabs my arm and pulls me to Kwihuu.

I am on her back, grabbing the reins without thinking, nudging her into the sky. The *zip-pew* of light arrows follows us, Kwihuu's blood trailing into the dusty wind behind us. Natka and Suu are up ahead. I cannot see if he still has the baby. I glance down below and see a boy pointing a handbow at me and staring. Our eyes lock for one moment and he drops the handbow, his mouth falling open.

It is Boone. Alive. In one piece. He looks skinny, but well.

I hiccup a relieved sob, not finding enough air, wanting to shout something to him, to apologize for everything that is happening, but I'm not conjuring any breath. Kwihuu moves faster, climbing high in the sky, away from light arrows and hunks of metal, away from the blood and pain and screaming, away from Boone, my friend from what feels like so long ago. I am gasping still, seeing stars through tears.

Another *Kwihuutsuu* pulls alongside us. It is Fist. He puts his hand out to my arm and squeezes. "Look ahead," he says. "Only ahead. Feel proud. *Oo'ta kon famalil naa paht toofa'a.*" It's not so tragic if you don't look down.

I say it to myself over and over as I try to calm my breathing.

It's not so tragic if you don't look down.

It's not so tragic if you don't look down.

It's not so tragic if you don't look down.

22

WE MAKE CAMP FOR THE NIGHT AND I FEEL that my whole body is numb. I have injuries I do not remember sustaining. I think this is the same for all of us.

Jo is pulled from her *Kwihuutsuu* and laid out on a blanket. She groans and mutters from the pain of her injury, but Fist applies a poultice and gives her sleeping scrub and it seems as though she will be okay. It is not a mortal wound if we can keep infection at bay.

The baby, a small thing, yet old enough to sit and hold up her bald head, cries and cries. I know the people from Origin Township have set out to recover her, even if they don't know where to look. Babies are prizes to be protected and nurtured. Old Man Dan will not let this happen without a fight.

Fist holds the baby, shushing her and rocking her in slow movements. He drips water from his claw-nails into the baby's mouth, and the baby greedily laps it up.

"Mayrikafsa," Fist says in a near whisper. "Come here." I do as he says, even though my mind reels at what has happened during this day.

When I reach them, Fist takes some sleeping scrub and mixes it with the water to form a paste. He puts this paste on my clawless finger and motions for me to put my finger into the baby's mouth. I do as he says, rubbing the child's gums, feeling little buds of sharp teeth poking through.

Within moments, the baby is asleep. Fist lays her on a blanket next to Jo and turns to me.

"Natka say you try to . . . stop him."

I nod. "I did not think he should take the baby," I say, still feeling numb. "That baby does not belong to the Cheese."

"It belongs with us," Natka says, coming up to us. "As do you. It was born of this moon, as were you. Mara wills it."

"Do I belong?" I run my hand over my face. When I pull it away, it is covered in smeared paint. "Have I ever really belonged?"

Fist puts his hand on my shoulder. "You my daughter, Mayrikafsa. You are Kihuut."

"But why?" I ask. "You already have a child. Why do you need another? Why do you want me taking part in these awful things?" I look at the paint, the dried blood on my hands. "Why *do* the Cheese take human girls? Is it because of Kailia? You know I cannot replace Klara's sister any more than I can be a true Kihuut."

Fist gazes to the stars and then back at my face. "Not enough *kakee*," he says simply. "No *kakoni*. No daughters. Kailia was the last." He turns to Natka, speaking in Cheese so quickly I cannot follow. Natka nods and looks hard into my eyes. "The Kihuut cannot die out," Natka says. "We must protect sacred land. So we take those born of this moon. Those who can feel A'akowitoa in bones. We must choose strong *kakoni*. Like you. Kalashava. Kamino."

Not enough Kihuut babies. I think back upon the village and realize I've not seen any children younger than six or seven summers. And the children that are there are very few, and none of them girls.

"Also, we teach a lesson," Natka says. "You humans come to our moon, take our lands; take what's not yours. Now you see how you like it."

"The *Origin* crashed here by *accident*," I say, feeling heat rise into my face, the numbness of the day finally wearing off. "We didn't steal land on *purpose*. We had no choice. We are stuck on this gum rock, dying off as well. Babies are sacred to *us*, too."

Natka shakes his head. "But you come to steal land from Hosani peoples." He points to the Red Crescent. "And instead you just kill them off. *Ro-ri-ta* hyoo-mans. How you get to Hosani if you kill the people *from* there?" Fist slaps his hand, hard, and hisses at him.

202

"My people weren't going to steal anything," I say. "The Star Farmers Act gave them lands found in the Outer Rim. The Old Earth government granted the lands."

Natka growls and slashes his fake hand through the air. "You cannot give land that is not yours!"

"*You* cannot take babies," I say. "I cannot abide stealing people." I go to Kwihuu, my head pounding, my heart pumping, and begin tying the bags closed on her saddle. I whip my blanket up off the dirt, shake it out, and tie it to her. "I do not want to be part of it."

"Where do you go, then, *looa'a kakee*?" Natka asks, his right fist clenching at his side. "You gum *pitar* hyoo-man?"

"I go home," I say, tightening Kwihuu's reins.

"To the village, then," Fist says with a long sigh. He touches his hip and winces. He is sweating and seems resigned to let me have my tantrum.

"I think she not mean village," Natka says, stepping so close to me that I can feel the heat coming off his body. "I think she mean to run away, back to hyoo-mans."

Fist looks up, startled.

Is this what I mean? That I am to take Kwihuu and go back to the township? To return home, a captive no more? To eat sweet cakes and feel Aunt Billie pat my head as she soothes my woes? I am so confused and angry.

"What is for you there, Mayrikafsa?" Fist asks. His voice is low and humming like Mara's soft breeze. "Work in fields. Heat. Dust." He gently pushes Natka aside and puts both hands on my sweating shoulders. "Your father

203

tell me to protect his *kakoni*. So this I did. I saw you bravery. I help you grow strong. Help Kihuut grow strong. This moon, Mayrikafsa, it is mother to us both."

Fist hugs me tight, then releases me, wincing again and quickly touching his hip where I see a small amount of blood seeping through his *peltan*. He stares at me hard. "You Kihuut now, Mayrikafsa." He puts one hand on the back of my neck, over the third eye, and pulls my forehead to rest upon his own. "You *Kihuutkafsa*. Warrior. As will be Kalashava, your sister." He puts more pressure on the back of my neck, forcing my eyes to meet his. "You *kaykalaa*. You family." Fist releases my neck and sweeps his hand to the side. "You *kaykalaa* not just to me, Klarakova, Natka, but to village, to Oonatka, Oonan, A'akow. Mara. You may be *krasnoakafsa* one day."

My chest tightens more than it has all day. I do not know what to say, but worse, I cannot speak. My throat closes in on itself, the stars fill my vision. I gasp for air. The breathing sickness has been threatening to take hold all day. Why now? Why after so long? I fall to my knees, clutching at my throat and chest. I start counting, trying to slow my gasps, but it's not helping.

"It looks like she is soon to be family to Ebibi," Natka says, brows furrowed. His hand goes to his chest, his eyes close and then open. He kneels next to me, scrabbling in a bag for something. He offers me a canteen, but I cannot stop gasping long enough to drink. I know it will not help anyway. I need the drops. I need Temple to hold my hands and count for me.

"B-breathing a-attack," I sputter. *"Naa mara."* I point to my chest. No wind.

Fist throws me over his shoulder and jumps on Kwihuu.

I gasp and cough and my lungs feel like dust and fire. The stars in my vision are so bright. I am not long for consciousness.

Natka and Suu are alongside us as Kwihuu streaks through the night sky. I reach out to the Red Crescent looming so close. Would this have been my home? Where is my home?

Fist is yelling in Cheese, Natka is yelling back. My head lolls on my neck as Kwihuu shrieks into the sky. Yes, Kwihuu, sweet dactyl. This is how I feel, too. Only, I cannot make a sound.

I open my eyes to blackness, then close them again because there is no such thing as true blackness on this moon. Not with the Red Crescent glowing through the nights and the suns scorching the days. My chest is still tight, my breath wheezing. I am alive. But . . . I open my eyes again and it is still black.

Now there are voices. Fist. Natka. Arguing.

"Mitan. Hee ta!"

"Naa. Bibiloka, ke ro-ri-ta kakono!"

Why are they yelling about roots and . . . what? I see an orange glow swirling in the distance like a star that has lost its way. I blink a few times and pull my hands off my chest so that I can push myself up to a sitting position. My hands touch the ground, and I yank them up. I am sitting on an animal. An immense beast.

"Fist!" I wheeze. "A'alanatka." The lost star bounces to me and as it gets closer I see that it lights up Fist's face.

I put my hands down again, feeling the soft fur under them, shocked at the coolness of this fur, of the total blackness surrounding me. I sit up as Fist kneels, holding a flameless flare up to my face. Natka kneels next to him and they talk about me in Cheese. I understand something about my coloring and Ebibi and how I am not dead.

"What is . . . this beast?" I wheeze. My chest is loosening some and I take a great gulp of air.

"Beast?" Fist asks, putting a hand to my forehead.

I reach out and grab his hand that is holding the flameless flare and point it at the ground. Then I realize my mistake. It is not fur. It is some kind of fine, soft scrub covering all of the ground. It even climbs the wall behind me. I have never seen anything like it. I wave my other hand over the soft scrub and Fist laughs.

"*Ebishava*," he says. "Plant of darkness." He takes his hand from my forehead and adjusts something that is tied tightly against my throat. "Is working," he says. "Ebibi *soka'a* show mercy." He touches his chest and closes his eyes.

"Ebibi's ghosts?" I say, my breath coming ever stronger. My head still beats along with my pulse, but my lungs have expanded. I feel as though I can breathe in all of the darkness. It is as if I am at the cooling flats again.

Through the sounds of trickling water, I hear Natka rummaging in a sack and then a blinding light sails up into the darkness. A true flare. And in the bright white glow that lasts only moments I can barely comprehend what surrounds me.

We are in an immense cave with countless tunnels leading to gods only know where. There are cooling crystals taller than four men standing on one another's shoulders, pools of water, sheer cliffs, clusters of more cooling crystals and other crystals that are white, green, gray. There are small plants, too, scattered throughout the fine, dense scrub that blankets the ground. These plants are heavy with brown fruit.

"Hashava!" I say. Natka and Fist smile.

The flare falls to the ground, its light dying out, but not before I see that littered under all the giant crystals and among the smaller clusters are even more cooling crystals. They lie everywhere, as if this cave is the belly of a beast that dines on—

The light is out. It is blackness again. I jump up, my heart buzzing. I have never been in such dark. Not even in the hiding pit. I feel it crawling all over me. I scratch at my eyes, gulp the air.

A hand reaches out to steady me. "We are in the caves of Ebibi," Natka says gently. And though I can't see him, I am sure he is doing that thing the Cheese do when they speak of Ebibi—touching his chest, closing his eyes.

"Life is plenty here," he continues. "If you welcome the dark."

This makes no sense to me, but I continue with my questions. "How did you stop the breathing attack? It usually takes special drops that only Aunt Billie has; that she found in short supply in the *Origin* wreckage and has been trying to replicate but with no—" A clawed finger rests against my lips.

"*Bibiloka*," Fist says, taking his finger from my lips and tapping the object twined around my neck. "What you say . . . coo-link cree-steel. But blessed by Ebibi."

My hand goes to my neck and I feel the crystal that is nestled in the soft divot between my collarbones. How did I never think of this? How did *Aunt Billie* never think of this? I always breathe so well at the cooling flats. It is such a simple answer that has eluded us.

"*Flotaka*," I whisper.

Fist laughs. "*Naa flotaka.* It is Wantosakaal magic. And Ebibi magic."

Fist cracks another flameless flare and his face shines orange in the light. Natka makes the silly hand gestures that Ben-ton does when he's doing his *ro-ri-ta* magic tricks.

This reminder of Ben-ton, another stolen human, opens the fresh wound in my memory. Natka. The baby. The awful raid. The poor homesteaders. Boone. It must show on my face because Natka's hand stills and his mouth goes small and tight in the orange glow.

"You are my sister," he says. "You wear the bibiloka because we save you."

I nod. "But I am also Temple's sister."

"You are Kihuut, Mayrikafsa," Natka says with force. "Kalashava is Kihuut. There is no more Tem-peel."

I look up, and for the first time I notice that we are not in complete blackness. Not really. My eyes have adjusted enough to notice the millions upon millions of tiny glowing specks on the ground and the walls. I blink hard. He is right about Temple. I have known this for weeks, but have not wanted to admit it. Temple is no longer Temple. She hasn't been for a long time. She is more Cheese than I will ever be. She loves it with them. She is free with them. Her spirit now whirls stronger than a devil spiral in the scrub. She is happy. She thrives.

And what about me? Do I thrive? Am I happy? Can I be both Rae and Mayrikafsa the mystery warrior? Do I have to give up one to be the other?

Human or Kihuut?

Physician's helper or . . . *krasnoakafsa*? Chieftess? Would either ever be possible? I sometimes think I could be happy being a healer, despite the restrictions of a settler's life. It would be interesting, familiar. I would reattach ears instead of take them.

But then . . . what about the Kihuut? What about the freedoms they offer? The respect. Could I ever leave Temple?

I stand on the edge of blackness and I do not know which way to turn.

○ ○ ○

Many hours go by as I walk the caves of Ebibi, marveling in the coolness and softness and dampness of all the things. Everything I touch seems to be alive, flourishing. I wonder what medicines hide in these plants. Aunt Billie could study this place for summers on end.

All this time, Papa's lessons of the moon never taught us of the balance it holds in space, how it hangs, unmoving, one side facing the heat of the suns and the judgment of the Red Crescent, the other side pocked in caves, facing a nearly naked sky.

I run my hand over a soft, fabriclike plant that glows a very light green in the blackness. Its veins illuminate themselves. It is magic how this plant has made its own way in the darkness, crawling blindly up the walls. I could do well to learn from this plant.

Natka and Fist have left me here with a bag of flameless flares and with Kwihuu happily munching the fine scrub at the entrance to the caves. They make their way back to the village while I try to make my way through my thoughts.

Is my heart with the Cheese? How can it be when they steal babies and ears with nothing but a shrug? Don't I have a duty to the humans? But then, what of these stories of so much killing when the *Origin* crashed? I hear Papa's words echoing in my mind—"a taste of our mighty strength"— and it makes me shiver.

The Cheese could not seriously consider a human girl-child as a possible leader one day. The idea is ridiculous.

When Ben-ton mentioned it months ago, I believed him to be trying to curry favor for some reason, to use me to find acceptance from Klara and Fist. But maybe he knew. I wonder if Rory knew? Did she speak of these things with Fist?

I sit in the darkness, pondering Fist's words about being born of this moon and how that makes us all the same. Maybe I am more Kihuut than I think. But no. I could never—will never—condone maiming and kidnapping.

Could I?

I will Ebibi to give me answers, but he only throws more questions at me.

What would Papa say to know I would even contemplate never coming home again? He would say I am selfish, I am weak as a woman is wont to be. But maybe Papa is with Ebibi. I shake my head. No. Papa is with his gods. The angry, punishing gods, not the sweet darkness of Ebibi. He would not like it here. He would not understand beauty in blackness.

And, gods, oh, gods, I miss Boone ever so much. Our secret horse racing and teasing, even our studying. I miss our clearing the fields while telling wild stories. I miss skinny Raj and Boone's nervous mama. What would Boone say if I never came home? Would he ever forgive me?

And what of Aunt Billie? Can I just leave her, never to return? She could teach me so many things, and I think now, I could teach her things as well. Is her heart broken, having lost both Temple and me on top of the old wounds of having lost Benny and Mama? Would her heart heal to see us again? Or break anew to see the Cheese that we are becoming? Or was it never broken by us in the first place, only relieved to have fewer mouths to feed?

The questions are too many. Ebibi has not shown me a path. I continue to wander in the darkness until I hear a *Kwihuutsuu* scream. I light a flameless flare and hold it over my head.

"You must come now, Tootie." It is Jo, her shouts carrying around the corner that hides the cave entrance. "There is trouble in the village." As I run to her I see her shoulder is bandaged, tinged red with blood and dirt.

Kwihuu is behind her, just outside the cave. She flaps her wings and lowers onto the soft, cool ground next to me. I climb into the saddle and grab the reins. "What trouble?" I ask.

"A'alanatka" is the only word I hear before Jo's *Kwihuutsuu* screams and flies up into the stars, Kwihuu right on her tail, the cool air of these lands of Ebibi blowing over us in whistling whispers.

23

FIST LIES SWEATING ON WANTOSAKAAL'S TABLE.
The gash on his hip is angry and seeping. He is muttering
with fever. Klara kneels next to him, chanting, her head
low, her ear membranes throbbing in and out slowly.

Wantosakaal spreads a poultice over the wound and
Fist grimaces, his eyes opening and then rolling back
in his head. She binds the wound and puts a hand on
Klara's shoulder. Klara stands and they go off in a corner. Wantosakaal's voice is quiet but still grating. I try to
understand the snippets I hear, but nothing makes sense.

Jo pulls me to the side. "She say *a'akow naa sonako*."

"Fire won't stop," I say. "You mean the fever?"

"*Ja.*"

I look at Fist, so big his feet hang off the edge of the

huge table. How could a strong Cheese like this be felled by a fever? It seems impossible.

"Is there anything that can help?" I ask, my brain buzzing. At Origin Township, fever is one of the most insidious killers. Aunt Billie creates tinctures and exhausts her limited supplies of medicines from the *Origin*, but more often than not there is no medicine that can overpower infection. Before I . . . left . . . I was learning some of the tinctures, but I don't remember the recipes. Maybe the Kihuut have a special herb, something.

"There is nothing," Jo says, her face lined, dark. "Only the mercy of Ebibi." She touches her chest and closes her eyes, then gives me a half smile. She traces the space on my right hand where my finger used to be. "We cannot cut off Fist's hip, Tootie."

"I know that," I say. "But there has to be some kind of . . ."

Klara walks to us. She nods slightly and Jo takes a protesting Wantosakaal outside of the cave, leaving me and Klara alone with Fist.

I walk to the table and put a hand on Fist's sweating arm, then look to Klara.

"*Owa'a*," she whispers. *"A'akow."*

"Yes," I say. "He's hurt. More badly than we thought. And feverish."

"Mayrikafsa," she chokes out, emotion strangling her words. She takes my hand. "Help."

"Tell me," I say, squeezing her hand. "I will do anything."

Klara looks to the ceiling and then back at me, her eyes glistening. She puts her other hand on Fist's arm.

"Whatever it is, Klarakova, please tell me. We must have time on our side. *Maa bali.*" "More time" is the best I can do in my translation.

She nods and swallows. "Medicine," she says. "Medicine in *Origin*. Medicine *a'akar* hyoo-mans long ago."

"There was medicine that helped the humans long ago? Well, the ship was stocked when it took its journey, but I don't think there's any left. And if there is . . . it might not be the right kind. It might not even help the Kihuut. The anatomies are so different." I can't tell if she understands me or not. Her eyes are black as the caves of Ebibi, and they are wild.

Klara tilts her head, putting her hand on my face, looking at me so lovingly that I feel my face flush. I think of the early days of my time with the Kihuut, the days when this same hand struck me many times, not out of malice, but instructing me in ways only the Kihuut could. It seems so long ago.

"Find medicine, Mayrikafsa. *A'akar* hyoo-mans. I saw it work. Go to *Origin*. Find *flotaka*."

"But, Klara. I don't know where to—wait. You've seen medicine help humans?"

"*Famalilta.*" It comes out as a whisper.

"Tragedy?" I whisper back. Klara puts her other hand on my face and stares into my eyes. It's as if she's trying to send her words into me through her palms.

"*Famalilta* to Kihuut. *Famalilta* to Hosani pea-pulls. *Ebiloti. Maa maa maa ebiloti.*"

"Many, many sickness?" I say, not fully understanding where this is going.

"*Ke'ekutaat* bring illness. *Ebiliki* in *mara.*" Her tears are flowing again.

"Death in the wind?" It makes me think of months ago when Ben-ton spoke of a plague brought by humans. I thought he was just being dramatic.

"Much death, Mayrikafsa." Klara blinks slowly. I wonder what she's seeing behind those closed eyes. "Hyoo-mans have medicine. Hyoo-mans not die. Hosani die. *Kihuut owa'a. Ebiliki* in *mara.*"

"The death in the wind killed people from Hosani, but only hurt the Kihuut? And the humans had their own medicine so they were okay? What does this mean, Klara?"

"Go, Mayrikafsa. Go!" Klara swallows hard, and lightly clacks her upper lip against her teeth. She not so gently pushes me. "Go. *Origin*! Go!"

I stand and stumble back a little. "Okay," I say. "I will try. But, Klara, I don't know where any medicine is. The *Origin* is as much a mystery to me as it is to you. It's huge. I wouldn't know where to look."

"Act like warrior, Mayrikafsa," Klara says, her voice sharp. "Gather supplies. Take Natka. Find medicine. Bring home." Her eyes narrow and I am afraid she might take her grief out on me physically.

"I would do this alone," I say, taking a short step back

from her. I have never seen her this undone. "It will be easier by myself." A plan is forming in my mind. A *ro-ri-ta* rockhead plan.

"We cannot trust her," Natka says, bursting into the cave with an armload of fragrant scrub. Jo follows after him, gesturing her apology at the interruption. Wantosakaal reenters the cave and motions for Natka to put his armload of scrub into a pot hanging over the fire. As he's cracking the branches and pushing the wad into the pot, his eyes narrow and he looks up at me.

"You feel too much still for the hyoo-mans. If you leave, you not come back." He smashes the lid onto the pot and Klara hisses at him. Fist moves his head back and forth on the table, moaning.

Wantosakaal takes the lid off the pot. She chatters at Natka in Cheese until he backs away from her, handing over the spoon he used to stir the scrub.

"I'm not going to run away," I say. "I would not leave Fist to die. And I would never leave Temple. You know that."

Jo looks from me to Natka and back again.

"You wish to leave?" she asks, her face creasing with hurt.

"If I am to try to save Fist, then yes. I wish to leave right now."

"*Naa.*" Jo waves her clawed hand through the air. "You wish to leave the Kihuut?" Her face is stricken and then she puffs out her cheeks, her eyes flaring.

"No." I say. "I mean, I don't know." I put my head in my hands and then look to her, trying to ignore Natka's angered breathing and fighting stance. "I don't know what to do. But I'm not going to think about that right now. You have to trust me, Jo. I want to save Fist."

"We cannot save him," Natka says simply, and Klara cries out angrily. "It is only the truth," he says. "We must prepare."

"Klara and I were talking, Natka. She thinks there might be something we can try."

Klara regards us both, her mouth tightening. I cannot read her expression. "Go now," she says. She points at me, then Natka. "Both. Go. Return safe. Mara watch over you."

I do not like this. Natka could ruin everything. I am about to protest when Fist cries out and Wantosakaal puts a rag over his face, trying to cool the fever.

Klara hugs us both tightly. "Go."

"Come," I say, grinding my teeth, grabbing both Natka and Jo and pulling them outside. My brain whirls with all of the new information and with the plan that is forming.

Outside, Natka runs to the *Kwihuutsuu* nests, but I stay for a moment.

"Tell me about this illness, Jo. This medicine." I tell her what Klara told me.

"It was a hunting germ, Mayrikafsa," Jo says. Her voice is a low hum. "An illness brought to A'akowitoa to hurt anyone not *ke'ekutaat*. To kill."

"But Klara said the humans grew ill, too. And why in

218

the name of the gods would the humans kill the Hosani people if they held the only escape from the moon?" None of this makes sense.

Jo shrugs. "*Ebiliki* in *mara* is difficult to control. Humans survived with medicine. Medicine did not work for Hosani peoples on A'akowitoa. Kihuut survive, but . . ." She pats low on her belly. "No more *kakoni.*"

"The illness brought by humans is why the Kihuut have no female children?" I don't know what to think. Could humans truly be so cunning and cruel? Suddenly, cutting off ears and stealing babies seems less brutal by comparison.

I mean, it should not surprise me, the brutality of humans. It also should not surprise me that they could be so dumb. Accidentally killing off their only salvation from the moon? Origin Township truly is a punishment from the gods.

"It is how they gave us the name they call us, you know," she says.

"The name?" I say, not understanding.

"Because we do not go to Ebibi from this germ, because we cheat death for so long. This is why the hyoo-mans call us the Cheats."

"The Cheats?" I say. Then my hands go to my hair. "The *Cheats?*" I start laughing uncontrolled hiccups. "All this time we have been saying it wrong?"

Jo nods. "They call us the Cheats. Because we cheat death. We do not go away. We do not play by rules." She smiles, showing off those teeth of hers. "You have this in common with us."

Yes, indeed. I am about to break nearly every rule there is.

"Jo, stay with Klara. Keep Fist alive. Natka and I will be back." I grab her in a tight hug and it's so nice to feel the strength and warmth of her body up against mine.

It doesn't take me long to gather what we will need. I am not sure how many days we'll be gone, but I plan for the fewest possible. I have one last thing to find and I will be ready to go.

The cave is dark when I walk inside. The Cheese woman is standing over a fire, Old Man Dan's baby sitting at her feet, playing with some rocks. I come up behind the woman so she can't see me and put my hand over both her mouth and her nose. She struggles with great force, scratching my arms as she reaches back to fight me off. But my warrior training has paid off and I am stronger than she is. Soon she is limp and I lay her carefully on the ground.

"I'm sorry," I whisper. "When you wake, please know that I am terribly sorry."

I pick up the baby, offer her a fingertip of sleeping root, and when she is asleep, I put her in the sack on my back.

I leave the cave, walking with purpose.

"Tootie!"

I whirl around, my heart banging in my chest. It is Temple.

220

"*Kehka ke ton?*" she asks.

What am I doing? I lick my lips, having not prepared a lie. "Uh . . . I'm just gathering some things for Wantosakaal."

"*Fist ebilot?*" she asks.

I nod. "*Ja.* He is ill. I am trying to help, but there is not much to do."

Temple's face is grave.

"Ben-ton says you hate us. That you plan to abandon the Kihuut, run back to Origin Township. Is this true?" She runs her tongue across her sharpened teeth and looks up at me with her huge blue eyes. Her face has grown narrower, her waist slimmer. She is growing taller and more like a woman.

I splutter, raising my upper lip. "You should not speak with Ben-ton. He is a troublemaker."

"But is he correct?"

"I have no time for this, Temple. We will talk soon, okay?" I put my hand on her arm and lean down to kiss her cheek, but she backs away.

"You would turn your back on the Kihuut? After everything they've done for us?" Her hand hovers over the knife at her waist.

"Temple, please," I say, backing up a step. "I am—right this moment—working to save Fist's life. How is that turning my back on the Kihuut? Please. Let's have this talk another day. I will be back as soon as I can."

"Where are you going?" she shouts after me as I begin walking quickly away.

"I will be back soon," I answer. I hear her huff, then run away in the opposite direction.

Good gods. This Ben-ton and his gum mouth.

I walk quickly away from the village and out to the *Kwihuutsuu* nests, feeling shame and guilt, but also knowing that this is our only chance.

"Too slow," Natka says when he sees me. He is already in his saddle, ready to go. He points to the suns. "We lose time."

I don't answer. I tie the meager supplies to Kwihuu's saddle, keeping the baby hidden on my back. I jump into the saddle and pray to any and all gods that the baby will be quiet on the journey.

Natka will not like my plan, and so I will not tell him of it.

24

WE AGREE THAT WE CANNOT AFFORD TO CAMP.
We will push the *Kwihuutsuu* to ride as far and as fast as
they can, carrying us even as we sleep. I lead the way, refusing to tell Natka what my plan is.

The nose of the broken *Origin* is splayed out under us
as we fly over *Maasakota*.

Natka is confused when we don't stop, but he follows.
It should be less than half a day now. Kwihuu is lathered,
I can tell, and will need to stop soon. I wish we could land
at the homestead, but at this time of day, Aunt Billie will
not be there. We are going to have to make a spectacle, I'm
afraid.

It is with relief that I see the Origin Township market
area coming into focus below us. That relief is immediately

replaced with trepidation, because I know this is a risky plan, and I also know that having Natka along makes it even riskier.

I hold up my hand and Natka slows. Our *Kwihuutsuu* hover over the outskirts of the market. We have come in slowly and quietly and no one has seen us yet.

"Cheese!" a woman yells, dropping her basket of cooling crystals. Homesteaders run to help her refill her basket as others run for weapons.

"*Naa sita*," I tell Natka as we lower the beasts to the ground. Do not speak.

He snaps his bony upper lip at me, but says nothing. Without his silver paint and warrior clothes, he looks young sitting astride the dactyl. I know this is deceiving, though, and if the homesteaders recognize him as the Cheese who took Virginia's baby and her ear, they will know this, too. I am hoping they will be frightened enough to listen to me before attacking, but this is probably foolish.

We land Kwihuu and Suu at the edge of the market, leaving them to rest and chew scrub. They will come to us if we need them. The whistle hangs low on my neck, just under the *bibiloka*. I pull the bag tightly against my back, feeling the baby squirm. At times during the journey, I would fall back behind Natka, claiming to need to relieve myself, but instead would give the baby water and crushed hashava fruit mixed with sleeping root. She is waking now, just in time. She will be angry, soiled, and hungry. Perhaps not in that order.

Natka walks briskly to my side, his good hand hovering over the knife holstered on his thigh. I stop walking. He goes a couple of steps ahead of me and then turns.

"*Kehka?*" he asks, looking irritated. What?

I walk quickly to him, and without stopping again, reach down, remove the knife from his holster, and throw it as hard as I can back behind us, toward the *Kwihuutsuu*.

Natka makes no sound for a moment, then runs to me. I am walking quickly. He is blinking rapidly and spluttering. Finally he manages to bark out my name and I put my finger to my lips to tell him to be quiet.

"We cannot go into the camp weaponless, Tootie," he seethes.

"Yes we can, and yes we will," I say. I keep walking but turn to look him in the eyes. "You will not be taking any ears or babies or starting any fights today, Natka. We aren't even supposed to be here! You will be silent, contrite. If you are lucky, they won't kill or imprison you. I told you it was a gum rockhead decision to come."

We are approaching the first booths of the market. All of the people have run elsewhere. It is empty now, and the wind is hot and brisk, blowing my long black horsetail over my shoulder.

Something crunches underfoot and I look down. A piece of cooling crystal that spilled from the woman's basket. I put my hand to my neck, feeling my necklace, happy that it's helping me breathe so clearly this hot, dusty day.

"Your bag," Natka says, pointing. His head tilts to the side. "It moves."

I nod. "Stay one step behind me. Do not speak." I pull the bag around to my front and wrestle the squirming baby from it. Natka gasps. He says nothing but his eyes flash and his fists clench.

"I have returned the Livingstons' daughter!" I shout into the wind. My human language sounds tinged with Cheese now, but I am not ashamed. "I have returned her as a trade."

A head appears from behind a metal counter in one of the open-air booths. Shortly thereafter the muzzle of a light rifle also appears.

"We are unarmed," I say. Not smart, Mayrikafsa, I chide myself. You should have said that part first. I hold the child over my head. "And the baby is unharmed."

Old Man Dan appears from a booth at the other side of the market. He is laden with a handbow and a light rifle, his gogs pulled tightly against his face. He is in no mood to negotiate, I can see.

I put the baby on my shoulders, bracing with a hand. She pulls my hair as she squirms. I hold up my other hand. "A simple trade. I would speak to Billie Darling. We seek medicine."

Old Man Dan begins to laugh. Harsh, barking noises, bouncing off the meager buildings and booths. He takes several quick steps closer to us, though he is still three *Kwihuutsuu* wingspans away.

"You seek counsel with Ms. Darling," he says, his voice mocking. "You seek medicine." He steps closer still, giving the light rifle a shake and activating its firing coil.

He has stopped laughing and more heads are now popping up from behind counters and doorways. These people are like prairie spiders testing to see if an electrical storm has finished or is beginning.

"For decades you raid us. Steal our supplies, our horses, equipment from our wreckage. And you steal our *ears*." He points the rifle at me. "You also steal our *children*. The very soul of our township. Now you want to *trade*?" He spits and shakes the rifle once more.

I swallow hard.

"Brother Livingston," I say. "We have not come to fight. We have come with contrition. We have brought your girl back. I only seek to give you your daughter and speak to Billie." I pause, never taking my eyes from him. "To my aunt."

Huge gasps go up from the booths and doorways and even Old Man Dan seems shaken, as the rifle drops a smidge.

I laugh because the reaction surprises me. "Did you all not see my ears?" I ask. "Not note the blackness of my hair?" Because it is true. While my language is tinged with Cheese, and I wear their clothes and decoration, I will never resemble them physically. I have no scales, no bony upper lip. I have no ear membranes. My hair is not red, though it has become ropelike over the months. And yet, everyone seems shocked that it is me.

"Rae?" A harsh voice has come up behind me. I turn, placing my hand up on the baby's back to keep her settled on my shoulders.

"Rae." It is no longer a question. Aunt Billie stands before me, dropping the handbow that must have been pointed at my back. She rushes at me and stops just short of hugging me. She seems smaller than I remember, but smells just the same—a mixture of herbs and sweat and soap.

"Aunt Billie," I whisper. I am taller than she is now.

She looks at me, scrutinizing my face, my *peltan*, my Cheese shoes. She sees the empty holster on my thigh, then looks up into my face again. She reaches up and gently runs her fingers through the hair hanging over my shoulder from the horsetail.

"You look just like one of them," she whispers, tears flowing freely down her face. "Benny? Is he . . . is Temple still . . ." She fights through her words, showing more emotion than I've ever seen, then calms herself. "Your sister, she is . . ."

"*Kela omma*," I say, with a small smile, then realize I have spoken Cheese. "They are well, Aunt Billie. Temple thrives, Benny is . . . Benny is well." I fear that Aunt Billie will collapse at these words, as the look of relief on her face has washed over her so quickly it has caused her eyes to close and her mouth to go slack.

"How fares Papa?" I ask, wanting to know, but also not wanting to hear her say it.

"He still recovers from his injuries," Aunt Billie says, grinding her jaw, staring at Natka. "He shall never walk again, but is alive, thank the gods."

"Mayrikafsa," Natka says in a low voice.

I turn and see that Old Man Dan is standing only a few hands away now, pointing his light rifle at my chest. A few other men and women have ventured from the booths and are also pointing weapons at us.

"We just want medicine," I say. "Then you have your daughter back and we leave."

"And in a few days, you're back," Old Man Dan sniffs. "With your beasts and your brethren. And you take more ears, more children, and do it faster and fiercer because those among you who need medicine are now stronger and healthy. You are indecent, inhuman creatures whose lives go against the gods in all respects." His eyes roam up and down my shape. "We do not do business with heathens. Besides. We have no medicine."

Old Man Dan steps closer to me and I clearly see his grizzled face dripping in swaths of skin around his neck, his red nose speckled with burst blood vessels. His gogs are old, the plastic cracked around the lenses. I doubt they work anymore. If they did, he would have seen immediately I was not Cheese. Or maybe that wouldn't have changed anything. Maybe his old-man eyes have stopped working as well. No. He is still looking me up and down, making me want to spit on him. His eyes work just fine.

"How stupid do you think I am?" he breathes, leaning

closer, his mouth curling into a frown, the yellow-white whiskers at its corners glinting in the suns.

"We will call a truce," I say, thankful that Natka must not know this word because he stays quiet.

Old Man Dan laughs. "A traitor, holding my daughter hostage, says her newly adopted people will call a truce. Who are you, girl, to make promises like this? What must they think of us to have sent a *girl-child* as a negotiator?" He fair spits the word "girl-child" at me.

Aunt Billie steps forward, her eyes narrowed to slits. "She is not a traitor, Brother Livingston. She is a captive. She has obviously been sent here in a nonthreatening gesture. She has no weapons. She has your child. She asks for a trade." She turns to me. "What kind of medicine do they need? For what illness?"

"Infection," I say. "Fever. I tried to remember some of the tinctures you were teaching me, but I couldn't." This doesn't seem like the time to bring up the fact that Klara and Jo believe humans have magical germs and medicines that they can use to kill and cure at their own whims and mercies.

Natka, who is two hands taller than me, so nearly three hands taller than Aunt Billie, looks over her head at me. His lip snaps up and his hand has flicked to his side even though his knife is no longer there. It rests on his hip, his fingers tapping. I shake my head ever so slightly to reassure him that there's no need for fighting or impatience. Not yet, anyway.

Aunt Billie walks past me, letting her hand squeeze mine as she passes by. This small move of affection tears at me, throwing my concentration, making my breath catch. My hand flies to the crystal around my neck. I am okay. Easy breathing. Just surprised.

"Let us speak, Brother Livingston," she says, placing a hand on Old Man Dan's arm, lowering the rifle. "In a private area." Then she raises her voice and speaks to the people who have come to surround us. "No harm will come to my niece and her companion while Brother Livingston and I have discussions. Or so help me."

Hearing Aunt Billie speak this way fills my throat with a rock that is difficult to swallow around.

Natka turns, his back to my back, so no one can sneak up on us again. The baby has wrenched free a handful of my hair, and from what I can tell, is sucking on it.

The air is stifling, the hot breeze not helping one bit. There is a flash of light in the distance. An electrical storm brewing. Oh, gods, if we are to make it home on the *Kwihuutsuu*, we will need to be in the air very soon.

The men who surround us are still, their weapons aimed and ready. They openly stare at me, their faces streaked with sweat and dirt, their beards wild in the wind, their eyes roaming. Some faces fill with pity, others with hatred, others with something more unspeakable. No one makes a sound and I can hear the quiet snuffles of the *Kwihuutsuu* carrying on the breeze. There are more flashes of light in the distance.

After the suns have begun their afternoon descent in the sky, and the roiling storm clouds have increased and moved closer, Aunt Billie and Old Man Dan emerge from the booth where they held counsel. Aunt Billie's jaw is set. She holds out her hands for the baby. My eyes search her face.

"And the medicine?" I ask.

"Once you turn over the child, I will take you to the medicine storage site."

I do not like this.

"Are there not herbs at the homestead?" I ask. "In your treatment room?"

Aunt Billie shakes her head. "Not the kind you seek." She holds her hands out for the baby again. "You must trust me, Ramona."

It has been so long since anyone has called me by that name, it takes me a moment to respond. I reach up to take the baby off my shoulders. Natka hisses.

"*Kehka ke ton?*" His eyes spark.

"What am I doing? I trust Aunt Billie," I say, wishing I felt those words as strongly as I used to.

"*E'e naa,*" he says. "I do not."

"*E'o.*" I tap my chest. "*Lonkah.*" I hold his angry stare. "You will have to trust me, then."

Aunt Billie takes the baby from me, kisses her soft head, looks her over quickly, nods once, and hands her to Old Man Dan. He holds the child in front of him like a shield and backs away from us.

"I will take you there," Aunt Billie says. "Follow me."

I motion for Natka to follow us. Aunt Billie walks out of the market and away from the center of the township. The wind is strong now, the electrical smell of a brewing storm has reached us. I look nervously to the blackening sky and worry that Aunt Billie is going the opposite direction of Maasakota. It will take us even longer to get to the *Kwihuutsuu* and get home now. We cannot get trapped here during a storm. We cannot.

"Aunt Billie," I say, and it feels strange, these words rolling off my tongue. I think of Klara keeping watch over Fist and crying over Natka's shine tree wound all those weeks ago, how she holds reign over a whole village and yet often allows her emotions to so quickly overcome her. Aunt Billie is the opposite of this, and yet . . . she is not weak.

"Where do you take us?"

Aunt Billie smiles, looking weary. "There are many things that have not been revealed to you, Rae."

We are just outside the market when Aunt Billie kneels, pushing aside a great boulder that should be nearly four times too heavy for her to move on her own. The wind whips her hair in great bands above her head.

When I approach, I see that the boulder has been hollowed out so that it holds its huge size, but is quite lightweight. Beneath the boulder is a hole with a staircase descending into darkness.

Aunt Billie begins climbing down the stairs, and I follow her. Natka makes a disgruntled sound, but follows us.

At the bottom of the stairs there is a rough fabric bag of flameless flares, the same sort with the Star Farmers stamp that the Cheese have also used. Aunt Billie cracks a flare.

"Mind the step," she says, gathering her skirt and jumping down onto a rectangular platform. I jump behind her, Natka behind me. The platform is big enough to hold the three of us plus more. There are metal railings on two sides and no railings in the front or back. The platform is stamped with the outline of a female figure with wings.

"Now, hold the rails," she instructs. I do as she says and Natka follows what I do. Then, like Mara has blown her hardest breath, the platform shoots forward, barreling through the tunnel on wheels and a track.

"What is this?" I cry. The movement is both exhilarating and sickening—like riding a dactyl for the first time. I run my foot over the etching of the winged woman.

I turn to Natka and he is grinning broadly, despite himself.

"There are a series of these tunnels within the moon," Aunt Billie shouts over the rumbling noise. "They were here when our people first landed, used for trading between the people of the Red Crescent and the Kihuut. This one leads to the cave where your grandparents first sheltered upon crashing. It will take us directly to the *Origin*."

Well, how about that?

The "wings of angels" aren't how I pictured them at all.

25

THE RAILS HAVE CARRIED US FAR IN A SHORT
amount of time. Aunt Billie leads us off the platform and
from the tunnel into a cave. There is a pool of water that
must be where Origin Township fills its barrels.

There are drawings on the cave walls that I can barely
make out with the orange light of the flameless flare. Crude
approximations of the Cheese and the *Kwihuutsuu*. Mara,
Oonatka and Oonan, Ebibi and A'akow are there, too.
There is another figure along with them who is painted a
bright red. I wonder if this is the god of Hosani, the Red
Crescent.

Aunt Billie walks past the cave paintings without a second look. I guess she's seen them so many times they mean
nothing to her now. I could stay for days, studying the

stories, learning more of the ceremonies I've already seen. Natka seems keen to stay on Aunt Billie's heels, so I have to run to catch up to them.

They stand at an opening that must lead to Maasakota, but the opening is dark and caged. Aunt Billie removes a set of keys from a pocket in her skirt and unlocks the crisscrossing metal door. She steps forward and rolls away a hollowed-out boulder that has been hiding the cage from the outside.

Natka's mouth is open. He seems surprised and impressed with the ingenuity of the *ro-ri-ta* humans.

We close the door and reposition the boulder and then follow Aunt Billie into the gorge, appearing right at the crushed nose of the *Origin*.

A flash of electricity sparks overhead and my belly sinks. We may have lost all time to outrun the storm.

Aunt Billie weaves through boulders and wreckage and takes us to a spot where the *Origin* has separated into two pieces, a great distance from where Temple and I and Fist and Jo camped so many months ago. Aunt Billie walks us through a curtain of ripped wires and unrecognizable debris, into a ruined section of the belly of the ship.

We move swiftly, light from the waning suns and the Red Crescent filtering in through the countless crumbling floors above us that are cracked and corroded and full of holes.

At last, Aunt Billie shoves away a boulder that has crashed through the weakened wall. There is a door behind it.

When I get closer I see that the boulder is another hollowed-out monster that is much lighter than it appears to be. Aunt Billie pulls the keys from her pocket again and unlocks the door.

Natka hisses and I have to agree. What is going on?

We follow her over the threshold and into a room that has been rebuilt. The floors, walls, ceiling are meticulously clean. There are mostly empty shelves, some boxes and drawers. In the far corner there is a machine that hums as if it is alive.

"This is where I store the real medicine," Aunt Billie says. "What's left of it."

Her face is unemotional, though she blinks slowly, looking tired. "This was not meant to be a secret from you, Rae," she says. "Just a place that you needn't worry yourself about. In time I would have told you. You would have needed to know, as my true apprentice."

Her true apprentice. She was teaching me small things here and there, tinctures and poultices, things like that. She was allowing me to watch treatments and procedures. But it was never explicitly stated that I would be her apprentice. I could have been the physician of Origin Township one day. Perhaps I still could be.

Natka has walked over to the humming box in the corner. He places his hand on top of it, then pulls at a little door handle on its front. When the front of the box opens he gasps and jumps back, and even across the room I can feel the cold air rolling from the machine.

I rush to him and we both peer into the box, seeing small vials and boxes among the fog that is now gathering and spilling from the cold box. Aunt Billie comes up behind me and puts a hand on my shoulder.

"It runs on power from the suns," she says. "Like your gogs."

"I haven't worn my gogs in nearly a full summer," I mutter, waving my hand back and forth in the fog. Natka picks up one of the vials.

"Don't touch that!" Aunt Billie says, her voice going sharp.

Natka's eyes narrow and he picks up another vial just to defy her, I guess.

"Natka, please," I say. *"Naa aka oo kakeela."* Do not be a child.

He puffs air through his upturned nose, but puts the vials back.

"I need this machine to keep certain medicines cold," Aunt Billie says.

There is a tremendous bang outside, rattling the shelves. We all jump.

It is difficult for me to think of what to say next. My mind is muddled with Klara's worry, Jo's words, the fear of the storm, fear for Fist's life, needing to get back to the village, but also struggling to comprehend this room, and how it's been hidden in this mess of a ship for all these years. So many secrets.

"All those times someone was dying of a fever, you could

have come here and found the medicine to save them?" My hands are on my hips, my breath coming hard.

"Ramona, it's not like that," Aunt Billie says. "There is a finite supply. We have to judge who is strong enough to fight the germs without medicine, who is so weak the medicine wouldn't work anyway. There is more to treating illness than just throwing medicine at it." She says this last part pointedly.

"I have warned the Cheese there is no such thing as miracle medication," I say. "But they seem convinced you have some on hand. That you've used it before to save your own skin while killing off visitors from the Red Crescent." I pause to watch her expression. "And that you used the germs to render the Kihuut nearly barren."

Aunt Billie licks her lips and says, "That was before my time, Rae." Then, as if her explanation is all I need, "What kind of infection is it that needs medication? I will find what you need and you can leave quickly. Before the storm gets worse." She rummages through a series of drawers that line a wall. "What caused the wound?"

I know she won't speak further of the history of this fabled medicine and the germ weapon. I can tell by the shape of her mouth, by the rigidity of her jaw.

"Metal," I say, wishing there were time to press her, to find out the truth. "At least I think so."

"Is this wounded person a child or an adult?" Aunt Billie turns to look at me, asking unsaid questions with her eyes.

"An adult," I say. "Adult Kihuut, not adult human."

She pulls two sealed packages from a drawer and hands them to me. "I do not know the physiology of the natives on this moon, so I cannot promise this medicine will work. Also, this medicine is very old, Rae. More than forty summers. And it spent some time buried in the ground while this room was fashioned, so it's been exposed to high heat. This Cheese will have to take much more of the medicine than he or she would if it weren't so old and potentially damaged. I'd say double the dose and hope that works."

I look at the packages: "500 mg twice daily, seven days" is stamped on the foil along with the seal of the Star Farmers Act. Little pills. That is all. Little pills that stand between the strongest man I know and the land of Ebibi.

"If his fever has not gone after two days, then the medicine is not working and there is nothing to be done. You would be good not to give him more of it so you can save the rest for someone else. Some medicines work for certain bacteria, others do not. I am only guessing that this will help. If his fever begins to go away, continue giving the pills until they are gone, even if he feels better. Do you understand?"

I nod.

"Go now, before the storm worsens." She puts her hand out, drops it, closes her eyes, then puts her hand back out and rests it gently on my cheek. I lean into it, despite myself. I relax a small amount at the feel of her callused hand. It is so different from the feel of Klara's scales and claws, and yet, just as familiar. It brings me back to the homestead, to sitting by the cooling grate telling stories in the evenings. It makes me think of nightly prayers and helping make biscuits. It makes me remember tying ribbons on birthday gifts for Temple. It makes me remember my life before.

I cannot leave without asking more questions. I cannot.

"Is this the same medicine that saved the humans when you were young?" I whisper. "The same medicine that doomed us to this moon by not working for the infected people of the Red Crescent?"

Aunt Billie's eyes open and fill with tears. She nods.

"And the humans released the germ on purpose?"

"Only the true elders knew the whole story, Ramona, and they have all perished. From what I understand, they trusted the medicine would work on all humanoid life forms. Releasing the germ could only have been meant as a last resort, Ramona, for bargaining in case the people proved to be unwilling to share their planet."

"Well. The humans got a lot more than they bargained for, didn't they?"

Aunt Billie doesn't smile. Neither do I. A moment passes. Then two. Natka gestures that we need to leave. I can hear the storm pounding outside.

"Why are you doing this, Aunt Billie? Why give precious medicine to a Cheese? You don't even know if he's strong or weak, whether these pills will work at all."

"You brought back the baby, Rae. I will not betray your peace offering. And maybe by cooperating, we can show the Cheese that we are not who we were. If we cannot compromise, then life on this moon is without hope. That's what I told Brother Livingston."

I nod, memorizing her hand on my cheek, thinking of that same hand braiding my hair, playfully swatting at Temple when she'd try to sneak biscuits before dinner.

I do not know if I will be back to see these hands again. I feel like I know so much, and yet so little. I take a deep breath to steady my emotions. Natka has already turned to leave.

"Rae," Aunt Billie says. "Please tell Benny that I've never stopped thinking of him, that I love him dearly. And Temple . . . make sure she knows how much I miss her, how much I love her. And you." She swallows hard. "As does your papa."

I nod again, unable to find my voice.

"Will you come home, Rae?" Aunt Billie asks, barely above a whisper. "For good?"

I don't know what I shall do. "I must see that Fist is healed," I say.

"Will you see that Temple comes home, at least? She is still so young, so impressionable." There is a deafening explosion outside.

"I can only do what the gods will," I say, my voice soft.

Aunt Billie closes her eyes and smiles and I feel a terrible wave of guilt. I do not think we speak of the same gods anymore.

She guides us out of the small room and back into the filthy wreckage. "Be careful, Rae," she says.

I grasp her in a tight hug. This time I am the one to kiss the top of her head.

"I love you, Aunt Billie," I say into her hair. "Thank you for your kindness today." I pull back and swallow hard. "Please give my regards to Papa."

Aunt Billie nods, then waves her hand, shooing us away. "Go. Now."

I nod, walking briskly through the wreckage and back into the gorge. Natka blows his whistle and a few seconds later Kwihuu and Suu swoop into the gorge, landing at our feet. I jump into Kwihuu's saddle and grab the reins. She nips at my feet.

"Hey, girl, it's nice to see you, too," I say, flicking the reins and giving her a quick pat.

Electricity arcs through the sky, raising the hair on my arms.

"Rae!" Aunt Billie calls to me. "Keep your sister safe!"

I nudge Kwihuu and we are in the sky, the *Origin* shrinking below us, the medicine for Fist safely in my hand, lightning flashing all around. I see Aunt Billie running to the cave. She disappears behind the fake boulder in a burst of wind and skirts and hair and it is a relief that she is safe within the rocks.

Kwihuu pulls at her reins, asking to climb higher through the clouds. "You lead the way," I shout to her, patting her neck. "You can outrun this storm. I believe in you."

But Natka is holding Suu back. "We must stay in

Maasakota," he yells between booms. "Let the beasts fly free. Storm will finish. Kwihuu and Suu will return for us."

I shake my head. "These storms can last for days sometimes, Natka. It will be faster if we just risk it and fly."

Natka snaps his bony lip angrily. He's tired, I know. And worried. I am as well.

I yell over the wind, "Please do not fight me. We can make it, *kotan*." Brother.

Natka snaps his bony lip once again, but I see a smile play at his eyes as he nudges Suu to move faster. "Gum *ro-ri-ta kotani* you are, Tootie," he says over his shoulder.

The *Kwihuutsuu* dart and dodge, making it above the clouds, the storm nipping at our feet like an angry beast.

We have the medicine. We can save Fist. We just have to get to him.

26

WE ARE EXHAUSTED, FILTHY, WHEN THE
Kwihuutsuu land in the village.

"Tootie!" It is Temple who runs to us first, ahead of a
crowd of Cheese. She throws her arms around me and I
hug her tightly. She steps back and hugs Natka. In the distance, I see Klara walking quickly toward us, coming from
Wantosakaal's cave.

Natka and I, pushing aside our exhaustion and hunger,
run to her, meeting halfway. Temple is right on my heels.

I thrust the packages of medicine at Klara, and in
between heaving gasps of air I say, "Two pills. Twice a day. If
his fever isn't gone in two days, the medicine will not work."

Klara holds the packages, stares at me.

I open a package and take out a pill. I hold it to my

mouth. "Two pills. One early in the day. One late in the day. Until there are no more pills." I nod, trying to get her to nod with me. I put the pill back in the package and hand it to her. She peers inside, clacks her mouth.

Then she grabs both me and Natka in a tight hug, her long arms crushing us together. "*Totan*," she whispers. "*Totan. Totan.*" Thank you. Thank you. Thank you. And she's off, taking long, quick strides in the other direction, back to Fist and Wantosakaal.

Natka and I follow. My legs are sore and heavy, my eyes feel as though they are filled with dirt, they are so tired. And my stomach. Oh.

As if she can read my mind, Temple runs up alongside us with bags of dried hashava fruit and bits of plini. Natka and I eat quickly as we walk, saying nothing. Temple slides her hand into mine.

"I saw Aunt Billie," I say when I have finished the fruit and meat. "She says to tell you she loves you and she wants you to come home."

Temple shakes her head. "But I am a captive." She sets her jaw. "It is not my choice."

I laugh long and hard, the wind carrying my chuckles. I touch her hair, her mouth, her *Kwihuutsuu*-skin dress. I run my hand down the altered handbow on her fist, the knife at her waist. I touch the spiraled paintings that flow across her arms.

"Of course," I say, the laughter leaving me even more exhausted. "Of course, Kalashava, She of Sweet Scrub, you are a captive." I squeeze her close to me. "As am I."

Natka steps in between us, throwing his arms over both our shoulders as we walk.

When we reach Wantosakaal's cave Temple nods and gives me one last hug. "Go to him. He has called out for you during these days you were gone. Klara told us how he missed you . . . and Natka." She smiles at Natka, who playfully pulls at her ear.

I squeeze Temple one more time and watch as she runs back to the center of the village. I enter the cave. It is just as warm and humid as before. Fist is still on the table, his scaly skin has lightened in color, his body has become more skeleton-like.

Wantosakaal is busy crushing the pills between two rocks, making a fine powder. Aunt Billie did not say if this is okay, but I say nothing. Medicine is medicine, and however he needs to take it will have to do. Wantosakaal mixes the powder with a small amount of water and then drips it into Fist's mouth. He grimaces at the taste and she holds his mouth shut, rubbing his neck, helping him swallow. His wound is covered with a poultice so I cannot see how it fares, though I suspect it must be even more gruesome than before.

When he has taken the medicine, we all stare at him silently, as if it will work immediately. After a moment, Klara, looking elegant even in her exhausted state, looks up from Fist to me to Natka.

"When I said supplies, I did not mean the *kakee*," she says in a quiet, firm voice.

I look to my feet, feeling heat rise up my neck. I swallow hard and look up, holding Klara's eye.

"I couldn't just go straight to the *Origin*. I had no idea where to go. I needed to make a trade," I say. Then I whisper, "I needed to learn more."

There is a long silence, then Klara nods once. She tells us how badly we smell and instructs us to go take a bath and a rest.

I am more than happy to comply.

When I wake, the Red Crescent glows in the night sky. How long have I been asleep? I sit up and my stomach growls angrily, telling me it has been a long while since the food from Temple.

I dress, noting that I am alone in the cave, and jog outside. There is a small crowd around Wantosakaal's cave, even though it is late in the night. My heart bangs until I think it will explode.

Fist is dead. The medicine has not worked. Why did no one fetch me?

I am prepared to push through the crowd, to fight my way into the cave, but when I arrive, the Cheese see me and part ways, creating a path. I run through them, and they pat my back, my shoulders, my ears. I burst into the cave, expecting to be knocked from my feet with the grief of Klara and Natka, but instead, I am met with shining smiles.

Fist is sitting up on the table. Klara holds a steaming

bowl to his lips and he drinks in slow, childlike slurps.

"What . . . ," I start, breathing hard from my running and panic. I rest my elbows on my thighs and dip my head to steady my breathing. I look up. "What's going on?"

"*Kundastaal*," Fist says, the broth dripping down his chin. Klara reaches over to wipe the drips but he beats her to it, swiping his chin with the back of his hand.

"*Kundastaal*," she says, smiling at me, her eyes bright.

"*Kundastaal*," Natka says, clapping me on the back.

"Breakfast," I say, laughing. "Of course."

Wantosakaal brings me a bowl of steaming broth and I drink it down, feeling the salty warmth race through my veins, waking me up, clearing my mind. It is so good.

I set the empty bowl on a stone counter and kneel by Fist. He puts a hand in my hair and kisses the top of my head.

I search for the right words to express how I am feeling, when I hear a distant scream and the distinct *zip-pew* of a handbow.

And another.

And another.

Natka and I are out of the cave like two bolts of lightning, running toward the sounds that clench my stomach. The crowd that was gathered outside of Wantosakaal's cave is also running, buzzing in various pitches. They are worried just as we are.

Up ahead I see fire glowing brightly in the red night; fire that is coming not just from the flames that are always kept alive in the center of the village. Small patches of light are scattered across the ground, as scrub burns in a haphazard pattern.

As we run closer I see Jo locked in hand-to-hand combat with someone. I cannot see who it is in the dark.

"What is this?" I yell as I run to the fighting. There are more hand-to-hand battles commencing in clumps all around the fire.

My stomach drops. The Cheese are fighting humans. *Ke'ekutaat.* Invaders. Homesteaders.

Cheese, with sleepy looks on their faces, peer from their caves, see the fighting, and then run outside. Men, women, warriors and nonwarriors alike, are fighting the invaders as quickly as they can find weapons. The Cheese are not dressed for battle—most don't even wear shoes.

I am momentarily struck dumb, just standing amid the battles, light arrows skimming my hair and arms. How did the homesteaders find the village? How did they get here? Did they somehow follow me and Natka? How could they? They have no way to fly. I fall to my knees, my face in my hands. So much for compromise, Aunt Billie. I take several gulps of air and steady myself.

Well.

They will get the fight they have come for. I am up on my feet now, pulling my knife from its sheath on my thigh. These *ke'ekutaat*, these *invaders*, they do not have a chance. I will not let this stand. Not while I have breath in my body. I will make it right.

As I charge, my vision tunneling, my scream echoing from the rocks, I marvel at how many men stream into the village. Did they bring every gum able-bodied man from the township? More and more run out and begin immediately shooting and fighting. Fires spark up everywhere from light arrows and the scorching balls of plasma that shoot from the light rifles. I hurdle over burning scrub and throw myself at the first man I see, a man who is locked in fisticuffs with the woman Cheese who plays Oonan in the ceremonies. She is a worthy warrior and holding her own well, even though she is in a loose-fitting robe and her hair flies free. She probably doesn't need my help, but I jump into the fight anyway, slashing and screaming. I hear only the clashing of weapons and the pounding of my blood in my ears. Slash, stab, pick up handbow from the ground, shoot, slash, search for Temple.

Someone shoots a weapon that has a loud concussive boom to it, and for a moment the fighting ceases. Old Man Dan stands on a rock bench and shouts, "Who is the leader here? I want to speak to your leader."

There is no sound or movement, save for dozens of men and Cheese gasping to catch their breath. After a moment, Jo steps forward. Her hair, too, flies free, making her look wilder and bigger. She is sweating, heaving with breaths, scratched and scorched, but not terribly wounded.

"I am the leader."

This is news to me, and probably Klara, too, but I keep my mouth shut as does everyone else.

Old Man Dan jumps off the bench and goes to Jo. He nods his head once and several men run to her. With a lucky kick, one of the men knocks the knife loose from her hand. They go in together, trying to subdue her, but she screams and lashes out with both arms, cutting each man across his cheek with her sharp talonlike nails. They stagger back, and she laughs, showing off her pointed teeth.

The *ke'ekutaat* are angry now, clutching at their shallow wounds. After having shown her strength, Jo does not fight back as the men knock her to the ground and hold her hands behind her back. This, of course, angers everyone else and the fighting begins anew, with many of the Cheese struggling to free Jo, while Jo yells, "*Naa!* Do not fight! Let them take me. End bloodshed!" She knows it is suicide to continue fighting. It's not that there are more men than Kihuut, it's that they are more heavily armed and have had the element of surprise. They caught us while we were sleeping. And their light rifles and handbows outnumber our spears and knives and altered handbows. Their weapons are also faster to cause injury.

Natka runs to Jo but is bludgeoned by a tall man whose name I can't remember. He sells sweets in the market. Natka crumples to the dirt, bleeding from his head, not moving. Two men grab him by the arms and pull him, facedown, to the edge of the village. I squint and in the distance there are . . . horses? How did the homesteaders get horses out here?

At this point, I am spinning in circles. I watch as Klara

walks into the fray. Her strides are long, purposeful. She does not run, she does not hurry her movements. Men leap at her and with barely an acknowledgment of her own motions she gracefully crushes the heel of her hand into a nose, knocking a man flat, while at the same time curling her long fingers around the neck of another man. She never stops walking as she does this, leaving broken men in her wake. I have never seen Klara as a warrior before. It is a sight both awe inspiring and bone chilling. She possesses a grace and ferocity I do not think I could ever emulate.

I do not know where to fight first. Should I work to free Jo? I think she is trying to create peace by sacrificing herself. Do I try to save Natka?

A man lunges at me and I bat him off with my forearm, slicing at him with my knife.

"Feisty, eh?" he says. "We been given permission to use force with *feisty* girls. You stay calm and I won't hafta hurt you."

I slash at him, taking off the tip of his pinkie finger as he grabs for me. His face contorts with rage as he screams and grips his hand.

Another man comes, holding ropes as if he wishes to bind me. He's moving cautiously, like I am an animal to be captured. I rush at him, pushing him away with my left foot to his stomach. He falls back across one of the benches that surround the fire.

My blood is pumping, my senses heightened. I feel as though I have the strength of ten Kihuut warriors. I march toward the horses in the distance, to help free Natka and Jo, when suddenly there are two more men, each grabbing hold of one of my arms. I struggle and lash out with my feet, but they are strong. One of the men smashes my knife hand against a stone until the pain makes me drop my knife. Gum *ro-ri-ta ke'ekutaat!*

I bend forward, flexing my arms and trying to launch the men into the dirt ahead of me. When one falls I think I have succeeded, but then I see the metal arrow sticking out of his neck. I swing my newly free arm around and connect with the second man's ear, but he holds fast to my wrist, dragging me. I dig my feet into the dirt, giving my arm a yank and causing him to stumble forward a little. He then picks up a large rock with his free hand and hauls his arm back as if to throw it at me.

"They told me to bring you back alive, but it won't be my fault if an altercation causes me to violate that request." He smiles, showing dirty teeth that barely peek through his bushy beard. I have seen this man around the village, working for Old Man Dan.

His arm is back, ready to brain me, when there is a whistle through the air, a gurgle, and he falls to his knees, a metal arrow jutting from his neck. He collapses to the ground, twitches once, and is still. I whirl around to see where this arrow came from and Temple waves from the other side of the fire.

Best shot in the village, my little sister.

I wave back and she grins. She holds up her altered

handbow, showing it off, when I see a man running up behind her.

"Temple!" I shout. I flail my arms to the side, motioning for her to run. "Move!" But the man lifts her from the ground. She kicks out, bites at his hands, and twists in his grip. He throws her over his shoulder and she puts up a mess of a fight. I run to them, slashing at anyone who gets in my way, but am intercepted just before I reach them.

It is Ben-ton of all people. He is clean, unsullied from not fighting. "Let them take her," he says, trying to pull me into the shelter of a cave. I rip my arm from his grip and push him hard in the chest. He stumbles, but keeps talking. "You should go, too. Me, you, Temple. We do not belong here. These men have come here for you, you know. They're killing Kihuut because of you. Let us go together. Let us leave with no more fight. Let us be with our people. This is our chance to end this madness."

"What do you know of *ending* madness?" I shout at him, brandishing my knife. "You have no power and so you seek it by *spreading* madness with your smooth words and sly tricks. You are a trouble stirrer, a gossiper, a failure."

"I am a failure because I do not belong, Ramona." His voice is calm. "But I am not powerless. You think some girl-child can come here and just take over? Not likely. Soon, you will be a failure, too, Ramona. Just like every other human taken by the Kihuut. You should get out while you can, before your inevitable fall from grace." He looks me up and down in a way that makes me want to stab him.

"Look at yourself, Ramona. Bruised, battered, beaten. This is the life you want?"

"The *humans* did this to me, you rockhead," I shout. "Not the Kihuut!"

I do not want to think of things now, even as Ben-ton's voice echoes in my head: "These men have come here for you, you know. They're killing Kihuut because of you." I shake my head as if that will rid it of his words.

The man who has Temple is hauling her to the horses. She is limp now and I do not know why. I missed whatever happened because of that *ro-ri-ta pitar* Ben-ton. I spin around, take two long steps to where Ben-ton still stands, and whip him across the face with the hilt of my knife. When he falls, I kick him again and again while he squeals. There are hands grabbing me now, pulling me away from him.

Klara turns me around, shakes me, slaps my face. She is covered in sweat, dirt, blood. She pulls me away from the squealing Ben-ton, shouting, "Mayrikafsa. *Keeto!*" Enough!

I take a deep breath and realize I have tears streaming down my face. Who is he to tell me this is all my fault? Who is he to tell me I will ruin everything one day? Why is everything always my fault?

I manage to splutter, "My fault. They have Jo. Natka. Temple. M-my fault. I am no warrior. I must have led them here. It is all my fault."

Ben-ton stands, making slurping noises as he sniffs his bloody nose. He glares at me and then walks toward the horses with his hands out to the sides, showing he is weaponless.

Klara's arms engulf me, holding me tight. "Mayrikafsa. Sweet *kakoni*." She wipes away my tears. "Give Mara your worry. You strong *Kihuutkafsa*. *Mayri* make you strong." She shows me my tears on her dusty, bloody hand.

"Mayri-kafsa," I whisper. "Crying Warrior? That's my name?"

"You fine *kakoni*. Fine Kihuut. You lead with . . ." She taps my head. "And with . . ." She taps my chest. She pushes me back and smiles through her own emotion. The pieces of metal in her hair sparkle under the glow of the nighttime Red Crescent.

And then time slows. Klara falls as her head whips to the side, a spray of blood flying from her mouth. Two men grab her and drag her to the remaining horses, while I am still focusing my eyes and trying to figure out what just happened.

My breathing is not steady. My head whirls around. There are still more men, coming for me. I blow my whistle for Kwihuu. The humans may have Temple, Jo, Natka, Klara, and others, but I have my *Kwihuutsuu* and I can outpace them, beat them to the gorge. I dodge and slash at the men.

The fight will continue. I will fix this.

I blow the whistle again, kicking out at the men who lunge and aim their weapons at me. Where is that gum beast?

257

All around me, Cheese lie wounded or worse in the dirt. The humans have mostly disappeared along the edge of the village, a few wounded stragglers have been caught by the Cheese and are being dragged outside of the village center. I hope they are being dragged to Wantosakaal so their injuries can be treated and Fist can question them. We must learn where they came from, how they knew where to find the village.

Kwihuu still has not come. I run, the men giving chase. There is a discarded light rifle in the scrub and I grab it, firing behind me. There are shouts and cries and then the only feet I hear running are my own.

I run as fast as I can to the *Kwihuutsuu* nests and . . . no. No. No. Nooooo!

It cannot be.

Kwihuu, Suu, all of the beasts lie dead. Shot. Sliced open.

I fall to my knees, stroking Kwihuu's head. Her ugly, ugly head, which saved me so many times. Her terrifying snout, which nudged me awake when I was falling off her back from exhaustion. Her strong wings, which kept me aloft, chased me, tormented me, taught me to be a *Kihuutkafsa*.

"Oh, Kwihuu," I cry, holding her limp head in my lap. "What have they done? What have they done?" Smoke from the fires around the village fills my nose, along with the humid mustiness of blood. "Kwihuu, Kwihuu, Kwihuu." I am crying truly now, pulling Kwihuu's head fully into my lap as I fall to the ground. Quite the crying warrior as I wail over my dead beast. Over all the dead beasts. "What have they done?" I say again, over and over, dripping ribbons of tears mingled with snot onto Kwihuu's unmoving head.

But I am afraid deep down in my heart that I know the question I ask is wrong. It is not, what have they done? It is, what have *I* done?

What *have* I done?

The blood on my hands is so red, I cannot tell from which beast it comes. *Kwihuutsuu*? Human? Kihuut?

I count. Rapid at first, but slowly as I calm down. I get to fifty before I wipe away my tears and breathe deeply. In keeping with Kihuut custom, I take my knife and slice carefully down Kwihuu's sternum, removing her heart. When I am finished, I hold it in my hands, still warm. I walk, slowly, dripping, to Wantosakaal's cave.

I tell Fist of the Kihuut who have been taken. I tell him what has happened to the *Kwihuutsuu*. Through our tears we each take a solemn bite of her warm heart. Kwihuu is now one with us.

And now. Now I will go to the township if I have to fly there with my own arms.

27

WHEN I RETURN TO THE VILLAGE CENTER after speaking with Fist, the energy and the rage from the fighting has worn off. I am exhausted, covered in blood and dirt, so filled with sadness that my legs feel as though they have doubled in weight. The suns are just beginning to rise and the village holds an eerie quiet—like the air has been squeezed into a thick layer of palpable sadness.

Fist says the humans will not hurt the Kihuut they have taken. They will hold them hostage until we come for them. Then we can trade our prisoners for their prisoners. Maybe if Papa were still in charge this could happen. But if Old Man Dan has taken over as Sheriff Reverend, I suspect the Kihuut are already murdered, laid out in the market as trophies.

I am numb. Bone weary. Sticky. I need a bath. But I want to lift my heavy legs, run to the township, screaming the entire way. I want to slaughter every last man with my bare hands. I understand now why the Kihuut were bent on vengeance after Kailia was murdered. These are frightening feelings, but they are the only thing keeping me from falling to the scrub and never getting up.

My mind will not settle on one thought for more than a few seconds. My hands shake. I walk past the scene of the battle, seeing the scorch marks, the blood in the dirt. There is something flapping in the breeze, momentarily caught between two rocks. I grab the ripped piece of canvas just before it blows away.

WANTED:

RED MOON NATIVES

for kidnapping, grave injury, murder.

Any Cheese man or woman is to be caught, tried, and sentenced.

REWARD

So that's it. There will be a trial. I sigh and feel my first real breath of the morning. Fist was right. The Kihuut prisoners must be alive. For now. This stills my mind a bit and I feel excruciatingly tired. Knowing my friends, my family, aren't being slaughtered right this very moment gives me a peace that will allow me to rest for just a bit. Then I will come up with a plan to save them. And gods help me if it is another failed Ramona Darling plan.

At least I will have tried.

I sleep fitfully for a few hours and then give up. I go back to Fist. He is still very weak, but sitting up straighter. He is drinking the broth on his own now, with Wantosakaal clucking at his side.

I, too, drink the broth, feeling it warm my numbness.

There are prisoners in the back of the cave, arms and legs bound. Mouths trussed. We talk over their groans.

"No time to break in new *Kwihuutsuu*," Fist says, his voice still scratchy, his brow angry, the skin around his eyes twitching. "We must beg Ebibi. Forgive us." His fist goes to his chest. His eyes close briefly.

"Ebibi's forgiveness?" I say, setting down my empty bowl. "For what?"

"For what you must do, Mayrikafsa." Fist slurps more broth, then hands his bowl to Wantosakaal. She refills it and prods him to drink more.

"Many moons ago Klarakova ask me. Find gift for Ebibi. A *krasnoa'a hubito* beast. A . . . beautiful black beast. I took beast as lesson to *ro-ri-ta* girl." He gently pushes my shoulder and smiles. "I offer beast to Ebibi. So Ebibi keep you safe."

"Heetle," I whisper. "My horse."

Fist nods. "You must go to Ebibi. Find *hubito* beast by

small pool of water, near *bibiloka* ten Kihuut tall."

I look up in alarm, but Fist raises his hand. "She eats, Mayrikafsa. We do not abandon her. She is your link to Ebibi." He again touches his hand to his chest, and closes his eyes. "She protect you. *Somar toktal.*"

"*Somar toktal?*" I work out the meaning of his words. "A living talisman," I breathe. All these months, having not heard or seen anything of Heetle, other than one brief mention that she was offered to Ebibi. I have been afraid to ask what truly became of her. I did not want to hear I was eating Heetle soup or sleeping upon Heetle blankets.

"I will keep *ke'ekutaat* safe . . . and scared." He scowls at them and I know he would hurt them if he could. But he's smarter than that. He understands his family, his friends, they are hostages, too.

"Wantosakaal say I am not strong. I not fight." Fist gives Wantosakaal a glowering look and she clucks her tongue. "Mayrikafsa. Find *hubito* beast. Guard village. We will train new *Kwihuutsuu* soon. We will gather raiding party soon. We return *maa owa'a* to *ke'ekutaat*. Soon."

My heart thrums at his words. Returning much hurt to the humans is an inclination I understand. I feel it, too. "Of course," I say. "Of course."

Fist nods and says, "Be safe, Mayrikafsa." He holds my hands and pulls me close. "Come back quickly."

I nod, unable to speak against the emotions I am feeling.

Fist sits up straighter and squeezes my hands tightly.

"You can do this, *kakoni*. I believe you can. You must believe, too." He pulls me to him, hugging me tightly, whispering in my ear, *"Ke tana al e'e bo tafanko ta."*

You are all I have left.

I break away from the hug and grasp his arms with both my hands. I sniff away the tears that threaten. "It is in Ebibi's hands," I say. And for the first time I touch my chest and close my eyes.

Fist smiles and shakes his head. "It is in *your* hands, Mayrikafsa."

And so it is.

We share one last hug, and I am out the door, a bag of supplies slung across my back.

The walk to the caves of Ebibi is long and lonely. It has given me time to think, though. I cannot sit idly by while Temple, Klara, Natka, Jo . . . everyone . . . are held at the township. Even if there are trials planned, who is to say they aren't happening right now? That everyone isn't being executed right now? No. I cannot stand by and guard the village and wait for Fist to grow stronger. I know it is dangerous, but I must take action to save the Kihuut. To find Temple. I must.

The bits and pieces of a plan wind their way through my brain like the plants growing on the walls in Ebibi's caves. This will be difficult to execute, and will take time. Going at this alone . . . I shake my head. Do I beg the gods for disaster? It feels as though this is what I am doing.

My energy is renewed, however, as I reach the opening to the caves. A flameless flare leads the way as I step into the cool blackness, keeping a lookout for the glowing pool by a *bibiloka* ten Kihuut tall. Should be easy to find, I think.

And it is. The crystal looms enormous in the blackness, like a shadow's shadow. The pool glows a light blue, showing ripples and dips where insects dance. There is a snuffle and I see her. Heetle. She is looking well after all this time, standing to the side of the crystal, munching on the soft, furlike scrub that coats the ground.

"Heetle," I say quietly. "It's me, girl." I walk slowly to her, my hand outstretched. I have picked some hashava fruit, and hold it in my palm. She sniffs my hand and eats the fruit. I pat her nose.

"How have you been? Do you like this place?" She rubs her head against the side of my face. "Were you lonely, girl?" She stamps her feet, which I take to mean yes.

She is without saddle, and has only simple reins tying her to the massive crystal. But that will do. I will ride bareback and we will go.

"I need your help," I say, trailing my hand along her side. "We're going back to the hot place, and for that, I'm sorry. We are also going to have to go far and fast. I am sorry for that, too. But I am glad to see you again. I have missed you."

I leap onto her back. It is so different from riding a *Kwihuutsuu*, and yet—I squeeze my knees, hold the reins—not so different. My heart aches for my sweet Kwihuu. I pat Heetle's soft hide, missing the feel of the slippery scales under my hand. I swallow hard and nudge Heetle forward. We will go slowly until we're out of the dark. I cannot risk her getting hurt.

It doesn't take long until we're out in the blinding suns again. Heetle bucks and whinnies at the sudden light and heat. I hop off and use the metal scraps and canvas in my pack to fashion blinders above and to the sides of her eyes. I pull out a blanket that has been woven with cooling crystals, and lay it across her neck. This seems to calm her. I climb back up and we are off, dust and scrub flying out behind us in great billowing clouds. I almost miss feeling my skirts flying out behind me. Almost.

I ride through the village without slowing down. My head spins as I think of the outrage Fist will surely feel. I am about to defy him. And leave the village unprotected. I am a fool. But we are all fools if we trust men like Old Man Dan to be honorable. A clock is ticking and it is ticking faster than my heartbeat, which threatens to shake me to pieces.

On the outskirts of the village I bring Heetle to a halt. Somewhere among these canyons, these rocks, lies the secret to how the settlers were able to find the village, and how they were able to get here so quickly. Be it bridge or tunnel or the true wings of angels, I must find it.

Heetle and I look along rock faces, climb into craters, and then . . . there it is. A trail of hoofprints leading to what looks like an unmarred rock face. I jump off Heetle and run my hands along the rock. Almost instantly an opening collapses under my hands. The humans have painted a strip of canvas to look just like the rock! It is ingenious, really.

I get back on Heetle and sweep the canvas to the side. I crack two flameless flares and hold one in each hand, along with the reins. The tunnel is dark and narrow, dusty. The cuts in the walls seem fresh. Is this a new tunnel cut into A'akowitoa? A fresh scar? How long have the settlers been working on it? Questions tear through my mind as Heetle and I fly through the darkness. Feeling Heetle's power as she runs energizes me. Aunt Billie and Papa would never let me run her at full gallop, worrying she would collapse from heat exhaustion or injury. But now, as we speed through the tunnel, and I feel her power under my legs, I do not doubt her strength or stamina.

We have not been galloping long when the interior of the tunnel changes. I slow Heetle down to look around more closely. The walls are narrower, smoother, and carved into them are the same female figures with wings as were on the platform in Aunt Billie's tunnel—the tunnel she said was created by the people of the Red Crescent. The homesteaders must have found this one, an unfinished work, and finished it on their own. I think on this a moment. There really could not have been a way for them to follow

Natka and me to the village. Somehow this revelation is not as much of a relief as I want it to be. I gently kick Heetle and she picks up speed.

We will make it to the township as fast as we can.

And, hopefully, my plan will work.

28

TIME PASSES YET ALSO SEEMS TO STAND STILL
as we fly through the darkness of the tunnel. When we find
the exit into *Maasakota*, the Red Crescent glows red in the
night. Heetle and I camp for a few hours, and then we set
out for the *Origin*. We will find a way to the homestead
from there.

Pushing aside the hollowed-out boulder, I kick at the caged
opening of the tunnel Aunt Billie led us through. I kick and
kick and kick, letting out all my angst and energy from the
past few days. Soon the metal bends and the lock cracks.
With a scream and a grunt I push the mangled cage open
and walk Heetle through the entrance.

We both drink deeply from the pool of water and then we're off again. We take a skittish ride on the moving platform, and a precarious walk up the stairs, but we make it aboveground.

Heetle is beyond exhausted when we emerge into the full heat of the summer suns. We gallop long and hard until we reach our destination. There is so much dust on my face, the sweat won't drip. I slow Heetle to a stop, jump from her back, and wipe my mucky face with my hands. I untie the horsetail at the top of my head, gather it again along with the loose hair that has come undone during the ride, and braid it. My fingers are clumsy, not just struggling to remember how this works, but fumbling to keep the thick, matted ropes of hair in the braid at all. This is as good as I can do to clean myself up as I lead Heetle to the Darling homestead.

I tie her under the same awning she was stolen from. The trough is dry. I will have to see to that. Making one more pass with my hands to clean my face, I am unsure whether I should knock at the door, or just walk in. I feel like a stranger here.

I knock and wait.

There is rustling behind the door, but no quick movement. No eye appears at the peephole, but the door opens a crack. I see no one. Then . . .

"Ramona?"

I look down to where the voice came from. Papa. In a makeshift chair with horse-cart wheels. He maneuvers the chair backward, moving the wheels with his hands, then opens the door wider.

"What are you doing here?" His face is lined, shadowed in the dim light of the cabin. His sunken eyes look wet. He cranes his head around me. He is again wearing the Sheriff Reverend star. My throat tightens as I realize it was Papa who must have ordered the raid. Not just Old Man Dan.

"I have come home," I say, swallowing my anger. Papa continues looking around me. He grips a light rifle across his lap. "I am alone," I say, stepping into the house and holding out my hands to show I hide nothing. As my hands move, his briefly reach out to me, as if I was attempting an embrace. There is an awkward moment as he realizes my intent. He snatches his hands back and once again grips the light rifle.

"What do you want?" he asks, his face flushing pink. His hair has grayed. There is a white stripe growing down his beard. His face is grizzled, blackness smudged under his eyes.

"I want nothing," I say, dropping my hands. "Well, other than water for Heetle and maybe some for myself." I take a step closer to him in the dim room. The wind blows outside, banging the awning rhythmically, as if our stiff conversation should be a song. "I am home, Papa. To stay. Where is Aunt Billie? Temple?"

Papa licks his lips and holds tight to the rifle. His eyes keep darting to my face, my *peltan*, my shoes, back up to my face. His expression is one I cannot read.

"I have heard there will be a trial," I say, speaking slowly. My hand dangles at my leg, in case I must grab my knife. "A trial for the Cheese who stole me and Temple." I smile even as my heart pounds, not knowing how the conversation will turn. "I can testify against them. I *want* to testify." It is terrifying how easily the lie comes.

The room is suffocating with pauses. "The trials are over."

I do my best to stifle the gasp shattering my chest. The trials are over?! But there would have been so many of them. How could that be possible?

"Why would you have testified against them anyhow?" Papa continues. His wet eyes have turned steely. "I heard you were one of them now. Fighting with them, like a man would. Creating unmentionable havoc." His eyes flash and I finally see a recognizable Papa in this mysterious form in front of me.

"This is what you want, isn't it?" I say. Neither of us moves closer to the other. The air between us could spark and explode like a flare at any moment. "Me? Home? I am not your enemy. I *did* return Brother Livingston's baby, remember."

"Why didn't you come back with the men, then?" Papa asks. "If you wanted to come home so badly? Why did you fight them so fiercely?"

It's a good question and I struggle for an answer. "It was mass confusion, Papa," I say, hoping I sound sincere. "The attack came at night. It was as if a dream had come alive.

How was I to know what was happening? I thought, at first, it was a native-upon-native fight."

The awning continues to tap in the wind, the stillness of the room crawling over my face, my arms, my hands, making my fingers twitch toward my knife again.

"Can you tell me about the trials? The outcomes?" I hope my questions seem reasonable, that my voice sounds less shaky than it feels.

Papa's hand goes to his beard in a gesture I know means frustration. "Guilty, of course. Now we sentence them."

"We?"

"The elders." Papa is watching my every move, my every expression. He does not trust me. I don't blame him. I do not trust him, either.

"Of course," I say. I drop my eyes, try to seem demure, hope he will give more information. I have lost more time than I thought.

"Take water from the basin in the back," Papa says finally. "For Heetle. And for the sake of the gods, Ramona, clean yourself."

"Water," I say, trying to keep my face as unreadable as his. "From the wings of angels."

Papa looks up and sniffs. "Yes. Thank the gods for all they bestow. Now go water your horse." He clears his rusty voice as I turn to walk away.

"Ramona."

I look over my shoulder at him, in the shadows, in his wheeled chair. "Yes?"

He clears his throat again and his eyes move from my face to the ceiling. "Thank the gods also that you are home." His eyes return to my face. I cannot tell if this is an order or a declaration. His hand clenches the gun.

Once Heetle is watered I go back inside and speak to Papa. "Aunt Billie and Temple," I say. "I wish to see them."

"You will not leave this homestead dressed like that," he says.

I step toward him. I could easily overpower this shell of a man. Throw him from his chair, march to the village center. But no. That is not how I will do things. That would, ultimately, accomplish nothing. Seeing him like this has cooled some of the vengeance roiling in my blood. There has to be a better way. There is always a better way. I take a breath.

"I do not think my old dresses will fit anymore," I say simply.

"Take something of Aunt Billie's. Now. Change. Then I will take you to them."

I walk past him through the shadows, and I see, sitting on the mantel over the cooling grate, next to the box that holds the rope of Cheese hair, my armless statue. I forgot it after all this time. I wonder who took it from my apron pocket and put it in such a place of prominence?

I look from the mantel to Papa, who is staring at me intently. His jaw works as if he's about to say something, but he says nothing.

In the bedroom I find a dress and put it on over my *peltan*, keeping my knife firmly strapped to my thigh. The skirts feel odd and heavy against my legs. The blouse is scratchy, the sleeves too short and too tight against my muscles. The whole outfit is so confining. How in the secrets of the gods did I ever survive wearing cumbersome, stifling clothes such as these?

I return to the front room and Papa nods, wheeling his chair past me, the light rifle still in his lap. "You may accompany me as I check on the prisoners. Then you will be delivered to Aunt Billie." He eyes me, again, hard but curious. "Hopefully, you have retained some of her teachings. Once you have proven your allegiance to the township, Aunt Billie will need extra help. The elders grow feeble. The workload is immeasurable."

His statements surprise me. He wants me to continue learning her healing ways? To attend to other homesteaders? I cannot help but remember Aunt Billie in the *Origin* wreckage, speaking of me becoming her apprentice.

I shake the thought from my mind. I want to ask how the Kihuut are faring, who is injured, whether they will all be sentenced to death or if there will be any clemency at all, but I bite my tongue. It will not do to seem too worried, to seem as though I care about them.

I follow Papa outside and watch as he expertly rigs his chair to the one-man and slides into the seat. The engine sputters stinkily to life and I go to Heetle.

Following a good distance behind Papa, we ride to

the center of the township. There is a clot of men stacking metal slats in the town square, with more men drilling holes into the ground. They are building something and my stomach turns as I imagine what it might be.

"Gallows work," Papa confirms, nodding his head toward the men. "Once the scaffolding is complete the sentencing will begin. I suspect it will be the largest hanging this moon will ever see."

Near the construction work, there is a crowd of people surrounding a pen that looks hastily built. It is taller than me, but not by much. The Kihuut are crammed inside. I see Jo, Natka, Klara, a few others. But not Temple. The townspeople jeer at them, some even throw things between the metal bars. Rotten food, trash. The Kihuut are quick to throw it back at them, riling up the crowd even more.

I jump from Heetle, a cloud of dust surrounding me. "What is this?" I say, marching up to the crowd, anger flushing my neck and cheeks. Natka sees me and yells, "Sister!" but he speaks in Cheese so the townspeople do not know he speaks of me. He is covered in dust and sweat and dried blood. He snaps his upper lip and I see confusion play at his tired eyes as he takes in my appearance.

Heads turn. Eyes take me in. There are gasps. Papa has removed himself from the one-man and wheeled up to the crowd. "Back away from the prisoners," he shouts. "Remember who you are. Remember the words of the gods. Are you animals, too? Of course not." The people back away, some looking ashamed, others looking angry.

Papa turns his attention to the two men doing a poor job of guarding the prisoners. "You." He points to the biggest one. "Take her to the schoolhouse." He then looks at me hard. "For her own protection." The man rushes at me, pinning my arms behind my back. I do not resist, so he doesn't have to drag me away. I hope Temple will also be at the schoolhouse.

The surly guard, armed with two handbows, pushes me into a cart.

"What?" I say. "Why so heavily armed against a mere girl-child?" I smile sweetly and then regret this taunting. Not smart, Mayrikafsa.

The guard sits beside me in the cart, and powers us through the scrub. Several minutes later we halt in front of the schoolhouse.

Before we even get inside, I hear shouts.

"You are a human, you gum child!" It is Old Man Dan yelling. "A HUMAN!" I hear a slap, and a cry.

The guard, who has me by the arm, pushes open the schoolhouse door. Temple holds her cheek and Aunt Billie stands in between her and Old Man Dan, face aflame, eyes sparking.

Her attention is diverted by the gust of hot wind that blows into the stifling building as we come through the door.

"Look who showed up today," the guard says, shattering the thick silence that has followed what I suspect now was Aunt Billie's cry. Temple's expression is so obstinate I

277

think I could set her hair on fire and she would not make a sound.

The guard pushes me toward Old Man Dan.

"So," Old Man Dan says. "You tired of playing native?"

I swallow all insults and retorts, look to the ground and say, "I came to testify against the Kihuut." I look up at him. "But discovered I was too late."

Temple shoots me a look that would melt rocks, and she snaps her sharpened teeth at me. Her hair has been cropped closely to her head. An unraveled ribbon falls against her cheek. Her clothes are clean, covering her arms and legs, and she fidgets, pushing the sleeves up and down, chewing at the buttons on her blouse with her teeth.

"Gone feral, that one," the guard says, taking a step back.

"I would have you keep a civil tongue around—and about—my nieces," Aunt Billie says, walking to me and looking me up and down.

"You should have accompanied me home, Ramona." Ben-ton speaks from where he is seated in the corner. I did not recognize him at first, dressed as he is in clean, well-fitting human clothes. His hair is trimmed and shines yellow. He stands and walks to me, his gait awkward, shuffling, as he approaches in his heavy boots. I wonder what has become of his *nantolas*.

"We could have watched the trials together. I have never seen justice served so justly—or swiftly." He smiles at me in such a condescending manner I would smack his mouth from his face if my actions would not land me in the pen with the Kihuut.

I swallow my hatred and work to keep my voice steady. "Seems a shame, then, letting them fester in that pen. Why not kill them now? Why waste time with gallows? End the misery. Forget these terrible times. Begin anew. Praise the gods."

The sarcasm in my voice needs to be tempered or I will ruin everything. I bite my lips together to keep from speaking more.

Old Man Dan is upon me suddenly, looking me over, walking circles around me. "At least *you* remember your natural language," he says, seeming to have missed my sarcasm completely. "Whether it's civil or not, at least it's not that godsforsaken slurry of clacks and bleats."

I tighten my jaw, but then release it. I know that Temple remembers human language, too, but she must be refusing to speak it. I say nothing more. Old Man Dan squeezes my cheeks so that my mouth opens.

"Brother Livingston!" Aunt Billie protests. "Remember your place!"

"You got pointy teeth in there, too?" he asks. I snarl at him, showing my one sharpened tooth and then shake my head loose from his hand.

"We'll take care of that soon enough," he says. "But first we remind you of human decency." He again looks me up and down, sneering in disgust.

"Go get the soap, Benny," he says. Ben-ton smiles and

nods at me as he walks out of the schoolhouse. "Welcome to rehabilitation," Ben-ton says as he glides past. The tone of his Cheese-accented voice has changed ever so slightly and I wonder if he has the brain capacity to realize things here might not be quite as lovely as he dreamed.

"When did you earn this position of importance?" I ask Old Man Dan, not responding to Ben-ton. I step forward, crossing my arms across my chest. "Smacking around the children of the Sheriff Reverend. That is a father's right, not yours. When did it become acceptable to go against the teachings of the gods?" I look to Aunt Billie. "Papa knows of this?"

"Of the violence?" She eyes Old Man Dan coldly. "No. But because of your papa's . . . predicament . . . the township sought an assistant for him. Someone to act in his place on days he is unwell." She looks to me, her eyes open, unblinking, communicating something. Is she telling me that Papa had nothing to do with ordering the raid on the village? Or is she telling me that this is all my fault?

"And they chose *him*?" I say, frowning, then regretting my impertinence. I must not cause trouble. It is not the time.

"I worked in his stead while he was being punished for violating the harvesting laws." Old Man Dan chews the inside of his cheek as he grins. "The township figured since I had a taste for the job, who better than me to help out now."

I feel many inappropriate retorts on the tip of my tongue.

"We shall rehabilitate in gentler ways, Brother Living-ston," Aunt Billie says, stepping toward him.

"Or I could just do it without you present." He gives a nod to the other man, who takes a step closer to Aunt Billie.

"I will rehabilitate," I say, holding up my hands. "No need to get pushy."

Temple spits on the floor right at my feet. She looks up at me through her glower and all I see is hatred. I remind myself that this is only temporary. She won't hate me for long. I hope.

Soon, Ben-ton is back with the soap and Old Man Dan takes me outside the schoolhouse.

"Strip. Now."

I stare at him hard, not moving. He sighs and goes into the schoolhouse. Aunt Billie comes out in his stead.

"Ramona, we only ask that you clean yourself up a bit." She is trying to speak softly, as if to a wounded animal.

"I will not remove my clothes where others might see."

I do not care a toot for modesty. Not anymore. But I will not strip so that they see my *peltan* and knife.

Aunt Billie sighs and returns to the schoolhouse without saying anything.

Old Man Dan returns with a metal seat. He motions at the stool and smirks. "You may stay stinking for now. But we will not stall the rehabilitation process. If you please, Ramona."

I practice my counting. Not to calm my breathing but

to calm my rage. I breathe deeply through my nose, filling my lungs, then exhaling slowly, counting, promising myself that if I beat Old Man Dan with his gum stool I will not succeed in anything except for momentary pleasure.

I sit on the stool.

There is the *shing* of a blade coming unsheathed and before I can react, a thump at my feet. I swallow, noting that I feel no pain. I look down and see my braid. My matted, roped black and dusty hair lies at my feet. Old Man Dan goes to work now, hacking at the rest of my hair until it is shorn as closely to my head as a newborn *kakee*. I feel naked without my horsetail.

"Much better," he mutters, sheathing his knife. "Now it will grow back long and shiny. As the gods intended." He dusts hair off my shoulders and squats in front of me. He wobbles and then steadies himself by grabbing my knees and squeezing. Hard. "You fought fiercely to just give up and come home now?" He sucks his mustache and rolls back on his heels. "Quite a change of heart you've had, huh?"

I shrug. "When you are a captive, you are treated better if you act as one with the tribe." I unbutton the top three buttons of my blouse and pull it, along with the strap of my *peltan*, over my right shoulder, showing off the scar from the *Kwihuutsuu* talons. "Do you not think I suffered? That I learned to do what a girl must do to survive?"

"I do not doubt you learned much," Old Man Dan says, pushing himself up to standing. He cracks his back. "I just

282

want to make sure you didn't forget anything important."

I stand, facing him. "I am sure you will find that I am still the Ramona Darling I've always been."

"Yes, well, we'll see about that."

I begin to walk to the schoolhouse door, but Old Man Dan stops me. "One more thing, Ramona." He reaches up and yanks the cooling crystal off my neck. It falls into his palm and he closes his hand around it. "No need to waste valuable resources." He puts the necklace in his pocket and walks into the schoolhouse.

Ben-ton moves out of his way, but stays in the doorway, where he must have been the whole time, watching everything. He blinks slowly, resting his closed eyes for a moment, then turns and goes back inside.

If Old Man Dan had struck a blow to my stomach I would have more breath in my lungs than I do now. I gasp once, twice, three times as my body adjusts. The dust and dirt and heat flow into my lungs, tightening them like dried plini skin.

I measure my breathing; try to calm down.

Without that necklace I am weakling Rae, but I must be Mayrikafsa, cunning warrior of the Kihuut. I *cannot* be weakling Rae. Not now.

Not ever again.

Breathe, Mayrikafsa. Breathe.

29

I AM SITTING IN THE SCRUB IN FRONT OF THE cabin, watching night beetles scurry around the rocks, when Temple sits down next to me. She has a blanket over her shoulders even though it is stiflingly hot.

The Red Crescent frowns above us, making the night glow.

"Can't sleep, either?" I ask.

Her frown is more evident than the Red Crescent itself. She is still angry with me. She doesn't speak.

We sit in silence for several moments. Temple puts her shorn head into her hands, then looks up at me, her blue eyes wide, desperate. "I cannot stay here, Tootie. I cannot do it." Her voice is a raspy whisper. She yanks at the sleeves of her nightdress until they rip at the seams. *"E'e naa fataka nee."* I do not belong here.

She rubs her hand over my nearly bald scalp. "But *you* seem to want to be here now. You came on your own? Why aren't you building a raiding party? Why aren't you trying to save everyone right now? This is a poor showing for a future chieftess, Mayrikafsa."

I shake my head and a bitter, quiet laugh seeps out. "I am no future chieftess. But I promise you I don't *want* to be here now." I stare at the Red Crescent.

"You seemed calm enough about it this afternoon." She is not looking at me while she talks, her eyes trained on the Red Crescent, too. "The trials are over, Rae. They are going to kill everyone. I'm sure you saw the building crew. It will only take a few days to build the gallows."

I reach for her hand and she lets me take it. "If I tell you there's a plan, would you believe me?" I whisper, turning to her. "That I am to get everyone back to the village?"

Temple squints at me. "By yourself? But how?"

I tap my head. "It's all up here."

Temple sighs. "That's what I'm afraid of. Do you have a way to stop time while you work out this plan of yours?" She pushes my shoulder, gives me a sad half smile, and she is the Temple I know. "Does Fist even know you're here?"

"Of course he does!" I lie, trying not to feel irritated at this interrogation. "He sent me, rockhead. He's watching over the human prisoners and recovering from his illness and injuries. I promised him I will . . . take care of everything." That is almost the truth.

"And then what?"

I shrug. "Then we will all be home. I haven't thought that far, Temple."

Temple nods.

"I think I can get everyone away from the township," I say. "But I am not sure how to get them back to the village. I am not sure how to do any of it quickly." I pause, feeling a storm of emotion threatening to engulf me. I cough it away. "Kwihuu is dead, Temple. All of the *Kwihuutsuu* were killed."

"Oh no," Temple says, and her head whips around. She stares at me, eyes going bright. "Oh, Rae, that's terrible."

"You just called me Rae."

She ignores me and stares back at the Red Crescent. "All the *Kwihuutsuu*." She shakes her head and says to herself, "So awful."

I swipe treacherous tears from my face. The Cheese would not mind the emotion from their Crying Warrior, but it feels strange to be back at the homestead and to allow such strong feelings to show.

I breathe deeply, the scratching of the dust in my throat distracting me from my sadness. "There are plenty of wild *Kwihuutsuu* out there, but I am not sure I can get to a nest and break in even one of them. You know, in all of the extra time I will have away from rehabilitation."

Temple gives me a rueful smile. She throws her blanket

out on the scrub and lies on it. "You'll think of something."

"Will I?" I stretch out in the scrub next to her.

"You always do." She closes her eyes. "You're so smart, Tootie. The smartest person I know."

"She wasn't that smart before."

We both jump up, ready to fight.

It is Boone. Taller now, skinny as a shine tree. I relax a little but see Temple does not. Boone laughs and holds up his hands.

"What are you doing here?" I ask, breathless. And how much has he heard?

He taps the gogs hanging around his neck. "Still smashed, but working well enough. I saw you two out here and I thought I would come say hello. It has been a long time, Rae." He smiles, but his eyes dip, looking sad.

"How did you get away?" I ask. "After the . . ."

Boone sits on the blanket. Temple finally seems to relax a little, though she stays standing as I sit next to Boone.

He shrugs. "There was a storm. The dactyl that was holding me balked after one of the electrical bolts. He dropped me, but luckily we were not that high off the ground. I twisted my ankle, but it wasn't that bad. As soon as I hit the ground I ran as fast as I could, even though my ankle was burning and I was bleeding everywhere." He drops his head in his hands for a moment and looks up. "I was closer to the township than to the cooling flats. I ran here first. Maybe if I had found your papa sooner he wouldn't be . . ."

I put a hand on his arm. "You could not have changed

287

anything to do with Papa," I say. "You probably saved him, even, by being able to tell everyone where he was."

Boone shakes his head, his eyes closed, his face creased, full of anguish. "I dream of the raid every night, Rae. Every gum night." He turns to look at me. "I am so glad you're home. Safe." There's a long stretch of silence as we all stare at the Red Crescent. There is so much to say, I can say nothing at all.

After several moments, Boone lightly touches the scar on the back of my neck. "Did they . . . did they do awful things to you?" He whispers the last part.

"They are not as bad as you would think," Temple says. There is a hard edge to her voice.

Boone's eyebrows go up.

"It's true," I say, shooting Temple a look. "Maybe we could show you sometime." I mean this as a joke, but as soon as it comes out of my mouth I regret it.

Boone pushes away from me. "What? You're not . . . you don't plan to go *back*, do you?"

Now it is Temple's turn to shoot me a look. "No, no," I say, forcing a quiet laugh. I shake my head. "It was just a joke, Boone. I am glad to be home."

It is drying my mouth and breaking my heart to lie to him, but he looks so broken, sitting here in the red light of nighttime. And as terrible as it is to admit to myself, I no longer know if I can trust Boone with my secrets. He does not know Mayrikafsa like he knows Rae. He does not know Mayrikafsa at all.

We are all quiet for a while, listening to the wind and the night beetles.

"Do you still enjoy making those small statues? The ones with the clapping hands? You were always so good at intricacies, Rae."

I shake my head. "No time. Too much training," I say, then regret the words.

Boone's mouth becomes a thin line and he goes silent. After several moments he clears his throat and from the way he tenses next to me, I can feel what his next question will be before he even asks it. "Did you learn anything of Rory?" he asks. Temple shakes her head because even she does not know the story Natka told me. Boone lowers his head and is quiet again, but I interrupt the silence.

"Actually, I did hear of Rory," I say, feeling a bittersweet melancholy. I tell him everything I know, leaving out the part where Rory was stripped of her Kihuut name for failing the flying test.

"Kamino," he says finally, with a small smile.

I nod. "Perfect, don't you think?"

He nods.

"And also perfect that you can see her shine tree from the fields. She is watching you, Boone. Every day."

He nods again, slower this time, then drops his head onto my shoulder and weeps. I wrap my arms around him and we rock slowly back and forth. It's contact we've never had—this kind of togetherness is not allowed among humans who aren't family, and often not even shared among family. But I've become so accustomed to it among the Cheese. It feels natural to hold him like this. Boone collapses further into me, and I blink back my own tears as I hold him and he cries and cries until he is asleep.

Temple and I give him time to rest, to be away from his grief, and then wake him so that he can get home before the suns come up. If anything is worse than having been stolen by the Kihuut and heathenized, it is getting discovered spending time with a boy after dark.

After a few hours of fitful sleep inside the homestead, I awake to the sounds of hammering. Mara brings the noises with her as she throws fistfuls of dust up against the Star Farmers window of the bedroom.

Temple sits at the foot of my bed, watching me.

"Storm's a-brewin'," she says in a whispery imitation of Papa.

I rub the dreams from my eyes. "Storm?"

Temple holds a finger to her mouth and points to the doorway. Voices carry over the threshold.

"It's ridiculous to continue construction," Papa says. "There is obviously a storm coming. You only waste energy and resources. Everything will be torn down with the first real gusts."

"We must show strength. We must show the seriousness of the impending sentencing. We *speed up* the construction, is what we do."

It is Old Man Dan. Of course.

"I do not suppose any of the Cheese doubt the serious-ness of the sentencing," Papa counters. "And the crews are working at capacity already. We do not need to waste man power building scaffolding that will likely be blown hap-hazardly around the entire township—"

There is the sound of a fist hitting the metal table. "This is important, Zeke. Not just to show the Cheese we mean business, but to show the townspeople as well. They do not abide the current delays, I can tell you that. Lest you seek a rash of vigilantism, I would show the people you mean to follow through. And if those Cheese are killed by accidental electrocution during a storm rather than justice served . . . gods help you, man."

"Why would there be doubt of follow-through?" Papa speaks low, through his teeth. "Who would seed their minds with this doubt?"

"You're up!" Aunt Billie bustles into the room, startling me and Temple. She claps her hands in a hurry-up man-ner. "We have much to do today. Get dressed." She thrusts dresses at us and marches back out of the room. Papa's and Old Man Dan's voices quiet to whispers.

"How long does it take to break in a *Kwihuutsuu*?" Temple whispers to me.

I shrug. "Depends on the *Kwihuutsuu*."

"How long you think before the storm comes?"

I shrug again. "Could be now, could be days. You know that."

Temple and I are surely thinking the same thing. They intend to hang as many Cheese as they can fit on that scaffold they're building. And if Old Man Dan gets his way . . . we are nearly out of time.

There is a loud gust that buffers the homestead, and the wind carries a crash and shouting.

"Waste of resources!" Papa shouts, and as Temple and I poke our heads through the doorway we see Old Man Dan rushing out the front door, with Papa in his chair, close behind.

I give Temple a hopeful look. Mara is on our side. If that was the scaffolding collapsing, the sentencing will be further delayed.

"I am the dumbest person alive," I say to myself as I hold a giant slab of dried plini meat over my head. It smells foul in the roasting suns. The horseshoe-shaped rock formation towers over me, looking the same as it did when we stopped here for lunch on our way to the cooling flats what feels like a hundred summers ago. The wind gusts are growing stronger every day, but still no signs of electrical bolts. I can only pray the *Kwihuutsuu* will break in quickly and we can wage an escape. Whether the Kihuut are hanged on the gallows or accidentally electrocuted in their pen, time is not on our side.

Two wild *Kwihuutsuu* circle above me. One is bright red, the other is yellow. I have never seen a yellow *Kwihuutsuu*, though I have seen yellow clothes made from the skins. The yellow one is enormous. Big enough to hold several full-grown men.

I give the meat a shake. The yellow one circles lower and lower. I tear off a piece of the meat and throw it at her. Mara catches it and it hits the beast's beak, falling to the scrub. She flies a little higher, but then comes closer again. I toss the meat back at her and this time she catches it. When she does, I blow the whistle. She circles higher into the sky now, shrieking.

I hope the whistle didn't scare her.

The other *Kwihuutsuu*, having seen the success of her companion, comes closer, and I throw a small piece of meat at her. She chomps it out of the air and I blow the whistle.

This has been my routine for two days. I beg Aunt Billie for "personal time to study herbs and roots, and also to spend alone time with the gods," and then I sneak off with Heetle and plini meat, and try to train these two *Kwihuutsuu* to come when they hear the whistle. If only I could get one of them to land so I could try to ride her. I know that won't be easy, but if they're to help us escape, they will have to learn more than just snapping meat from the sky.

This time with the *Kwihuutsuu* is keeping me from losing my mind, but it has gone on too long today and I must rush back to the schoolhouse. Heetle is more than happy to comply, galloping through the scrub, kicking up clouds of dust, and I have to pull my blouse over my nose and mouth to try to prevent a breathing attack.

We fly through the center of the township. The scaffolding is nearly complete, but a strong gust of wind has pushed the whole thing precariously to one side. It leans as if wanting to kneel in the scrub. Men wander around it, measuring, discussing.

I whisper my thanks to Mara and nudge Heetle faster. We are soon at the front of the schoolhouse. I tie her up and walk in wheezing. Temple looks up from her tablet, worry passing over her face. Aunt Billie hands me a bottle of the breathing drops, but I shake my head. I do not want them. I want to be able to take care of this on my own.

"How did you survive without the drops?" Aunt Billie asks. She has softened since we first arrived and kneels, placing a hand on my knee.

"My necklace," I gasp. "The one Old Man Dan took away from me. It had a *bibiloka* on it—a cooling crystal. Something about the crystal helps me breathe."

"Well, how about that?" Aunt Billie says to herself. She puts the vial of drops in front of me on the table and goes to a corner of the schoolhouse, where the cooling grate is. She reaches in and takes out a crystal. She holds her hand up to my face, the crystal gleaming in her palm.

"Better?"

I take as deep a breath as I can muster but something is not quite right. I shake my head. The crystal is only barely working to soothe my wheezing and now I'm coughing. "Maybe it needs to be hanging in this part of my neck," I gasp, pointing to the soft spot where an area of skin has gone white, having been protected from the suns while the crystal hung there.

Aunt Billie hands me the crystal and I hold it to the spot, but still it doesn't seem to be working.

"Take the drops, Rae," Aunt Billie says, her eyebrows dipping in worry. Temple puts down her tablet and comes over to us. "Please. For me."

I do as Aunt Billie says, and feel a bit of relief but nothing like having the *bibiloka* around my neck. It is strange that one crystal would work, when another would not.

Temple points to my neck. "The *bibiloka* came from the caves of Ebibi, not the cooling flats. Maybe that's the difference."

"You have found the caves?" Aunt Billie's eyes sparkle. "I have only heard tales of them. Of how there are cooling crystals the size of grown men. Of the healing powers of plants that grow right on the walls." She is looking back and forth, from me to Temple, her eyes as wide as mine when I first learned of Old Settlement. "With those ingredients, Rae, we could create many new medicines. Think of it . . . you working by my side, learning the ways of generations of physicians. We'd work together keeping the township's health in robust shape."

Her smile is bright and her words interest me more than I would like to admit, but it doesn't feel right to discuss

Ebibi's caves with Aunt Billie. I can tell by the way she bites her cheek, Temple wishes she had said nothing.

"I easily brought the men to the village before. I could organize a scouting party," Ben-ton says from the corner where he always sits. "Take some men to the caves."

"Could you?" Aunt Billie's face glows with pride until it crumbles at the sound I can't help but make.

The men he brought to the village? The men he . . . that traitorous, treacherous . . .

I stand quickly, knocking my chair over. "You have never been to the caves of Ebibi, Ben-*ton*," I spit. "You could find the caves no more easily than you could find your own *pitar* with two hands and a flameless flare. But *I* could send you there, if you wish."

My hand dangles at my thigh, where my knife is hidden in the folds of my dress. He stands quickly, smart to take my threat seriously.

"It was easy, you know." The words slide from his mouth, smooth, oily. "The homesteaders were bumbling about, having broken through stone. They dug nearly a whole tunnel on their own. Did you know that? Just to find you and Temple. Did anyone dig a tunnel to find me?" He casts a pointed look at Aunt Billie. "No." Ben-ton takes a step closer to me, and my fingers tingle as they rest on my thigh. "I came upon them, dusty and squinting in the suns. And I offered them passage to the village in return for reuniting the entire Darling family."

Temple spits at him. I feint a lunge and he jumps back, always the coward.

Aunt Billie clears her throat and places a gentle hand on my shoulder. I take several deep breaths, right my chair, and sit down. This is not the place to send Ben-ton to Ebibi. I know that. Though my heart hammers.

Ben-ton returns to his seat as well and languidly eats a biscuit. I shoot knives from my eyes as I imagine all the ways I would enjoy eviscerating him.

The lesson begins. And apparently, rehabilitation means repetition, because we have learned all of this before.

"What act brought the settlers to this moon?" Aunt Billie asks in a voice just as bored as I feel.

"The Star Farmers Act," I say. Temple does not speak during lessons, unless it's to me, and always in Kihuut.

"Why are the natives of this planet doomed to spend eternity adrift?" Aunt Billie intones.

I tamp down the urge to argue, biting my bottom lip. Then I say, "Because they do not believe in the same gods we do."

"Close," Aunt Billie says. "The correct answer is because they believe in the *wrong* gods."

It is *ro-ri-ta* trash straight from my *pitar*, what she says. I want to spit at these lessons. But I do not. I take notes on my slate, answer questions, keep my head low. I want so badly to argue that this is wrong, but instead I say nothing, waiting for the next in the endless string of questions. If I can get them all right, maybe rehabilitation will end faster and I can spend more time training the wild *Kwihuutsuu*.

There are several more exhausting hours of rehabilitation in this day, but then the suns begin to sink in the sky and Temple and I are released. We run straight to the pen in the market so we can visit with the Kihuut. Well, so Temple can visit with the Kihuut. She tells them about our horrible studies and makes them laugh with profane jokes about humans. She also tells them of Ben-ton's treachery and that I am working on a way to get them free and back home. She tells them that they should pretend to hate me so that the homesteaders do not get suspicious.

Natka, for one, is all too happy to comply with this request, and enjoys shouting Kihuut profanities at me and lunging at me through the bars. Some days I wonder if he isn't acting a little too well. He has caught hold of my sleeve and is in the process of growling and ripping it off me when I shout, "*Peltan!*" as a warning. He can't tear off my sleeve or my Cheese clothes will be revealed.

Papa wheels out of his office toward us. "I don't know why you continue to come here, Ramona," he says. "They obviously do not care for you now."

"I am only trying to teach them of our gods, Papa," I say, dipping my eyes to the ground. Temple begins coughing loudly. As she turns her back I can see that she is trying not to laugh. "I weep for anyone who cannot see the glories of the proper gods." My words make me want to roll my eyes, but they seem to placate Papa. He even smiles.

"Good work, Rae. Perhaps one day they will hear you."

"Perhaps," I say.

"Pare-haaps," Natka mocks, giving my sleeve another yank.

"*Peltan!*" I yell at him again. He is going to expose me in more ways than one if he does not stop.

"Pare-haaaps," he taunts. "Pare-haaps. Pare-haaps."

Papa points his handbow at Natka. I put my hand on his bow to lower it, my heart suddenly leaping to my throat. "Don't worry, Papa. These beasts do not speak our language, nor understand our ways. No matter how much I try to teach them. They only mimic." I stare hard at Natka. "Like animals."

Papa pats my arm. He smiles again. Two smiles in one day! "Do not stay long with your beasts, Rae. It will be dinnertime, soon." He wheels over to his one-man.

For a moment I am filled with pride that Papa seems pleased with me. But then I realize why he is pleased with me and I am disgusted.

"Don't take it too far, Rae," Temple whispers to me in Kihuut. "Even Papa will only believe so much."

"People believe what they want to believe," I say. I wave to the Kihuut, who all spit at me and yell curses. Jo winks, then rubs her eye as if something has flown into it.

"Come," I say, holding my arm out for Temple. "We will be late for dinner."

We turn to walk away, and when we do, I hold my hand out behind me and stick it quickly through the bars of the pen. It is full of dried plini. Not much to share among everyone, but still something other than biscuits and water. I feel a quick pat on my shoulder and then Temple and I walk quickly to Heetle and head back to the homestead.

There is food cooking when we arrive home. I sit at the table and say the prayer of forgiveness for my daily mistakes, and Papa watches me closely as he drinks his before-dinner chicory. Ben is at the table, too, also drinking chicory. He looks up at us, with no expression. I am tempted to take off my boots and pummel him with them.

Papa asks, "You have been home how long now, Ramona? Temple? Ben?"

Temple snarls at Papa, but I smile and say, "For me, nearly a week."

Papa nods. "It feels longer than that. In a good way. Your rehabilitation is going well. Billie speaks of starting up your physician studies again soon."

My eyes fly to Aunt Billie, who smiles at me. Ben sighs deeply. His expressionless face now looks lined and his mouth dips in a small frown. He fidgets in his long sleeves and vest, sweat seeping through.

Aunt Billie says, "I look forward to having enough help that I can take a day of rest every now and then." She and Papa and I laugh quietly, while Temple broods and Ben slurps his drink.

"I've been thinking," Papa says, rubbing his palm over the scarred metal of the table and then looking up at me.

"With the success of your rehabilitation . . . maybe it's time to bring you back into the fold in other ways as well. Not just with your healing studies, but to publicly show the people you are still Ramona Darling, not some Cheese beast. Maybe you could help pray with the homesteaders, Rae? You seem to have dedicated yourself to the gods since you've been away."

I am stunned silent. Aunt Billie beams as she brings the stew to the table.

"I think that is a lovely idea," she says, sitting. "And maybe . . ." She gives Papa a hopeful look. "Maybe it would also be good for Benny to see the day-to-day action of the sheriff, as well?" We all look at Ben-ton, shifting uneasily in his seat. Sheriff Reverend one day? As likely as baby *Kwihuutsuu* flying from my ear.

Papa pulls a silver star from his pocket and spins it on the table.

I reach out and take the star. It's heavy and sharp, with the words "Reverend Apprentice" stamped on it.

"Papa, I . . ." But I have no words. Truly. Allowing a girl-child to not only learn physician work, but to lead prayers? I would never have foreseen this. I am not even sure that Papa's gods allow this. He is . . . trusting me. Reaching out to me.

Papa holds up a hand. "No need to get emotional, Rae. Just pin the star on your shirt in the morning, and we will get to work. You'll be able to divide your time between prayer studies and healing studies."

"Where is my star?" Ben asks. Then, before anyone answers, he has lost focus on the conversation and is gazing out the window.

I spin the star on the table, around and around, and watch as it mimics the thoughts spinning in my head.

30

"THE TIME IS NIGH," OLD MAN DAN SAYS. HIS face has been the color of the Red Crescent ever since he saw me walk in the office with my reverend apprentice badge.

The wind beats on the walls of the office with impressive force.

"Nigh, I tell you!" he repeats. "It has been too long since the trials. The storm will be here any moment and the people grow restless. If you do not sentence and execute, you will have homesteaders taking private revenge upon the Cheese. And as much as I would love to put down the beast who stole my Virginia's ear, I do not believe in shooting penned animals. I believe in justice."

Papa rolls his eyes sky high. "You. Justice." He moves

his wheeled chair closer to Old Man Dan. "If you put those Cheese on that windblown, poorly constructed scaffolding, it will take one unified push and the whole contraption will come tumbling down. They will all escape. You know that."

"And if, when they escape, the townspeople are ready with light rifles to execute the fair and just sentences . . . is there anything wrong with that?"

Papa curls his lip in disgust. "I remind you, yet again, Brother Livingston, I am the Sheriff Reverend of this township. I will mete out the law as I see fit."

Old Man Dan leans down into Papa's face and says in a hard, quiet voice, "You have gone soft because of your new weaknesses, Zeke. You are not fit to be Sheriff Reverend of this township."

I do my very best to keep quiet.

"This is a civilized community, Brother Livingston. Fair sentencing is imperative. Do you not recall they have prisoners of their own? That loved ones of our people are being held in the Cheese village?"

"If you think any of those men are still alive, then you are more dumb than you look, Zeke."

"They will be properly sentenced," Papa says. His stubborn tone sounds so much like Temple it makes my heart ache a little. "We have been over and over this, Brother Livingston. I will not budge my stance."

"Why not trade?" I say, my mouth dry. "Our prisoners for theirs? Surely the gods would find this fair and—"

"Her wicked tongue tries to lead us to a trap," Old Man Dan snarls.

Papa holds up his hand. "Rae is rehabilitating at an impressive pace and I would ask that you keep your tongue civil."

Buoyed, I continue, "Why not give their people back unharmed so we can ensure we get ours? There need not be more bloodshed. How does this eye-for-an-eye mentality really work? In the end everyone is blind."

Surprisingly, Papa appears to consider this, but Old Man Dan shakes his head. "These heathens have killed our men already. I'm sure of it." He narrows his eyes at me. "Besides, who are you to counsel us, girl? I don't trust you as far as I can throw you."

"Brother Livingston, please," Papa says. "She lived with them for a great long while. She knows them better than we do. Besides, she brought back your daughter. You can't forget that."

"Do you think the gods would really approve of a girl-child offering counsel to the leadership of this township, Zeke? I have never heard of such nonsense." Old Man Dan's face goes even redder, which I thought to be impossible.

Papa looks at me and then to Old Man Dan. There is a great gust of wind that blows a line of dust into the office from under the door. Mara is outside howling her displeasure at this day.

"*If* the scaffolding proves sturdy," Papa says, looking out the window at the swirling dust, "we may proceed with sentencing. That has always been my opinion. As soon as you prove to me it can hold the prisoners, I will begin the sentencing."

"I can have that proof to you in one hour's time."

"May the gods be with you, then, Brother Livingston."

Old Man Dan huffs his approval. He pulls his bandanna over his nose and mouth and bangs out the door into the blistering wind.

"Surely we won't kill them *all*?" I say, finding my voice.

Papa shakes his head. "What did you think we would do, Rae? We don't have the facilities to hold them long-term and we certainly can't let them go." He shakes his head. "Their fates lie with their gods now, and we both know how that will turn out." He looks to the ceiling for a moment, and then wheels himself to the doorway. "I will go check on the scaffolding as well. We can't risk an escape, but Brother Livingston is right. If we don't end this soon I will have a pen full of electrocuted natives, and a mutiny on my hands."

I nod and Papa wheels out the door leaving me alone.

I have to get the Kihuut out tonight. The storm is imminent. And Old Man Dan will ensure that the scaffolding holds even if he has to bolster it with his own hands.

How am I going to do this? I have yet to get either of the *Kwihuutsuu* to let me ride them and we cannot outpace a legion of one-mans and horses when we are only on foot.

There is nothing else to do but hope for the best. If we are to die, at least it will be fighting.

The day is torturous. Hot. Long. There are sparks of light-ning on the horizon. It's as if the moon itself feels the energy seething within the township.

There is not time for me to get away to tell Temple what is going to happen tonight. There isn't even time for me to get to the pen to tell the Kihuut.

When finally, finally, the suns begin to dip in the sky and Papa stops droning on and on about religious law and says it is time to leave for supper, I am so beside myself I want to hug him tightly. Then I remember I am about to defy him in a way that will be unforgivable, and so I nod once and say, "Excellent. I will be there shortly. I—I want to look something up about neighborly compassion."

I keep my expression serious, my mouth a straight line, and Papa nods. He wheels out to his one-man and I hear it putter away.

I try not to ransack the office as I search for the key to the pen. I know there must be one even though I have never seen anyone open the door. I am rummaging through Papa's desk drawer when Old Man Dan bursts in and then stops, seeing me.

"What is this?" he says, his hand going to the light rifle slung over his shoulder.

"What does it look like?" I say, trying to keep my voice from shaking. Think quick, Mayrikafsa. "I-I'm looking for Papa's reading glass. He *is* getting old, you know."

"Isn't that his reading glass right there?" Old Man Dan

asks, pointing to the circle of glass that magnifies everything. It is sitting right on Papa's desk. Right in front of me.

"Of course," I say, grabbing it and shoving it in my skirt pocket. "How silly of me." I push past the grizzled hulk of a man and walk quickly to Heetle.

I have no key.

This will not do.

The evening is interminable. I try to communicate with Temple via eyebrow wiggles and impatient taps on the table, but this only results in Aunt Billie taking my temperature and wondering if I am suffering from heat stroke.

Ben-ton arrives briefly and announces he will be sleeping at the schoolhouse. No one says anything. I think that he, too, is having trouble adjusting to the hot confines of the cabin and needs the open space we have learned to enjoy from the Kihuut. Maybe he will not admit this, but it's what I believe.

It is finally bedtime and we say our family prayers. As soon as Papa's snores begin, I make my way to the kitchen. As I force down a biscuit, fuel for the journey to come, I am seized with a moment of doubt. Would it be so bad to stay here? To be a healer? I am not sure I could truly be a reverend as I do not think I believe in these gods anymore, but . . . to be able to help Aunt Billie? To achieve a place of sanctioned prominence within the township, as a woman? It seems an impossible idea.

My armless figurine gazes at me from the mantel,

glowing a light blue from the haze of the cooling grate. I think of my dexterous hands creating new ways to save lives. I think of Aunt Billie's praise. I take the statue and rub my thumb over the nose, the eyes, the lips. And then I notice the box. The box I've never been allowed to touch. I put the statue in my *peltan*, which is hidden under my nightdress, and carefully unclasp the lid. Coiled inside is one reddish-brown rope of hair. Could this hair have belonged to Kailia? I rub my thumb over it and think of the Kihuut I've come to love. Their strength, their brutality, their fierce devotion.

It's true that I could still help them escape while choosing to stay here. I could eat my meals at a table instead of on the floor. Boone and I could resume our secret horse races. Aunt Billie and I could study together once again. It's just . . . I am not that Rae anymore. With the Cheese, it took being lost to start finding myself. I am discovering the true Rae, and I think her name is Mayrikafsa.

I put the rope of hair back into Papa's box, and I make my way outside.

Temple is already outside, throwing her blanket to the scrub, preparing to sleep. I take her hand. "Not tonight, Temple. Tonight we run."

Her eyes go as wide as I've ever seen. "Tonight? But why?"

"Papa is afraid there will be a rebellion if they don't get to the sentencing right away. The people are restless. The electrical storm nears. If the townspeople do not have their revenge quenched they will turn on him."

"Then Old Man Dan will seize control of the township." Temple's brow furrows.

I nod. "He may well do that anyway, if we succeed, but at least the Kihuut will be momentarily safe."

"They will come after us, Rae." Temple's voice is low, hard. She sounds like Papa.

"I know."

"They will never give up."

"*I know.* But at least the Kihuut will have avoided the gallows."

"For now." Temple's ominous tone crawls down my spine.

Together, we move quietly to Heetle, and lead her from the homestead, walking far enough from the cabin that we can climb on and gallop away without waking anyone.

When we get to the pen, the Kihuut are asleep, even among the dust and debris swirling in the ever-increasing winds. But after fierce whispers from me and Temple they are soon awake and alert.

"Have you seen a key anywhere?" I whisper to them in Kihuut.

"*Ke'ekutaat* with wheels. He wear it. Like your *bibiloka*," Natka says.

How have I never noticed this before? Papa wears the key. Not smart, Mayrikafsa.

"Does the other man have a copy?" I ask. Not that it matters. Going back to the homestead or to Old Man Dan's homestead to steal a necklace from around his or Papa's neck is beyond impossible.

Natka shakes his head. "I have only seen one."

"We have to get you out of here tonight," I say. "They are going to kill you."

Klara walks to the bars and puts her hands over mine. "You risk much, Mayrikafsa." Hearing my Kihuut name washes over me like a healing salve. "Ebibi smile at you bravery." Klara touches her chest and closes her eyes. I do the same.

I push at the bars. They are heavy and built deep into the ground. I do not have the tools to cut through the metal or the strength to push even one bar to the side. I think about the heavy boulders I used to push every day and I whirl around.

"Temple. We need rope." She runs behind the scaffolding and finds a length of rope. I tie one end to a connector that is holding together the roof and bars of the pen. I tie the other end around Heetle's middle.

"When Heetle pulls, you push," I instruct. "All of you!"

They do as I say. But just as my heart swells with the movement of the pen, there's an unmistakable stink and the growling of an engine. A bright light shines in my eyes.

"I knew you were up to something!" Old Man Dan shouts, jumping from his one-man. His rangy son, Pete, jumps down at his side, both training light rifles at me and Temple. "You were acting mighty cagey this afternoon. I knew I was right to trust my gut and come down here."

"Keep pushing," I yell, ignoring him. If the Kihuut can escape we can easily overpower Old Man Dan and Pete, even with their light rifles.

"Stop that!" Old Man Dan yells. "Or I'll shoot you all here and now." He shakes the rifle, as does Pete, and I hear the coils activate.

I slap Heetle's hind end and she rears up just as a brutal gust of wind nearly knocks everyone from their feet. Between Mara, Heetle, and the weight of the Kihuut being blown into the side of the pen, there is just enough power to pull the left-hand wall down. The Kihuut stream out, cheering.

Horses and one-man vehicles appear in clouds of dust in the township center. It appears Old Man Dan did not keep his suspicions about my actions to himself. Suddenly there are weapons everywhere and we're surrounded.

"Just give up now, girl," Old Man Dan says. "You and your sister will be spared."

Another one-man flies into the group, nearly running over several people, who jump out of the way. It is Papa, with Aunt Billie on his lap. She leaps from the one-man even before it is fully stopped. She is still in her nightclothes, her long hair streaming out to the side from the wind.

"Ramona! Temple! You were not in your beds. What are you doing here? What is happening?"

"We are leaving," I say, my handbow pointed at Old Man Dan. "And we are taking our friends with us." A lightning bolt crashes not too far away and for a moment, the crowd crouches down.

"But . . . ," Aunt Billie yells over the growing wind. "I don't understand."

"They're going to kill the Kihuut, Aunt Billie," Temple says. "All of them!"

"But these . . . Kihuut . . . they've visited so much pain on us, Temple," Aunt Billie says, her voice high pitched, pleading. "They are not without guilt."

"They are not," I say. Red dust swirls around my skirts, making them billow and heave, the air around us electrified with the coming storm. The Kihuut, Temple, and I all stand in a kind of horseshoe, facing the homesteaders.

I shout over the wind, "They raid us in the most brutal ways, I agree." Natka moves next to me and takes my hand.

"They steal horses, supplies, ears, girls," I continue. Klara moves to stand behind me. She puts her hands on my shoulders. I show everyone my scar from the *Kwihuutsuu* talons.

"They are violent and seem to take pride in their viciousness." Jo moves to take my other hand. She squeezes it tight and I squeeze back.

"But they are also kind and welcoming." Temple climbs Jo like a boulder and perches on her shoulders. "The Kihuut are proud to share this moon with others who also feel its strength coursing through their bodies."

"*Kaykalaka*," Klara intones, her voice a beautiful hum we can all feel in our chests.

"She says 'mother,'" I say to the homesteaders. "This place, this moon, it is their mother, *our* mother, and they love her and protect her."

"What about *your* mother, Ramona Darling?" The voice is strong, loud, coming from the back of the crowd of homesteaders. The crowd parts as Virginia walks forward, the side of her head still bandaged. She holds her baby girl to her chest. "These . . . these creatures killed your mother in cold blood. They took my girl. They took my ear. And you care not? You join their vicious band with no thought about what they've taken from *you*? Do you not comprehend that you grew up without a mother's love and protection—because of them?"

"My mother was killed as an act of retribution after the homesteaders murdered a Kihuut warrior. If the home-steaders had not been vicious in their own right, my mother would still be alive. Did any of *you* care for her love and protection, or did you all put her at risk—put everyone at risk—by continuing to seek an eye for an eye?"

"False logic!" someone shouts from the crowd. "Are we to just stand by? Give them every girl-child? Give them every ear?"

The crowd is getting noisy, moving closer to us. I look up and see Temple idly tossing a stone from one hand to the next, as she remains perched on Jo's shoulders. The look on her face tells me she is settling on a target. That would be a poor choice at this moment.

"I am not saying that at all," I answer the crowd. "I

understand the impulse for vengeance. Believe me." My mouth is going dry. I am losing them. I do not want to fight, not like I did when I first got here. I do not want there to be bloodshed. It just begets more bloodshed. There has to be a way to stop it. Or at least pause it.

In this moment, though, how can I get them to understand what I'm trying to say, when I barely understand it myself?

"What I'm trying to say is that we all should be able to live harmoniously on this moon. Humans, Kihuut . . . we have been here for enough generations that we are all born of the same place now. We all have this moon flowing in our blood. We should be able to communicate and help one another."

"With cursed bleats and clacks? I think not." It is shouted from the crowd and there are loud murmurs of agreement.

As the crowd pushes toward us, Jo and Natka and the other Cheese all hold themselves tense, ready to fight. I feel like A'akowitoa is urging me on, pushing me to tell these homesteaders the truths they must know.

"It's interesting how violence begets violence, don't you think?" I continue, trying to ignore the angry shouts, trying to ignore the quickening pulses, trying to ignore the fact that I am losing the Kihuut, too. Their happiness at being free is being rapidly replaced by rage. They are ready to take ears at a moment's notice.

I cast a wary look at my brethren. "Perhaps, the Kihuut

would not steal ears or girls if they had been afforded common human decency when our people crashed onto this moon." Natka clacks his lip to his teeth, sneering at the crowd. Many in the crowd sneer back.

"Common decency?" a man shouts. "Our people landed on this moon and were then immediately and unceremoniously fed to devilish beasts! Our supplies are constantly raided. Our fields ransacked." ·

"Perhaps they would not steal supplies if the humans had not ruined their trading customs by killing off and scaring away the surviving people of the Red Crescent." I try to keep my answers calm. But it is difficult, especially as I watch the crowd shuffle closer, and I hear the constant *thwap-thwap* of Temple continuing to toss her stone from hand to hand.

"They steal our girls, Ramona," Virginia cries out, clutching her baby daughter. "They stole *you*. How can you support that? How?"

"I don't support it. I promise I don't. But please think about this: Perhaps the Kihuut would not target female children born of this moon if they were still able to bear their own female children." Klara squeezes my shoulders. "Did you know that they were rendered nearly barren by a germ unleashed by humans? The same germ that accidentally killed the people of the Red Crescent? That killed all chances of the Kihuut's continued trade and communication with that planet? Perhaps they would be more amenable to sharing this moon if humans had not stolen so much from them."

There is a murmur growing in the crowd at these revelations, and then the crash of another bolt sends half the crowd scurrying for cover.

"So, yes, Virginia. Yes, Aunt Billie. Yes, everyone," I yell over the wind. "The Cheese, the Kihuut . . . they are violent. They are angry. They are not without guilt. But neither are we." I let go of Jo's hand, pointing at the crowd now, and as another bolt strikes dangerously close by, I yell, "You do not get to judge, lest you be judged as well."

A noise comes up from the crowd, and people regard each other with confused looks.

"Enough of this," Papa says. Aunt Billie stands next to him, her hand on his shoulder, almost protective. His face is pale. He opens his mouth to say something, closes it, and then says loudly, for the entire crowd to hear, "I am so disappointed. I thought you'd enjoyed your rehabilitation. I thought you'd made your choice to stand by my side." He looks to Aunt Billie and then to me. "To stand by *our* side. To grow as a healer. To rise up as a leader of this red moon. I guess I was mistaken." He wheels closer to me and holds out his hand. "Give me the handbow." I reach into my *peltan* and remove the reverend apprentice star I was intending to bring with me, to remind me of what could have been. I place it in the palm of his hand and close both my hands around his.

"You can have the pin back, but I'm keeping the bow." My voice is low. His hands are warm in mine. I feel them relax ever so slightly before he pulls me close to him. He whispers, "I heard the boy Cheese call you sister, you know. You forget I used to speak with his father quite often." He releases me and I stand back, startled.

We regard each other for a moment, and I think I see a flicker of something in his eyes. Not hatred. Not mistrust. But maybe the tiny spark that led him to secretly befriend Fist all those summers ago. Papa might not admit it publicly, but I think deep down he, too, would see a peace between our two peoples.

I pull the whistle from my pocket and blow.

"What was that she said about killing people of the Red Crescent?" someone from the crowd shouts at Papa. Other people follow, shouting, "Yes! What did she say? Germs as weapons?"

Everyone is suddenly just as restless as the wind. The humans still have their weapons aimed at us, but are now distracted and murmuring among themselves. They outnumber us and outarm us, but they are losing focus as my words settle over them and as the electrical bolts increase.

I blow the whistle again.

"I promise this will not be the last time you see me," I say over the noise. I know not everyone can hear me, or wants to hear me, but for those who can, I try to speak loudly.

Someone shouts, "Don't you threaten us, girl!" and I am mortified.

"No, no! I don't mean that as a threat," I say. "I mean that, if you will have us, Temple and I will come back to visit."

"Speak for yourself," Temple huffs. I shoot her a look.

"You'll come back for more babies!" a woman shouts. "More ears!"

Have they not been listening? "No! Not for more babies or ears! We brought *back* the baby. I will do my best to stop the raids. You have to believe me." I hear angry bursts of breath from many of the Cheese. Natka regards me like my hair is on fire.

There is stony silence from the humans who are listening.

"Is it too naive to think humans and Kihuut can put aside decades of eye-for-an-eye fighting and work together?" Everyone is restless. I am not sure they are listening anymore. Jo looks at me and gives a rueful shake of her head.

Everyone, Kihuut included, ducks from a loud crashing boom. The storm is nearly here. I lean over to Papa and say, "I can still grow to be a leader of this red moon, Papa. Truly I can try."

There is a series of deafening shrieks as the largest *Kwihuutsuu* any of these people have likely ever seen dives into the group. The people scatter, screaming, powering up weapons.

Then there is another shriek and the second *Kwihuutsuu* arrives.

"On the wings of angels, Papa," I say as he wheels his

319

chair far away from the snapping, still mostly wild crea-tures. "So many answers are found on the wings of angels."

The Kihuut and Temple are already clamoring onto the beasts, and much to my pleased surprise, the beasts are allowing it. I hop on, too, and we are all barely hanging on to each other as the *Kwihuutsuu* take to the skies amid electrical bolts.

"I'm sorry for leaving, Aunt Billie," I yell down, not knowing if she can hear me. "But please find solace in the fact that this time it is of my own choosing. I'm trying to make everything better for everyone. Please trust me."

Through the swirling red dust, I see Ben-ton looking up at us. He waggles his fingers, reaches behind his ear, and then throws something at me. I reach down and pull it from the air. My *bibiloka* necklace. I tie it around my neck and hold my hand up in thanks.

Perhaps he has seen why it is not best for me and Temple to stay here. Perhaps he realizes the township does not afford the life he dreamed it would.

I nudge the huge *Kwihuutsuu* with my knees and she takes to the sky, the *whoomph* of her wings adding even more swirls in the clouds of dust on the ground.

Natka claps me on the back, smiling. Klara reaches over his shoulder to squeeze mine. Temple is on the smaller *Kwihuutsuu*, waving madly at us, shrieking along with the beasts as they climb higher and higher.

I tear at my nightdress, ripping it off, exposing the

peltan, feeling the wind whip over my arms and neck. Feeling free. Just as it should be. We steer the *Kwihuutsuu* toward *Maasakota*, catching a glimpse of the Darling homestead and its field. There is a boy, wearing gogs, looking up at us. Boone. It must be.

As soon as I make the decision, I know it's reckless. The storm is upon us, I know this, but I kick at the *Kwihuutsuu*, slowing her down and skidding her to land several hands from Boone. He does not run as we approach. He does not aim his weapon. He stands motionless, gogs still smashed on one side, arms hanging loose.

I leap from the animal, ignoring the cries of protest from the Kihuut, and run to Boone. Before he can say anything I grasp him tightly in a hug. I smell the fields on him, the dirt in his hair. I smell his Boone-ness, his boyness. A smell I have missed so much.

"I am going back," I say in his ear. "I will try to live up to Kamino's memory."

I pull the armless statue from my *peltan* and press it into his hands.

"Fix her for me, please? I promise to come back for her."

Boone nods, his eyes full, his lips quirked into a frown on one side and a smile on the other. "Always so bossy," he says.

I nod, a rock growing in my throat.

And then I am back on the *Kwihuutsuu*. And we are over the ruined *Origin*. And over the lone shine tree. And over to the other side of the moon.

My hand grips the *bibiloka* around my neck and I breathe deeply.

Oo'ta kon famalil naa paht toofa'a.

It's not so tragic if you don't look down.

I am so glad to be going home.